SAFE HAVEN
FOR
BETH

By

KAREN CARR

Published in 2018

ISBN- 13:9781090354020

Enjoy Beth's journey

Karen Carr

This is a historical Christian novel taking place in 1876 Wyoming Territory. The town of Mustang Ridge, the Mustang Mountains, and the characters are products of the author's imagination. However, I have used realistic dates, products, prices, procedures, processes, etc. Any resemblance to actual persons, living or dead, is entirely coincidental.

No part of this book may be copied without the author's permission.

Scripture quotations are taken from the King James translation, public domain

Cover design by Karen Carr
Cover photo of display at Archway, Kearney, NE

Dedication

I thank my Heavenly Father without Whose guidance and leading this book would never have been written.

Secondly, to my four awesome grandchildren, Sarah, Dan, Joe, and Piper who have supported me throughout my writing process, including helping at my book signing events.

Thirdly, to my two children, Jeff and Darcy, and their spouses, who passed down my genes so I could have those awesome grandchildren!

Worry looks around, regret looks behind, faith looks ahead.
Unknown Author

Acknowledgements

Many, many thanks to those who have had such a big part in getting *Safe Haven for Beth* into the hands of the readers.

Thank you, Sarah Hovinga, for traveling with me to Nebraska and Wyoming to do on-the-spot research.

To Kayla Schmidt, your help in getting the right information to me regarding proper hitching of teams of horses was invaluable.

To mybeta readers who have helped me is such a big way; Carol Schmidt, Kayla Schmidt, Chrystal Berche, Margaret Smolik, Kathy Stauffer, Juliette Beaudry, Cady Windish, Sue Daugherty, Sarah Hovinga, Jed Magee, and Rhea Bender.

To my two writing groups, Alpha Writers and FHB Writer's Group for your amazing advice and tutelage in helping me in my writing.

SAFE HAVEN FOR BETH
Boston in the year of our Lord 1876

Thaddeus was injured, and his mother knew it. She could tell by the look on his face, and she felt the shudder of his pain when she put her arm across his shoulder. He didn't want her to see because he was afraid of what she would do when she found out. Then she would be in danger of being hurt too.

Elizabeth made him sit down while she gently removed his jacket. He closed his eyes as she softly touched the moist spots on the back of his shirt. He heard her gasp when she beheld the bloody gashes on his back made by his grandfather's whip.

"How did this happen?"

"It was my fault," he replied. "I stopped my work in the barn and was napping. Grandfather says laziness is of the devil. I shouldn't have done it."

His mother rinsed the ugly wounds on his back and gently smoothed on an ointment that relieved the throbbing pain. He felt better, but he was still fearful of what his mother might do.

"You won't tell him that you know what happened, will you?"

"No, son, I won't say anything to him, but has this happened before?"

"Yes." He hung his head. "I've disobeyed him before and he has used the whip."

"Why haven't you told me?"

"I didn't want him to send you away like he said he would do," he had replied. "I'm a man; I can take it."

She hugged him then. "But a young man of sixteen should not have to take on such a burden alone."

A few days later, his mother pulled aside Thaddeus and his younger sister, eleven-year-old Rebecca. She told them that after much prayer, she had made the decision that they must leave Grandfather's home. They would have to be very secretive about it. They had to leave without his knowledge or he would take them away from her. For that reason, their younger brother, Nathaniel, would not be told of the plans. Nathaniel would never be able to keep such a secret even though he had just turned six.

It was difficult for them to go through their daily routines as though nothing had changed, as though they really weren't planning to run away from this prison that their grandfather had made for them. But Thaddeus knew he could count on his mother to make it happen. He trusted her to get them to safety. He just wished they were already there, wherever safety might be.

CHAPTER ONE
Mustang Ridge, Wyoming Territory

Beth Eastman had a good feeling as she and her three children approached the small settlement of Mustang Ridge in the middle of the afternoon. Mustang Ridge was nestled between mountain peaks in the center of the Wyoming Territory. Beth pulled back a strand of blond hair which had been tugged lose by the wind and tucked it back into her bonnet. As she drove the covered wagon down the main thoroughfare of the western town, she scanned the few buildings on both sides of the street. The building fronts were clean and well-kept. Yes, she had a good feeling about this town.

Beth pulled up to the hitching rail just past the building with a sign over the door that read: Mustang Ridge Mercantile, Sam Garrison, Proprietor. "Thad, look at that letter again and double check to see if we are at the right place."

Seventeen-year-old Thad rode his horse beside the wagon and pulled the letter from his pocket. Glancing at it, he said, "This says we need to talk to the Proprietor, Sam Garrison. We are here, Ma."

Beth pushed the brake lever forward, wound the reins around the side of the seat, and climbed down. She turned and helped six-year-old Nate to the board sidewalk. Thad took the weight from under the wagon seat and fastened it to the lead horses to keep the three teams in place.

"We need to purchase some supplies," Beth said. "We'll start with the things we need the most and go from there."

"Do you have a list, Ma?" Thad asked.

Her hand disappeared into the pocket in the folds of her skirt. She handed him a piece of brown wrapping paper on which she had written down the needed supplies.

Thad took the paper from his mother and said, "Come on, Nate. You come with me." The two boys entered the mercantile to take care of the family purchases. Nate eagerly jumped up and down. Inwardly Beth smiled as she watched the two "men" in her little family. *They are so grown up,* she thought. Especially little Nate, who really was just acting grown up at age six, while Thad had matured beyond his years over the last few months. Beth's inward smile faded as her thoughts dwelt on the cause for their flight to this small town in the Wyoming Territory.

When Beth's husband, Jackson, was thrown from his horse and struck his head on a rock, he was killed instantly. She knew their Texas ranch, although not as large as other ranches in the area, would be a lot for her to handle by herself. She believed God was telling her to sell though it was the last thing she wanted to do. She really would have liked to keep the ranch where they had been so happy. And to be reminded of Jackson.

God provided a buyer with a very good offer, so she sold the ranch. With the proceeds from the sale, she felt pretty comfortable, but knew it wouldn't last them forever, so she obtained work in the bank of a nearby town. She found a small home in town to rent and tucked the money away in her sewing basket, just in case. Little did Beth know how her job in the bank would lead to the worst year of their lives.

Carlyle Caruthers was a banker back in Boston, well-known, influential, and well-healed. Texas was one area in the west which had banks, and it was in his capacity as a banker that he happened upon the little Texas town and Beth's particular bank. Discovering her name being the same as his own, he did some investigating and discovered that his late son had been her husband.

Before they knew what hit them, he had taken them back to his home in Boston, where he ruled their lives with an iron fist. Caruthers was an extremely cruel and domineering man. He made no effort to soften the blow when he informed Beth the children would live with him and if she wanted to be a part of their lives, she could live there too. But he would tolerate no interference from her regarding his care of her children. If she did, he would bring charges against her as an unfit mother and seek guardianship of her children. He had the wealth to back this up. Beth consented to his dictatorship, hoping her children would be in good hands. But when he began ruling their lives, not allowing the children to see their little friends, making them do grueling work on the estate, which was hard for adults let alone children, well, she quickly changed my mind.

The final straw came the day when Thad confessed that his grandfather had taken a whip to him because he caught him napping in the barn instead of mucking out the horse stalls.

Further questioning revealed it was not the first time it had happened. Beth was appalled. Why on earth had Thad not told her about these occurrences? Thad admitted he kept it from his mother because he was afraid of what his grandfather might do to her. That he might send her away and she would never see her children again, nor they their mother.

If only her husband, Jackson, had not been killed when his horse threw him and he struck his head on a rock. If only she hadn't been forced to sell their Texas cattle ranch. If only Jackson's father had not learned of their location and forced them to come back to Boston to live with him. If only she had stood up to her father-in-law and refused to let him take the children. If only.

Beth shook herself to be rid of the gloomy thoughts. *Enough of this. I can't dwell on that now.* Aloud she said, "Come, Becca." She helped eleven-year old Becca out of the back of the wagon. Becca removed her dusty bonnet and hand-brushed her long hair, which was the same color as her mother's golden blond hair. She let her bonnet hang by its ribbon and together they entered the store.

The interior of the mercantile had a wondrous smell. The pleasant aroma of dried herbs hanging in bunches from the rafters permeated the air within. Beth inhaled deeply and the memories tumbled back, memories of herbs grown on their ranch, tumbled in. Memories of Jackson helping her sow the seed and dig the plants.

She loved everything about herbs, from growing them to cooking with them, not to mention the delightful aroma they provided in her kitchen where she hung the herbs to dry.

When they left the ranch to move into town, it had been hard for her to leave the herb patch. She had brought cuttings and transplanted them at their house in town, but those plants were left behind when Carlyle Caruthers carted Beth and her family off to his Boston home. But she was thankful that tucked away in one of her bags were seeds she had saved from the original patch. She hoped someday soon she would be able to plant them at their new home.

"Mama, are you all right?" Becca inquired.

"What? Oh, oh yes. Guess I was just woolgathering," Beth answered. "I was recalling the herbs your father and I had planted."

Becca clasped her mother's hand. "Love you, Mama."

"Me too."

Beth paid for the supplies Thad had placed on the counter. As the clerk behind the counter handed Beth her change, she took a deep breath, thinking, *direct my words, dear Father.*

"Are you Sam Garrison?" she inquired.

"No, Mr. Garrison is in his office. I'm George. Can I help you with something?"

"I'm Mrs. Jack Eastman. We're answering his ad for a stagecoach station operator," Beth informed him.

"Wait just a moment and I will ask if he can see you now."

When George returned, he directed her, "He can see you now. I'll take you to him. Follow me please."

"Thank you." Beth trailed George to the back of the store with her children following her.

"Mr. Garrison," he said poking his head into the room. "This lady would like to speak to you."

"I'm Sam Garrison," said the man behind the desk. As he rose, he reached over the desk to shake her hand. "How can I help you?"

"I'm Mrs. Jack Eastman," she said. "You should have received a telegram from my husband regarding the opening for the stagecoach station manager."

They could not afford to have the same thing happen with Caruthers again. Beth had sent the telegram in Jack Eastman's name after Thad discovered a flier in Fort Kearny when their wagon train had stopped there.

"Ah, yes, yes," Garrison acknowledged looking behind her.

"Oh," Beth said. "These are my -- our children, Thad, Becca, and Nate."

"And where is Mr. Eastman," he asked.

"Well, that's the thing. Jack wasn't able to finish the trip with us. Something unexpected came up, but he will get here as soon as he can. In the meantime, I - he hoped we could go ahead and make any necessary arrangements."

"Well, this is a bit unusual. The first stage will come through in a little over a week," he mused. "I don't have anyone else interested. How long before he would be able to get here?"

"Oh, it might be as much as three weeks. I hope it won't be a problem."

"I see. Well, as I said, I did like Mr. Eastman's experience, and we are running out of time. Have a seat and we'll fill out the necessary papers."

Stepping to the office door, he called out, "George, get a couple more chairs for the rest of the family, would you?"

"Right away, sir," replied George.

"Now then, Mrs. Eastman, let's talk business details here. This position involves the signing of a contract later, but we would like to have the station operator on the job for a couple of months first, just to make sure it works for everyone involved. On kind of a trial basis, so to speak. That will work well for the stage line since Mr. Eastman…"

"Jack," Beth supplied.

"What, oh yes. Since Jack is not here today to sign any papers anyway, I'll just have you sign a temporary contract. However, I do have a concern about handling the horses. It takes a strong man to change out the teams. "

Thad spoke up for the first time. "I may be young, but my dad taught me about horses on our ranch. How far away is the station, Mr. Garrison?" Thad attempted to steer the subject away from handling of the horses.

"It's about a half hour northeast of town," Mr. Garrison answered him. "I guess we can give it a try. We'll have you and your family settled right away, though Deer Creek Ranch has been empty for some time."

"It's a ranch then?" Beth inquired.

"Yes. As agent for this division, I have made the necessary arrangements to rent the empty ranch to be used for stagecoach services. The stage company has contracted several ranch owners along what will be the Deadwood to Cheyenne route to provide services to the stagecoaches. Hunton's Ranch, Rawhide Ranch, Coffee Siding, Square 3 Bar, and 10 Bar Ranch are a few of them."

The agent removed some papers from his desk. "This is a temporary contract for the resident of Deer Creek Ranch. That, of course, will be you and your husband. In lieu of your husband's signature, we can accept your signature for the two months." He handed Beth a pen. Beth dipped the pen in the ink and placed her signature at the bottom of the document.

Mr. Garrison pulled his watch from his vest watch pocket. "It's too late to take you to the ranch today, but you can stay in town tonight and someone will take you out there in the morning. It will need some cleaning before you can stay there, so you will need several hours of daylight for such work."

Beth looked at her children. She couldn't very well tell him they had planned to camp out on the trail overnight. But how would they find the ranch without someone to show them the way? She had not seen a hotel as they came into town, and she didn't want to spend the money anyway.

Mr. Garrison added. "I'm afraid there is no hotel in town. Just rooms over the saloon which would not be appropriate for a family. In fact, why don't you and your children come and stay with my wife and me for the night. My Martha always wants an excuse to entertain people and she doesn't get much opportunity way out here. She'll love to have you."

"Oh, that's not necessary," Beth insisted.

"Not a problem. We were just about to close here, so let me lock up my office, and I can lead you there. George can finish closing the store."

As Beth and her family left the mercantile, she collided with a man walking on the board sidewalk.

"I'm so sorry," she said. "I wasn't watching where I was going."

"That's quite all right, ma'am," he said doffing his hat.

As she looked from his cowboy boots to his hat, her eyes were drawn to the sheriff's star on his vest. She gasped and grabbed a hold of the railing. She found it hard to breathe.

It appeared the lawman was about to say something else but Beth, having regained her composure, hustled her children down the sidewalk. "Come children. To the wagon," she said hurriedly, noting that Thad had placed the supplies in the wagon and waited to help her up.

They boarded the wagon and waited for Garrison so they could follow him to his home. Beth looked back over her shoulder and saw the lawman turn into the mercantile. She drew a jagged breath of relief.

Sam Garrison soon exited the mercantile and mounted his horse tied up at the hitch in front. He came alongside their wagon and motioned for them to follow him around the corner. Looking ahead Beth saw that the Garrison home was nestled at the end of the street surrounded by the most beautiful flower bed she had seen for a long time.

CHAPTER TWO
JOURNAL ENTRIES

Beth thought back to their time on the trail. She had kept a journal of their travels and experiences after leaving Boston. Sometimes written by the light of the campfire, sometimes in their tents before dark set in. She reflected on these journal entries now.

March in the year of our Lord 1876

We had been on the road for several weeks. After escaping from the Caruthers' estate in Boston March 7, we took a stagecoach to a nearby town and boarded a train to Cincinnati. There we purchased a wagon with a team of horses and a canvas cover, a horse for Thad to ride, two tents, food supplies, and cooking gear. Since we didn't have anything except our bags - even the purchase of these supplies didn't take up much room- two horses were able to pull the wagon with no trouble. We also obtained a second-hand rifle and a good hunting knife. I put Thad in charge of those because he is such a talented hunter.

While purchasing our supplies, I noticed a newspaper from Boston, and I read the front page. My eye caught the headline, "Woman Kidnaps Three Children." I snatched up the paper and read the article. The article addressed the fact that Carlyle Caruthers' grandchildren had been abducted by the lady who was in charge of their care. A reward was offered for information. How could I kidnap my own children? I don't know which emotion, fear or anger ruled, but we left that town immediately. I prayed for God to protect us.

Through the zig-zag process between the stage, train, and wagon, I hoped to put many untraceable miles between Caruthers and my family. We made our way by wagon from Cincinnati to St. Louis. We camped along the way, avoiding towns where Boston newspapers may have reached. Thad kept us in fresh meat by hunting as we traveled. His father taught him how to handle fire arms and how to hunt and it came in handy. Pheasant and rabbit provided several meals, which I cooked on our campfire. When we were near a river, Nate caught fish for our meals. Between Thad and Nate, we had food to eat. I'm so proud of my boys. I think being able to fish anytime he wanted is what kept Nate from tiring of our journey. Father in Heaven, I'm grateful for your provisions.

March 14 in the year of our Lord 1876

Whenever we camped nights, we slept in two small tents next to the wagon. Becca and I in one, and Thad and Nate in the other. It was early spring; however, we noticed the nights were still cool, and in fact, it felt like snow. Being March still it would not be unusual to wake up to snow. Thad thought we should find a sheltered place to camp for the night just in case.

Thad noticed a grove of trees up ahead and reasoned that it would be a good place to pull off and be out of sight. While we unhitched the horses, he heard water nearby and went off to investigate. He soon came back, telling us he had found a shack by a stream. It appeared it was used by travelers, but no one was there. We could use it and maybe we could even have a fire to cook with.

I couldn't believe my eyes when I saw it. There was a lean-to by a corral where the horses could be sheltered in the coming bad weather. Inside, the shack was a little dusty, but it would still be dry and warmer than sleeping on the ground by the wagon. There was even a pile of dry wood next to the fireplace and I had previously noted the woodpile under the lean-to.

I lighted the fire in the fireplace while Thad took the horses to the stream to water before turning them out into the small corral. Then he hauled water by bucket both for the horses and for the cabin. Becca helped out by cleaning the table and chairs. We wanted to get as much done in the remaining light as possible.

We slept in our bedrolls around the fire as we did on the trail. This time we would be inside a warm building instead of a tent outside.

Becca was excited to have a place inside to cook and she began warming up the beans and making some biscuits in the fireplace. She said she missed Grandfather's kitchen, but then she realized what she was saying. She said she was sorry: she knew what grandfather had done to Thad, but she still missed his house.

Hearing what his sister said, Nate asked what Grandfather did to Thad, and Becca clamped her hand over her mouth. I said the time had come to let Nate know the truth. He had earned the right. Thad explained to him how really mean Grandfather had been and had whipped him more than once, and threatened to take them away from Ma. That was why we ran away. Nate's little voice told Thad he was sorry, and there were tears in his eyes.

We put the steaming hot beans and biscuits on the table then sat down, waiting for the blessing. I prayed, "Father in heaven, we thank Thee for Thy faithfulness and Thy loving kindness to us. We thank Thee for Thy goodness in providing food, warmth, and shelter for us. Father, we don't know what lies ahead, but we ask for Thy divine intervention on our behalf. We know Thou art leading us. Continue to protect us, we pray. Amen"

March 15 in the year of our Lord 1876

The next morning there was snow on the ground. I heard the wind howling in the night, so I was thankful we were inside. Becca said she was afraid Grandfather would find us and make me go away. I told her we needed to trust that God would take care of us. She said she'd try to trust God, but it was so hard to do when we had to live out of our wagon. She missed not having a tub and her hair needed washing.

We spent the day in the shack resting. The first thing we did after a breakfast of beans, bacon, and biscuits, was to see to the horses. Then we had our devotions. God has provided for us in many ways since we escaped and not least of all was leading us to this shelter when the snow came. I knew that spending time in God's Word would calm our spirits and allow Him to continue showing us the way.

'Be still and know that I am God.' As Thad read that verse from Psalm 46, we were all quiet as we contemplated how to be still as God directed us. As we continued to read, trust became the underlying theme in the verses. They told us that God knows what was needed and would provide for us. We just needed to rely on Him to take care of us as He has already promised. My trust in Him had faltered at times lately. It seemed we were always on the run, and I expected God would have brought us to the end of our journey by now. Still, God's word says we must continue to trust in Him and I plan to do just that.

After devotions, we played several games of Hide the Thimble. Becca and I did some mending while Thad played checkers with Nate then both went and got more firewood while checking on the horses and the wagon.

During the night as I lay awake, I believed God was speaking to me about what we should do next. He put into my mind to join up with a wagon train at St. Jo. We would head west and put many more frontier miles between us and Boston. We would head to St Louis.

March 16 in the year of our Lord 1876

The following day began with the sun shining brightly and the snow was already melting, but we waited one more day for the ground to dry off. The muddy trail would be hard for the wagon to pull through. While we waited, I set about cooking some sour dough biscuits to take on the trail. Thad was able to take the rifle out and brought back a rabbit and a pheasant. I made rabbit stew and dried the rest of the meat in the fireplace to take on the trail.

The morning we left, I fixed sour dough flapjacks and used some of the left-over sorghum for breakfast. I made extra flapjacks to take in the wagon. We would wrap them around the pheasant meat to eat mid-day.

Thad hauled in some of the wood from outside to replace what we had used. He also took several cans of our beans to replace the ones we had used. Becca wondered why, and he told her that is what his father had done at the line shack on our ranch. Always replace if you are able, his father had taught him.

It was a cold meal on the way that day. We had spent enough time in one place. We had to make up time. Nate didn't want to go and became stubborn. He was tired and wanted to stay where we were. Poor Nate, little did he know how much traveling we had yet to do. Father, help my children as we travel.

CHAPTER THREE
Sheriff Tucker

Sheriff Tucker returned his hat to his head and sighed. He had been surprised when a woman hurtled into him coming out of Sam's Mercantile. She was comely and slender. He could tell her hair was the color of straw by the locks pushing out from the confines of her bonnet. At first, he thought she might have been hurt as she appeared faint and grabbed hold of the rail. But then he was sure he caught a look of fear when she looked at the star pinned on his vest. She seemed to be afraid of him. He wondered what that was all about.

The sheriff sauntered into the mercantile holding the door for Sam Garrison, who was just leaving.

"Howdy, Sam."

"Howdy yourself, Tuck. You are coming tonight for supper, right?"

"Sure am," he said. "Just stopped in to let you know I was coming. Say, who was that lady coming out just now? Somebody new in town?"

"You'll meet her tonight at my house. She and her family will be there. New stage station operator. But I have to get on home now. I'll see you tonight."

Tuck continued down the street to his office. He had one prisoner he needed to check on before he headed to the Garrison's home. The prisoner was not a hardened criminal. They had arrested him for disorderly conduct, and he had one more night to serve on his sentence. Charlie, the deputy, would be in any minute to take the night shift and bring him a meal from the Silver Star Saloon, the only place in Mustang Ridge to get food.

The prisoner woke from his slumber when he heard Tuck enter. "Howdy, Sheriff. Time for supper yet?"

"Just about, Cletus. Charlie is on his way with it."

"There's my supper now," Cletus pointed out as Deputy Charlie Yates entered carrying a parcel. "Sure smells good."

"That's what I thought, so I ordered one for me too," Charlie said. He deposited his meal on the desk and strode to the cell where the sheriff had opened the door. Cletus eagerly took the plate and sat on his bunk to dig into his meal.

"Sheriff, anything happen that I need to know about?" Charlie asked.

"No," Tuck answered. "Everything's about the same. If you need me, I'll be at the Garrison's."

"Your usual supper invite?" Cletus was smiling.

"Yeah. I'll stop back on my way home." He didn't mention to Cletus about the new family for the stage station, but he was looking forward to meeting them. He had not seen a man, just the children with her. He was eager to get to the Garrison's house.

"Sure thing. I have it under control."

"Cletus, how about a game of checkers when we finish eating?" Charlie invited.

"Fine by me," answered the prisoner.

CHAPTER FOUR
JOURNAL ENTRIES
March 20 in the year of our Lord 1876

I wanted to get another team of horses and supplies at St Louis but was advised to wait until St. Jo because of the extra cost of another team of horses on the steam ship. We were taking the steam ship up the Missouri River to St. Jo. I was told that since I didn't want oxen because we wouldn't be going over the mountains, I should have three teams of horses. My plan was to settle somewhere in the Wyoming Territory. I'll see when we get to St. Jo.

At St. Louis, I purchased passage for us, our wagon, and three horses on the steamship using my bank notes. I also traded in some of my bank notes for gold coins which are more accepted in the western frontier as there are no banks where we are going. We had banks in Texas, but they had not moved into some of the Western territories yet.

I learned once we arrived in St. Louis, mid-April is the latest they dare leave because of the weather. Too early and there would not be enough grass for the livestock; too late and there would be snow when the wagon trains reached the mountains. We would have plenty of time and may be able to leave before April. We had a few days to get to St. Jo and to prepare before they departed. Thank you, Father, that we will have plenty of time.

March 25 in the year of our Lord 1876

Nate was awed by the river and even the steamship. Indeed, as we traveled the river, he kept to the railing, watching everything with wonder as it passed by. He wasn't so tired of travel if we went by steamship instead. Five days after leaving St. Louis, we arrived at St. Jo. Many wagons were already camped outside the town waiting to start on the westward trail. I went to the wagon master and was told they would depart Monday, the 27th of March.

I gave the wagon master, Captain Josh Barton, our names. We changed our last name to Eastman, my father's middle name, and shortened our first names to Beth, Thad, Becca, and Nate. I told him I was a widow and was traveling west to meet up with family.

I signed the necessary papers and paid the cost of such an undertaking. I was so glad I had put aside the money from the sale of our ranch before Caruthers came and spirited us away to Boston. I was still able to use my bank notes to make the purchases of additional horses and supplies. Captain Barton told me if I was going to use horses, I would need three teams, so I guess that answered that question. There would be a lot of sandy ground to travel and the heavy wagon could bog down. So I purchased two more teams of horses making it a 6-up (as they called a set-up of six horses) or a six-in-hand and it would leave one for Thad to ride. Captain Barton told me I should include an extra axel, spokes, extra bows for the wagon top, and other things to repair broken wheels along the way. He said he had a daughter who was Becca's age and he hoped that someone would help his family as he was helping us.

I purchased the needed supplies and was amazed at how much food we needed; 600# of flour, 400# of bacon, 200# of lard, 100# of sugar, 10# of cornmeal, 60# of coffee, and 4# of tea. There were also sacks of beans and rice, a spade, carpentry tools, Dutch oven, clothing. 2000 pounds of food and supplies and we were ready to head west. We spent Sunday worshipping in a tent church set up specifically for the wagon people.

CHAPTER FIVE
Supper at the Garrison's

Beth guessed the Garrison's were perhaps in their mid-forties. With Martha's hair pulled back in a bun and Sam's gray at the temples and his salt and pepper beard, they made a striking couple. Martha Garrison was so warm and friendly to her and the children, not at all put out at having extra people to feed at the last minute. Beth was grateful for the welcome she received from her and hoped they would be good friends.

"Adam Tucker will be coming for supper too," Mrs. Garrison explained. "I'll just peel some more potatoes and there will be plenty for all."

"Well, if you insist," Beth replied. She thought more strangers might not be a good idea for them and was a little concerned about sharing a meal with someone new. "I just don't want to put you out since you already have company coming."

"Oh, Tuck's not company, he's more like family. He comes over for a home-cooked meal once a week as well as on Sundays. He's a widower and probably the worst cook in the Wyoming Territory! It's my contribution to the well-being of Mustang Ridge." Mrs. Garrison smiled.

Beth found humor in Mrs. Garrison's description of this Adam Tucker. Inwardly she recalled what a disaster Jackson had been at kitchen detail. She would tease him that he married her only for her cooking, saying he was on the road to starvation before she came along.

Jackson would laugh and hold her tight and say it was true, but still there were other qualities about her besides her expertise with food. *Oh, Jackson. How I miss you.*

"Is something wrong, Mrs. Eastman?" Mrs. Garrison inquired.

Beth's thoughts reluctantly returned to the present. "Oh, I was just thinking about my husband," she answered.

"Miss him, do you?"

"Oh, very much," replied Beth and wiped away a tear. She was relieved that for once she could answer truthfully.

"When will he join you?"

"Uh... I... uh, don't know for sure," Beth stammered. "He had something come up. He can't come just yet." Beth felt so low, lying to this kindly woman.

Mrs. Garrison patted Beth's arm. "I'm sure he'll come as soon as he can," she said, seeing the tears fill Beth's eyes.

"Mrs. Garrison, you are too kind. Here, let me peel those potatoes for you."

"All right, but call me Martha. It makes me feel even older than I am to be called Mrs. Garrison." She handed Beth the knife.

Beth straightened and taking the knife offered her she said, "And you can call me Beth."

"Well, Beth, I just know we are going to be best of friends. Now let's get the rest of those potatoes on to cook. The first pan is about ready and I will make the gravy. Then we can dish up the roast. Tuck will be along before we know it and when he comes, he comes hungry!"

Adam Tucker was not at all what Beth had expected. Aware he was a widower, she pictured him in the same general age category as the Garrison's, perhaps older. She also pictured him as a gaunt-looking, underfed man. But most of all, she was surprised to see that he was the man she had collided with in front of the mercantile, and he wasn't gaunt or underfed. He was a handsome, muscular, strong-looking man closer to Beth's age. As he removed his hat, revealing his dark brown hair, Beth drew in a deep breath as she again noted the star on his vest.

Martha said, "Beth, this is our Sheriff, Adam Tucker. But everyone calls him Tuck. Tuck, this is Beth Eastman and her family, Thad, Becca and Nate. They are going to take over operating the station for the stage line. Her husband, Jack, will join them later."

"So nice to meet you folks," said Tuck as he took Beth's proffered hand. "Real pleased to know someone will be out at Deer Creek Ranch and operating the new station."

"Thank you, Sheriff" Beth responded. "Has it been empty for very long?"

"Going nigh unto one and a half years now," Tucker answered her. "Looking forward to having the stage come through so near to town."

"Yes, the route has been bought out by the Deadwood Stage Line which will run from Cheyenne to Deadwood and back," informed Sam.

"We are a little excited about it ourselves. It is a bit of a change for us."

"Oh, what does your husband do?" he asked.

"Umm, we had a ranch down in Texas, but Jack...but we don't anymore," Beth finished, embarrassed. *My goodness*, she thought. *I almost said that Jackson was killed. Oh, I can hardly wait to get out to the station where we won't have to talk to people and lie any more to them.*

"Sheriff," Thad interjected, "Have you always lived here in Mustang Ridge?"

"Well, now. To be truthful, not in Mustang Ridge itself. My folks had settled on a cattle ranch not far from here. They came by wagon train also. They both have passed on."

Beth had felt herself cringe when Sheriff Tucker said "truthful." *If I can just get through this evening, then we will be way out in the middle of nowhere and I can forget about this deceit I'm involved in*, she thought.

"In fact," said Tucker, warming to his subject. "I need to go out that way on my rounds and check on things one of these days. In the meantime, I can get you settled in Deer Creek Ranch stagecoach station tomorrow. Save Sam here from having to close down the store to take you out there himself," he said with a grin directed toward Sam.

"Now, Tuck. You know I don't do that," Garrison complained with a grin. "George is very capable. He could probably do without me

for a day, and there would certainly be no need to close the store."

Sam explained to Beth, "But I do think that is an excellent suggestion. Martha and I can go along because there will need to be work done out there, cleaning and things. We have stored some of the nicer furniture here in town, so we could take that out in our wagon."

"Oh, yes," Martha agreed. "That would be perfect. I'll pack a basket for us to take some food to eat when we get there. I know how hungry Tuck gets, and I'm sure growing children would need some food."

"Sounds good," Garrison agreed. "We'll plan for tomorrow. That's settled then. Tomorrow we will head over there. Tuck, I could use your help loading the furniture into my wagon first thing in the morning"

"Sure Sam. I'll be glad to help you with that," Tuck said rising from his chair. "I best be getting back to the office. Thanks for supper, Martha. It was nice meeting you and the children, Mrs. Eastman. See you tomorrow."

Oh, dear, thought Beth. *This could be a big problem.* She was not looking forward to having a lawman around, even if he was nice.

CHAPTER SIX
JOURNAL ENTRIES

March 31 in the year of our Lord 1876

The wagons were ferried across the river from Banks Ferry at St Jo to Belmont Landing on the opposite shore. It was a smaller train than usual, I was told and I was glad because it took a week to cross as it was. I didn't enjoy sitting and doing nothing when time was of the essence. Wagons pulled by horses were first in line followed by mules, and lastly the oxen. Oxen's hooves cut up the trail and cause more dust, but I think it was also because they were slower than horses. Once we were on the opposite shore in Nebraska Territory, I looked back and said to myself, goodbye United States.

I am learning the routine of a wagon train. The daily schedule is

4:00 a.m. – The bugle is played by the night guard to wake up the camp

5:00 a.m. – Livestock is rounded up

5:30 a.m. – Women and children fix breakfast

6:00 a.m. – Women rinse dishes and stow bedding. Men roll up tents and put in wagons

7:00 a.m. – After every family has gathered team and hitched to wagons, bugler signals 'Wagons Ho'' to start. Average per day is 15 miles on a good day, 20 miles could be traveled.

Nooning time – animals and people stop to eat, drink, and rest

1:00 p.m. – back on trail

5:00 p.m. – when campsite with water and grass is found, set up camp. Wagons are formed in a corral

6:00 p.m. – families unpack and make supper

7:00 p.m. – women do chores, men talk, young people dance

8:00 p.m. – camp settles down for the night, guards go out on duty

Midnight – night guards are changed

Another thing we learned was that most of the time everyone except for the driver of the wagon walked. It was less for the horses to haul and there really was not that much room in the wagon with all of the supplies and it was quite a bumpy ride. Thad and I took turns driving the teams, or riding his horse. Quite often, Nate also rode because his short legs didn't allow him to move very fast. Sometimes he rode the horse with one of us. Becca mostly walked. She didn't like the bumpy ride in the wagon and only hitched a ride when she was too tired to travel on her feet. We got very dusty traveling in such a manner and I longed for a hot bath. But that wouldn't happen for a long time.

April 4 in the year of our Lord 1876

On this night, Thad reacted rather badly to the treatment he received from the men of the wagon train. I was sitting by our campfire cooking supper when Thad entered our camp. He came stomping in and threw the horse bridle against the wagon wheel. When I asked what the matter was, he said he was tired of being treated like a boy by the men of the camp. They wouldn't let him go along on the hunts. He believed he was a better shot than they were, so he felt put upon that they would not take him. He said they had several misses causing a waste of ammunition and startling the game away. He knew he couldn't go by himself; it was against the rules of the wagon train. Not to mention my rules.

I suggested he talk to one of the family men whose wagon was near to ours about the two of them going out together on a hunt and then take it from there. He did so the next day and Mr. Bolan agreed to take Thad that very afternoon. When they came back from their hunt, there was an antelope draped across Thad's saddle. The beam on my son's face told me the whole story. I think Mr. Bolan must have been instrumental in spreading the word to the men because they began asking Thad to come with them. I said to him that his childish fit didn't help to show his maturity, but I understood. He had been thrown into the position of the man of the family and then on the wagon train, they treated him like the sixteen-year-old that he really was. I think Thad learned from his experience: having a fit doesn't get a person anywhere. Address the matter in a calm and cool manner. Father, thank you for helping Thad to learn this lesson.

April 9, in the year of our Lord 1876

Once we left St. Jo, we traveled a distance of 267 miles before we reached Fort Kearny. We crossed several small streams and forded the Big Blue River, which caused some problems with some of the wagons. Someone's wheel axle was broken and one wagon was lost all together, but we were fortunate as we crossed unscathed. Shortly after leaving the Big Blue, we came upon the Little Blue. We followed this for some time and enjoyed the fresh water it provided. When it turned south, we left it. Fifty miles to the Platte River. That meant no source of water until then, so we had to conserve. We used the water in the barrels strapped to the side of the wagon for the horses. We had our canteens for our personal use.

On the first Sunday on the trail, Captain Barton called for a layover, so we could observe the Lord's Day though we would not be doing that every Sunday. He thought a time of worship would benefit us all.

Captain Barton read Scripture and we sang hymns. Then prayer was offered. On that day, we sang "Come Thou Fount."

CHAPTER SEVEN
Traveling to the Station

"Mama, how much longer?" Nate implored for the third time. They had not even left the Garrison's yet, but Nate was really anxious to get to their new home at the ranch and stagecoach station.

Beth looked fondly at her youngest son. She hugged him close and said, "Why are you so anxious, Nate?"

"I'm tired of traveling and I want to be home. Besides, I'm hungry. When are we going to eat?" Nate was thinking about the lunch basket furnished by Martha Garrison.

Beth laughed. Yesterday they had a lunch of cold flapjacks and dried apples before coming to Mustang Ridge. The meal Martha had prepared last night really gave her family a chance to enjoy eating a well-prepared meal. Beth looked forward to the home-cooked meals she would cook for her family in the stage station.

"It won't take us long to get to the ranch," Tuck announced. "Deer Creek Ranch is only eight miles from town. You boys, come help me give the horses one last drink before we go. Then we can mount up and get on the road."

Nate and Thad eagerly jumped to do his bidding. Thad grabbed the reins of Sheriff Tucker's horse and led the animal to the trough. When the horse had finished drinking, Thad led him to the wagon and handed the reins to the sheriff.

"Thanks, young fella. You are sure good with horses," the sheriff said as he tightened the saddle. "You'll be an asset to your father in running the stage station"

"Pa was the one who taught me about horses when we were on our ranch. I'll never forget what he taught me," Thad reminisced with a slight quiver in his voice.

Beth caught her breath as she noted the sheriff eyeing Thad curiously.

"Yes," Beth said quickly to prevent further discussion. "Thad misses working with horses, but he will soon be at it again."

"That's right," the sheriff agreed. "Say there, Thad, would you like to ride my horse to the station? That is, if it's all right with your ma."

"Oh, can I, Ma? I'll be careful," Thad inquired eagerly.

"I don't see why not, if it is acceptable with Sheriff Tucker," Beth replied.

The sheriff said, patting his horse on the neck. "His name is Irish. That's because of his red coat, not his temper." Everyone laughed and took turns patting Irish on the neck.

"What is the name of your mount?" the sheriff asked Thad.

"Buck," replied Thad, "because he is the color of buckskin."

"Well, now," Sheriff Tucker said, nodding, "and what are the names of your 6-up?"

"Bullet and Lightning are the lead team and next is Star and Blackie. The third team is Blaze and Copper," Thad answered.

"Ah," the sheriff said, "I see where Star and Blackie and Blaze and Copper get their names just from looking at them. Am I right so far?"

"Yes, Sheriff," Becca answered.

"The other two because they are fast, no doubt?"

Three heads shook a negative answer.

"No. Well, Lightning is pretty fast," said Becca, the spokesperson for the children, "but the reason for her name is on the other side of her neck."

Tuck walked around the horse in question, and then nodded. The jagged white on her neck did resemble a lightning bolt.

"And Bullet? Is he fast then?" Tucker asked.

"Uh, no," answered Thad. "We thought if we named him something fast, he'd think he had to live up to it."

Sheriff Tucker laughed heartily. "That's a good one," he said. "Well, time to get on the road. Why don't I ride Thad's Buck if that is satisfactory with you, Thad?" Thad handed the sheriff the reins to his horse and mounted Irish. There was no need to change the stirrups, as Thad and the sheriff were the same height.

The Garrisons invited Nate to ride in their wagon with them, and he settled in between the two of them. All agreed to the arrangement and Beth drove the wagon with Becca seated next to her. They were soon on their way to their new home with the Garrison wagon leading the way. The excitement was building within Beth and she could see it in her children as well. *I hope this is the right thing to do. Once we have had a chance to prove ourselves, I will tell the Garrisons and the sheriff the truth. I don't like being dishonest.*

Beth glanced at the Garrison's wagon piled high with furniture. Her anxiety to being around Sheriff Tucker somewhat dissipated when she saw all of that.

"Sheriff Tucker, Sheriff Tucker," Nate called excitedly.

"What is it young fella?" the sheriff asked as he pulled Thad's horse closer to the Garrison's wagon.

"How much longer before we can eat?" Nate asked, hungrily eying the basket packed by Martha Garrison.

"Nate, we really should get to the ranch first," Beth advised.

"But how lo-o-ong?" Nate asked again.

He really has a one-track mind when it comes to food, Beth thought.

"Sheriff, what does the ranch-house look like?" Beth asked, successfully sidetracking her youngest from his subject of eating.

Tuck looked over at Beth in the wagon and appeared to be thinking her question over before answering. "Guess it's been a while since I've seen it. Inside anyway. It's made out of logs. Looks right nice on the outside. Got a porch all across the front."

"How big is it inside?" she asked.

"The great room is the biggest one. Includes kitchen and eating area. Also, a living area," he said. "There are two other rooms for sleeping, a storage room, and even a loft. Long table with benches. Need that space for the people from the stage to come in to eat."

"I'm anxious to see it," Beth said.

"When can we eat, Tuck?" Nate asked of Sheriff Tucker.

"Well now. Let me just take a look at my daddy's watch and see if it is time to eat yet." Taking his watch out of the pocket in the front of his vest, Sheriff Tucker said, "Well now, Nate, my daddy's watch says its one hour before high noon."

"Oh goody.

"Can we eat now, can we? Huh?"

The sheriff laughed. "Let's at least wait until we get to Deer Creek Ranch."

"Are we almost there?" Nate asked of Sheriff Tucker.

"Nate, do you see those trees up ahead by the buildings? That is the ranch."

"Yippee!"

They all lapsed into silence as the last leg of their journey was completed. Beth began to think of their trip to Mustang Ridge and how they came to choose this town. She believed it was an intervention by God that they answer the ad for the stage station operator. And now here they were, on their way to the stage station. Beth felt really blessed.

As their wagons pulled into the yard in front of the Deer Creek Ranch, Beth called to the lead team as she reined in the lead horses next to the ranch house. "Whoa, there, Lightning, Bullet."

Beth climbed down from the wagon and looked at their new home. It was a large log building with a railed front porch just as Tuck had described. The horse corral stood next to the barn across from the ranch house. She was momentarily speechless. "It's beautiful," she murmured.

Tuck looked at the plain building that was the ranch house, then back to Beth to make sure they were looking at the same place. But Beth saw the building through different eyes than Tuck. She saw the front porch with its railings full of her herbs and colorful flowers. She saw her family playing on the porch, herself sitting on one of the willow chairs, which was covered with her father's old Indian blanket. She saw gingham curtains at the windows. She saw a home. She saw her safe haven.

Sheriff Tucker dismounted from Thad's horse and went to help Nate down from the Garrison's buckboard. "Here you go, young Nate. Down you go."

As Beth observed the sheriff handing Nate down, she noticed the look of elation in her younger son's eyes. *He seems to have found a friend.*

The sheriff and Thad unsaddled their horses and turned them into the corral, making sure the water trough was filled with fresh water from the well.

"This well is fed by mountain springs and tastes really good," Tuck informed Beth. "Clear and cold. Good for people as well as animals. We best get your wagon unloaded. Then we can get started on that dinner Nate is so anxious to eat." The sheriff opened the door and stepped aside for Beth to enter. She walked into the building, looked around and suddenly stopped. Tuck followed her in to see where she was looking. The sight of the brown bear skin rug on the floor with the teeth formed in a snarl, brought to mind the day on their journey when they met up with a real live bear. *After we had eaten our breakfast cooked over the campfire, we loaded our things into the wagon. Thad was hitching the horses to the wagon. Buck was saddled and waiting when all of the horses suddenly became panicky. We scrambled to quickly get into the wagon. Thad took up his rifle when we saw a bear cub heading purposefully into our camp area. Thad began firing at the ground in front of the cub hoping to scare it off. The cub stopped in his tracks. Thad said he heard the mother bear growling and running our way so we needed to get going. I wasted no more time and drove the wagon as fast as I could to get away. There is nothing more terrifying than an angry mother bear protecting her cub. It was such a terrifying moment for us that I don't think I was breathing normally until we camped later that night. Thank God for Thad and his rifle. Even so, my dreams were pervaded by that vicious mother bear for several nights to follow. I have no doubt it was the same for my children.*

Seeing her stop, Tucker asked, "Is something wrong, Mrs. Eastman?"

Beth was jolted back to awareness by the sheriff's question. "Yes, I was just remembering an experience we had with a bear on our journey here." She briefly described the encounter to Tuck.

"Uh... I'll... uh, drag that ratty old thing out in the yard and burn it," he said, and he grabbed a hold of the bearskin rug in front of the fireplace and dragged it into the yard.

Beth shuddered as memories of the bear pervaded her thoughts. She took her things back out onto the porch.

"My goodness, Beth," Martha said. "How terrifying for you and the children."

"Well, sounds like Thad had things under control," Sam said, "but you were fortunate. Bears are nothing to fool around with. It's good that you got out of there as soon as possible. Around here we see grizzly bears, which are much bigger. Shooting doesn't seem to stop them unless you get them in the right spot."

"I think before we unload, we need to clean inside," Beth suggested. She went to the wagon and got out her cleaning supplies. "Becca, you get started with this straw broom and sweep the cobwebs from the walls, then sweep the floor. Thad, you can find a small limb from the grove out back, so I can make a rag mop."

Martha took the rags and one of the buckets she had brought, and when the sweeping was done, she started to clean. Tuck built a fire in the cast iron stove so they could heat the water for cleaning. Then he and Sam went to look at the corral and repair any damage that had been done while it stood empty. Some of the gate posts were falling down, but otherwise it was in good shape.

Beth retrieved her bag of rags and began tearing strips to make a mop. She noticed her youngest standing just inside the door looking a little lost. "Mama, what can I do?" asked Nate.

"My, there are so many things we need to do. I have to think a minute about which one needs to be done first. Before you get started on one of these chores inside, I would like to have you go outside. If you would walk around the house and see if you can find a place that would be a good spot for a garden, you would be a big help to me. Then you can come back and tell me what you have found."

"I will, Mama," he said excitedly and he eagerly took off to find the ideal garden spot for his mother. Of course, once he began looking around, he forgot he was looking for a garden and began a game of "explorer." Which was precisely what Beth had in mind in the first place.

CHAPTER EIGHT
JOURNAL ENTRIES

April 11 in the year of our Lord 1876

On this day we arrived at Fort Kearny. I was surprised to see Fort Kearny had no walls of fortification. It was called a palisaded fort and was surrounded by a row of cottonwood trees instead. All the buildings were adobe, made out of prairie sod. Fort Kearny consisted of soldiers' quarters, a blacksmith, and a well-supplied trading post, which we travelers descended upon. Captain Barton suggested we fill our supplies here, because it would be some time before we could do this again and it would be much costlier. We were there for two or three days to get everything done, including resting, making needed repairs, purchasing goods, and to await the wagon train from Omaha, which was to join up with us. Fort Kearny is where the road west began; it was a meeting place for the wagon trains coming from different directions. I was excited, yet still fearful that Caruthers would find us. His wealth allowed him to afford to search for us.

While we were inside the store getting our supplies, Thad took one of our wagon wheels to the blacksmith to have the metal rim repaired. Crossing the Big Blue must have bent it a little and time and wear on it would only make it worse.

Becca looked around and wondered if we could go inside and look for something special to cook for our family. As Becca searched throughout the supply store, she found it! A bright orange pumpkin sat on the floor by the counter. She thought pumpkin pie would be that something special. That would indeed have been special, but I wasn't sure about making a pie on an open campfire. After giving it some more thought though, I decided on making a pudding in the cast iron Dutch oven. It would be like pumpkin pie without the crust. Becca was pleased and helped me make it and the boys were delighted to help us eat it. The pudding was tasty!

After we returned to our wagon with our arms loaded with provisions, Thad showed me a flier he had obtained. I read the first few lines and caught my breath:

> **"Wanted – able-bodied man to manage stagecoach station near Mustang Ridge. New stagecoach run from Cheyenne to Deadwood. Family man preferred, as meals need to be provided during short stopovers. He must care for change of horses for the coach. Living quarters are included at the station."**

I told Thad it sounded wonderful, but the flier said they wanted a man. How could this be something for us? But Thad thought we could do it. He said his dad had taught him all about horses on the ranch in Texas. He was as good with horses as the other ranch hands and he wasn't quite fifteen at the time. Besides, he had been working with our three teams for the covered wagon. All we needed to do was go and check it out. The flier said to send a letter to Sam Garrison at the Mustang Ridge Mercantile. I closed my eyes and silently asked for God's leading.

Later, after we had prayed about it, I told my children we had some business to take care of. Thad asked if we were going to do it, and I said yes. We would send a letter in reply with God's blessing and see where it took us. They were all happy with this decision. I guess it gave us all a goal to work toward. Before, we had just been heading west with no particular place in mind.

I wrote a letter to Mr. Garrison applying for the position in the name of Jack Eastman. The Pony Express rider went through Fort Kearny twice a week. The rider came through that afternoon, and my letter to Sam Garrison was on its way.

As the wagons prepared to head out from Fort Kearny, Nate looked at our wagon and stubbornly refused to get up on it. He said he was tired of riding in that old wagon and wanted to go home. He didn't want to ride on Buck with one of us either. I hugged him and knelt on the ground next to him. I told him we needed to find a new home. That was why we were traveling in this wagon. I said I had a secret.

Nate sniffled and asked me what my secret was. I whispered to him that I was tired of riding in the wagon too, but it was just our secret. He laughed, and I asked him if he would like to ride on the wagon with me? He was soon bouncing on the seat beside me. Of course, it was dustier setting up there, not to mention quite bumpy, so before long, he asked if he could ride on Thad's horse with him.

Sunday April 16 in the year of our Lord 1876– Resurrection Sunday

We observed the Resurrection of Jesus Christ. It began as a solemn occasion, but as we ended with joyful singing, I was reminded of how much our Creator loved us. There was a minister of God who was on the train for a short time and he shared Scripture and prayer with us. He taught us a new hymn saying it had just been written earlier in the year. "Christ Arose" was the name of it. I liked the message of that hymn and wrote the words down here that I might remember and teach it to my children.

Low in the grave He lay, Jesus my Savior!
Waiting the coming day Jesus my Lord!
Up from the grave He arose
With a mighty triumph o'er His foes;
He arose a Victor from the dark domain,
And He lives forever with His saints to reign.
He arose, He arose! Hallelujah! Christ arose!

As we sat around our wagons and campfires worshipping our Lord, it was hard to keep still when we came to this song. One just had to jump up and sing it.

CHAPTER NINE
Lunch with Friends at the Station

"While the inside dries, let's take our food out back under that shade tree and have our lunch. I think we deserve it," Sam said.

Sheriff Tucker agreed, saying, "I think that will definitely make Nate happy. Here, Nate, give me a hand with Martha's basket. She has so much food in this basket; I think I'm going to need your help to carry it."

Beth watched the sheriff as he "helped" Nate carry the basket. She was very much impressed by the sheriff. "Becca, take this canvas tarp out there so we will have something to sit on," Beth said.

"Oh look, Mama," Becca said. "There is a creek out back."

"Deer Creek. My – uh the ranch is named after it. It's a mountain stream," Sheriff Tucker commented.

Beth basked in the sunshine and the bucolic scene of the mountain stream with the Mustang Mountains in the background. *Beautiful, Lord. I thank Thee for Thy creation.*

"My, I guess I was rather hungry myself," Beth commented as she leaned back after enjoying the cold chicken, biscuits, and apple pie supplied by Martha Garrison. "This was absolutely wonderful of you, Martha, and the water from the well is cool and refreshing."

"Yes," Tuck agreed. "Martha is an excellent cook. Fortunately for me, she likes to cook for others, so at least I get a good meal once or twice a week. I lucked out this week."

"Oh, Tuck," Martha smiled, blushing.

Beth nodded. "Yes, Martha told me that you are a regular guest at their table."

"My mama is a good cook too," Becca interjected. "You just wait until she gets in a real kitchen, and you'll see."

Beth cast a curious look at her daughter. *What brought that on?*

"I've no doubt she is a great cook," Tuck agreed. "I can see by how healthy you all are that she is a wonder in the kitchen."

Beth felt her face growing hot. *I must be bright red*, she thought. "So, Sheriff Tucker," she asked, changing the subject. "What made you decide to be a sheriff?"

"That's a good question," Tuck laughed, "but I guess it was because I needed to be around when my folks were getting older and this opportunity came up, so I moved back to the area."

"Oh, you weren't living here then?" she asked.

"I had signed on with a big ranch when I got old enough to leave home. Always on the move, on cattle drives."

"I see. Are you happy doing this now?"

"Sure. I like the town. Mustang Ridge is a good town to settle in. You'll like the people once you get acquainted even though you are almost an hour from town."

Sheriff Tucker and Sam helped Beth and Thad move some of the heavier things into the station. Then Tuck announced that he needed to get back to town.

"Thank you, Sheriff," Beth told him. "We sure appreciate all your help."

"No problem, Mrs. Eastman," he said. "It was nice meeting you and your family. Looking forward to meeting your husband, too."

With that said, he mounted Irish and with a wave to Nate, he rode off in the direction of Mustang Ridge.

Sam and Martha also packed up their wagon and left for their home in town shortly after him. But not before Martha had invited Beth and her family to church Sunday and dinner afterwards.

"We'll be there," Thad accepted eagerly, looking to his mother for conformation.

"Yes, thank you, Martha," Beth said. "I so appreciate all that you and Mr. Garrison have done to help us out."

"See you Sunday."

After Beth watched her new friends disappear in a cloud of dust, she turned to her children.

"We have more work to do. We need to prove ourselves capable here quickly, so we can call a halt to this deceit that I have started. I feel really bad about lying to these good people, and the bad role model I am to you children."

"Does that mean we have to go back to our given names?" Nate evidently liked being called Nate instead of Nathaniel.

"No, we can keep our new names," his mother assured him. "After all that is how Mr. Caruthers found us in the first place. Becca, once you are done cleaning that area, you can get started on supper. At least we won't have to cook it on a campfire."

The warmth issuing from the cast iron stove was strangely comforting to Beth. She wrapped her arms around herself and sighed. *We are home*, she thought.

That night seated around the table in their new home, the family enjoyed the usual sour dough biscuits and bacon and beans. But the apple pie from the dried apples from Fort Laramie gave a festive feel to the gathering, which had not been present at meals since they had left Boston. Beth and the children each gave thanks before partaking. Each one voiced gratefulness to God in his and her own way.

Beth and Becca shared one of the bedrooms while Thad and Nate shared the other. It felt so good to be in their own beds in their own home. Later, they would fix up the loft for the boys. There would be plenty of room for them up there and Becca could have her own room. Beth hoped and prayed they could prove their worth here, so they could stay. She soon fell asleep but dreams pervaded her rest, dreams of the frightful journey from Boston.

CHAPTER TEN
JOURNAL ENTRIES

April 19, in the year of our Lord 1876

We had been following the Platte River since leaving Fort Kearny. It was always on our right. The river was very wide but not very deep. It provided water for our use, though a bit muddy. We could use it to drink if we let it set for a time in the bucket, then the silt went to the bottom. However, I preferred to boil it. We had heard about cholera along the Platte in years past, and I believed it might have been because the water didn't move in the river. Making coffee with it hid the alkali taste, plus the boiling of the coffee water may help purify it. Though I shared this idea with the other women, they thought I was being foolish.

Water from the Platte also provided drinking water for our livestock on the wagon train. Besides the oxen or mules used to pull the wagons, some families have brought beef cattle and some dairy cows which provided milk for the young ones.

We made friends with the Wells family, who are from Ohio. They joined up at Fort Kearny on the train from Omaha. Jacob and Sarah have two children, Benjamin, age eight, and Isabelle, who had just turned twelve. She prefers the name Izzy. They are one of the families with a milk cow, and they gave us some of the milk when they had too much to use. Sometimes we hung a small covered pail under the wagon with the separated cream in it. By the end of the day, the bouncing motion of the wagon had churned it into butter. It was delicious on our dry biscuits and flapjacks. The children enjoyed getting to know each other, and it was good for me to have Sarah as a friend. It helped to pass the long days on the dusty trail. And dusty it was. I was so tired of it coating my skin, matting my hair, making my dress stiff. I knew I shouldn't complain considering all of the bounty God had given us.

April 21, in the year of our Lord 1876

It was so hot and dry; a body could barely breathe. I longed for cooler weather and it had not rained since we left St. Jo. One thing I had noticed was how quickly nice people became irritable and downright mean when the weather blazed so hot for days on end.

My family and I are no exception. Becca became increasingly irritable as the hot days continued and Nate whined and cried with barely a pause. I felt like crying myself. Thad had not been unduly affected by the heat so I was thankful one of us was in a good frame of mind.

The Platte River was a God-send in this weather. It was so shallow that once the members of the wagon train filled their water barrels and canteens, and the livestock was watered, we all waded into it. The children had fun running and splashing in the water. I even tied my skirts up and waded in as several other women did. The bank of the river was lined with our shoes and stockings. It was muddy, but it was wet and felt good in the awful heat.

One day, Captain Barton had us pull over to make camp earlier than usual due to an impending storm and also because it was the Lord's Day. Most of the people from the wagon train gathered in a circle. We read from the Scriptures, sang hymns, and offered up prayers to our faithful God.

You could feel the coming storm in the heat we had been experiencing in prior days. We no sooner finished supper and were putting away the cooking utensils than a cool wind picked up and blew in a pelting rain. We even had hail at one point and we feared our wagon covers would be torn. Ours survived but others did not fare as well. When the morning came and the weather settled down, those with torn tops took to repairing them. Everyone was wearing their overcoats as the temperature had dropped considerably following the storm.

It amazed me how the weather out here changed so quickly. The wind was so strong at times it was hard to walk on the trail. One minute it whipped the sand up and around us and into our hair, even our mouths, eyes and any fold in our skin or fabric. The next minute, it was cool and still.

The children gathered buffalo chips as they walked. Earlier in our trek, Captain Barton had suggested the use of the well-dried buffalo dung to use for fuel for our campfires as wood was scarce. We hadn't seen any buffalo, but Captain Barton said the buffalo tend to stay away from any commotion.

April 23 in the year of our Lord 1876

Nate got the stomach sickness just before supper along with four of his friends. Once the wagons are circled for camp, he plays with boys around his age. We mothers thought it strange all five became sick at the same time but no one else on the train did. We began questioning our little ones as to what they might have eaten or drank. Meanwhile, the men of the train were sure it was from the water in the Platte river and that they had contracted cholera as a result.

I was sure it wasn't cholera as I boil the water my family consumes. The other mothers said they do as well after I had convinced them. We discovered our boys had found a bush with berries on it just outside the circle of wagons and they had sat down and pretty much devoured all the berries. I don't know if they were poisoned or just got sick from eating too much. Either way they were lucky as they had recovered by morning. I told Nate to always check with an adult before eating or drinking anything out here. I thanked God that it wasn't cholera.

CHAPTER ELEVEN
Safe Haven

There was plenty to keep the family busy the next week or so. Even Nate. Beth enlisted his aid in several small errands. They had their time occupied enough, so they didn't dwell on the lie they were living. Well, not as much anyway. But God does have a way of causing us to think on our sin until we are convicted by His Spirit.

At the end of the first week their new home looked just that: like home. Beth was pleased that she had taken up a bag just to bring such things as family pictures and doilies when they fled Boston. As she placed the tintype of her and Jackson in their wedding costumes, on a shelf, a tear slid down her cheek.

"Oh, Jackson," she whispered, "I miss you so much." Her finger lovingly traced the outline of his handsome face. "Am I doing the right thing, am I? I know you would never be this deceitful, but what else could I do without you here to protect us?"

Beth thought she could hear Jackson's voice saying, "The truth, Beth. Always the truth."

"But we needed to find a place to live and be safe. I had to provide for the children. You had said to avoid your father at all costs. Oh, Jackson, what am I going to do?"

Falling to her knees by her bed, she prayed, "Oh, Father God, help me. Help me to do the right thing and still keep my family safe."

"Mama, Mama. Where are you?" Nate called to her.

Beth rose from her position of prayer and called, "I'm in here, Nate. What is it?"

"Look, Mama. See what I found for you behind the house," he cried eagerly placing something in her hand, "and there's more too."

She knew from the aroma that he had found some wild sage. She was pleased that he had recognized it as an herb that she used in her cooking.

"That's wonderful, Nate. Show me where you found it."

Nate took her by the hand and led her out back, past some trees and to what once must have been a nice little herb patch. He was right; there was more.

"This is a wonderful find, Nate. Why don't you help me pick some more of this sage and we will hang it to dry," she said. As they picked the pungent herb, Beth asked Nate, "Did you know that this was your Papa's favorite herb? We always had a lot of it drying at the ranch."

Nate nodded wisely for a boy of such few years. He knew his mother was remembering his Papa and said nothing to interrupt that flow. In fact, Nate was trying really hard to remember Papa himself. He was only four and a half when Papa was killed.

Sam Garrison had given Beth a date for when the first stage would stop. The first run would begin in Deadwood and stop at Deer Creek Ranch on Thursday. It would continue on its journey to Cheyenne and turn around to head back to Deadwood. That meant the return stage would come to the ranch on Tuesday. Beth felt she was ready with the station. Just one thing missing: the horses and feed for them. Sam said he was sending men to bring them out along with feed and supplies so soon they would be up and running.

Becca and Beth were hanging the wet clothes on a clothesline Thad had set up for them in the yard near the station. Another symbol of something more permanent, thought Beth.

"Mama, what made Grandfather so mean? Was he always that way?" Becca asked while hanging a towel on the line.

"No, I don't think he was always that way. Your Papa told me once that when Grandmother Alice passed away, Grandfather became that way. So, I guess that answers your question about why. Your Papa was six when his mother died, but he remembers her gentleness of spirit. I guess Grandfather's grief was so great, he turned on everyone."

"It's sad when grief does that to someone," Becca pointed out.

"Yes, it is," agreed her mother.

Nate's excited voice came to them as they were finishing the job. "Mama, Mama," he called to her.

"What is it, Nate?" she asked as he came running to where they were working.

"Horses. They're bringing the horses," he gasped.

"Slow down and take a deep breath."

After he was able to talk again, he shared with her and Becca that the men were bringing the horses up the valley road.

"Wonderful," Beth said. "Let's go see them."

Beth and her two younger children came from behind the station and headed for the barn and corrals. As they arrived, the herd of horses was driven into the corral where Thad had an opened gate awaiting them. Following the horses was a wagon loaded with hay. The men and Thad got busy right away forking the hay into the barn.

Now the place has come to life, thought Beth. A real honest - to - goodness stagecoach station. It was exciting to watch the horses prancing around as they were placed in the corral. They too seemed to feel the excitement. Nate sat on the fence watching the horses. Beth stood behind Nate as she thought he was too young to be seated up there, especially since he couldn't seem to sit still.

"Hey, little man," Beth said as she put an arm around him, "may I stand here with you?"

Nate nodded, but his attention still remained fixed upon the glorious sight of the horses in the corral. He grew even more excited when he discovered that among the men herding the horses was his new friend, Sheriff Tucker.

"Tuck! Hey, Tuck," Nate cried out. Nate stood up waving and were it not for his mother standing there in readiness, young Nate would have taken a nose-dive into the corral full of horses. Beth had noticed the sheriff even before Nate and was watching him as he moved his horse with skill and agility in the saddle.

Sheriff Tucker rode his horse through the horses to the corral fence where Nate was setting, "Howdy there, Mr. Eastman," he said to Nate.

"Tuck, that's not my name. My name is Nate. Remember?"

"Sure do," the Sheriff responded. "Morning, Mrs. Eastman," he said doffing his hat. "Starting to look like a stagecoach station, isn't it?"

"It certainly is, Sheriff. Do we know definitely that the first sage will come this week?"

"Yep, got a letter here for you from Sam giving you the schedule, but the first one will come this Thursday. This station is about midway from Deadwood to Cheyenne."

"Tuck, Mama made some apple pie this morning. You've got to try it. She's the best apple pie baker in the whole West!" invited Nate.

"Well now, that's quite an endorsement. I just might have to try some if it's all right with your Mama," the Sheriff said.

"Is it, Mama?" Nate implored his mother.

"Well, of course it is. I was going to ask Sheriff Tucker to do just that when he had finished with the horses."

Later, as they were seated inside the station and each enjoying a piece of Beth's apple pie, the sheriff answered questions posed by the four of them regarding the stage.

"Will the stage always come on Thursdays?" Beth asked Tuck.

"Yes, it will be on Thursdays and Tuesdays. It will stop here on Thursdays as it comes from Deadwood. Then at Cheyenne, it turns around to come back and will stop here on Tuesdays."

"Do you know yet when Mr. Eastman might be coming?" Tuck looked at Beth.

"No, Sheriff. I don't," she answered. "Would you like your coffee refilled?"

"Don't mind if I do," he responded, holding his cup to get the refill. "Mighty good coffee and this pie is real tasty too."

"I made it with the dried apples Thad bartered for at Fort Laramie. He traded his antelope hides to the Indians for dried fruits and vegetables."

"Thad, sounds like you were a big help to your folks on the wagon train. Good job," Tuck praised.

When Tuck finished eating his pie and had drained the last of the coffee from his cup, he rose from the table saying, "Got to be getting back to town. Oh, almost forgot. Sam and Martha wanted me to remind you about lunch on Sunday following church."

"What time is the Sunday service?" Beth asked.

"Ten o'clock."

"Tell the Garrisons that we'll be there," Beth promised

Tuck rose from the table amidst cries from Nate and Becca, "Aw, Tuck, don't go yet! Can't you stay a little longer?"

"Nope. Got to get back on the trail. Should get back to town before dark if I leave now. Irish here, he's getting kind of funny about the dark ever since a bad storm we had a while back. Don't want him getting skittish on the way back."

"Afternoon, Mrs. Eastman," Tuck said tipping his hat. "Mighty fine tasting apple pie."

"Thank you, Sheriff. You can tell Martha that I will bring one on Sunday."

"I can hardly wait," Tuck responded, "but your pie is worth waiting for. I'll see you folks in church too."

Tuck went to the corral followed by the three children. Thad helped to saddle Irish while Becca fed the horse some hay by hand.

Smiling from the porch of the station, Beth waved farewell along with her children. *They are developing a good relationship with the sheriff, she thought. They need someone to look up to. I pray, Father, that his influence will be a godly one. He is such a kind man, too. He evidently goes to* church, *but I know that doesn't necessarily mean that he knows Thy Son.*

Nate ran back to the house calling, "Mama, Mama. How many times until Sunday? Tuck said he'd see us on Sunday, and he said to be sure to bring my Bible."

Lifting her youngest up to give him a hug, Beth replied, "Today is Tuesday so that means we have five more bedtimes. Then on Sunday, after an early breakfast and chores are done, we will leave for town."

Squirming his little body to get down he said, "Mama, let me down. I need to get my Bible ready to go."

"Is this the first sign, Father? Help us to follow Thee," Beth said to herself.

After Tuck had gone, Beth sat down with the letter from Sam Garrison. He said basically what Sheriff Tucker had told her. In addition, he had inserted a list of rules for the stagecoaches and for the stations.

DEADWOOD STAGE RULES FOR PASSENGERS

1. Abstinence from liquor is requested, but if you must drink, share the bottle. To do otherwise makes you appear selfish and unneighborly.

2. If ladies are present, gentlemen are urged to forego smoking cigars and pipes as the odor of same is repugnant to the Gentle Sex. Chewing tobacco is permitted but spit WITH the wind, not against it.

3. Gentlemen must refrain from the use of rough language in the presence of ladies and children.

4. Buffalo robes are provided for your comfort during cold weather. Hogging robes will not be tolerated and the offender will be made to ride with the driver.

5. Don't snore loudly while sleeping or use your fellow passenger's shoulder for a pillow; he or she may not understand and friction may result.

6. Firearms may be kept on your person for use in emergencies. Do not fire them for pleasure or shoot at wild animals as the sound riles the horses.

7. In the event of runaway horses, remain calm. Leaping from the coach in panic will leave you injured, at the mercy of the elements, hostile Indians and hungry coyotes.

8. Forbidden topics of discussion are stagecoach robberies and Indian uprisings.

9. Gents guilty of unchivalrous behavior toward lady passengers will be put off the stage.

The image is a black-and-white photograph.

Beth chuckled as she read the rules. Reading on, she found that she would be supplied the food needed to prepare for the meals by the stage company. She could buy what she needed at the mercantile in town by putting it on the company's bill. She would be paid $1.00 per meal by the passengers.

"Thad, I wonder if you would be able to make a leaching barrel for me," Beth said.

"What's a leaching barrel," he asked.

"It's a barrel to make lye water for soap making. You can use the big water barrel from the covered wagon. Here, I will try to draw you a picture."

Beth sketched a simple drawing of what she wanted him to build. "Build a platform, so the barrel sets about three or four feet off the ground. Then build a sloping trough under the barrel to funnel the lye water into a bucket as it seeps out."

"Then when the base is done I can help you hoist the barrel up on it. You will need to cut holes in the bottom first though. Then we will put in a layer of pebbles in the bottom. Maybe Nate can help you collect them from the creek. Then you will need to put two or three inches of straw or dried grass on top of the little pebbles. Nate can help with that also. Then it will be ready to dump the ashes in which I have been saving."

"I think I can do that, Ma. Do you want me to start right away?" Thad inquired.

"Yes, I want to get started on making the lye water. It could take three or four weeks."

"Nate and I will get started on this project first thing after morning chores," Thad said. "Right Nate? You can take a pail and collect some pebbles."

"Yeah, but can we go fishing when we are done?" Nate asked him.

"Sure can."

CHAPTER TWELVE
JOURNAL ENTRIES

April 28 in the year of our Lord 1876

We had been seeing Cheyenne and Pawnee Indians along the trail since we left Fort Kearny. The people on the wagon train were fearful of being attacked. However, they were helpful to us, sometimes helping when a wagon became stuck and trading dried foods with us. Captain Barton explained that they were not hostiles, but it was wise to keep our children close to us. At first, I didn't understand what he was referring to, but one day something terrible happened that made it very clear to me.

I was walking with Becca while Nate rode on the wagon with Thad. We had Buck tied behind the wagon to let him rest. Suddenly a couple of Pawnee braves rode up, one of them dismounting. He came up to Becca and before we could do anything about it, he reached out and touched Becca's golden hair. She was terrified, though not as much as I was. I tried to remain calm and thereby to calm my daughter.

"Trade," said the brave. He handed me the reins to his pony and reached for Becca's arm.

"No!" I said. "No trade! Mine!" I was surprised at my own quick thinking and boldness. I turned away, taking Becca to the wagon. I motioned for Thad to help her up to ride with him and Nate. I turned and faced the Indian with my hands on my hips. I don't think I had made him very happy but he did turn and mounting his horse, led his pony away. Maybe it was because Captain Barton was riding up to see what was going on, or maybe it was my firmly telling him no. Most likely it was God.

"Everything going well, Mrs. Eastman?" he asked, watching the Indian ride away.

"I think so, Captain Barton. That Indian brave wanted to trade his pony for Becca, but I told him no trade, that she was mine. Do you think he will leave us alone now?"

"Maybe, but it would be best to keep Becca on the wagon until we are away from them just to be safe. Becca, sorry you had to experience this."

April 29 in the year of our Lord 1876

Captain Barton ordered the wagon train to stop and make camp early in the afternoon. Word spread along the wagon train about a Mrs. Trenton who was in labor and having trouble. There was no doctor on the train, so Captain Barton looked for a woman to help her. He came to our wagon and asked if I had ever birthed a baby and could I help. Though I had helped once I didn't know that much about it, but as I was the only one, I said I'd come. I told Thad to watch Becca and Nate while I was gone.

It was a long night- one I don't want to relive anytime soon. It was a very hard labor for Mrs. Trenton. She had started with severe back pain early in the morning. Finally, her husband rode up to Captain Barton and told him he needed to stop his wagon, so Captain Barton ordered the wagon train pulled over. The birthing pains grabbed at her so hard, and she had lost so much blood that I silently lifted her up to God. By sun up, the baby was stillborn and Mrs. Trenton, weak from the loss of so much blood, asked to hold her baby. I put the wrapped baby girl in her arms and let her husband in to sit with her. She died peacefully holding her baby. I felt wretched that I had not been able to help her and her baby. Her young husband was grief stricken, as one would expect. I went back to my wagon and hugged my children. Thank you, Lord for my children and for their safety, I prayed.

Before the wagons moved out, a service was held at which Captain Barton presided. Then the bodies of the young mother and her baby were wrapped in blankets and buried in the sandy ground. Following his prayer, we sang "Abide With Me" and "I Need Thee Every Hour.

The wagons continued on their trek, running over the graves, packing the soil in hard. It seemed to me an awful way to treat their graves, but I found out it was to protect the bodies from wild animals that would dig up the graves if the ground was not packed hard. Oh, what a wild country this is, Lord.

April 30 in the year of our Lord 1876

As the wagons bogged down in the sandy soil and got stuck in the shallow Platte, the travelers had to lighten their wagons. Some had so over-loaded their wagons with furniture and silly things that even their oxen could not pull the wagons. Because of that, I saw a lot of things along the trail, from organs to heavy wardrobes. The travelers were learning what was really important. Our wagon was fine because we didn't have any large pieces of furniture. Just the bare essentials.

CHAPTER THIRTEEN
The First Stage Arrives

Thursday morning of the following week found the inhabitants of the new stagecoach station anticipating the arrival of the first stage. Beth had been informed it should arrive at midday and a warm dinner would need to be served for the passengers and the two stage employees. They would not know until the last minute how many passengers would be on the stage, so they had to have enough food prepared to feed however many came. This stage line used a stage which had two seats, each holding three passengers; sometimes four if a child was included. In addition to those six passengers, several second-class passengers could be riding on top with the baggage.

According to the rules, the stage coach driver would blow a trumpet or small bugle as they neared the stage stop. This would give Beth and the children a warning to be ready.

Rabbit stew was on the menu along with some of Beth's fabulous sourdough bread. An apple pie topped off the meal. The children all helped with the preparation. Thad obtained the rabbit for the stew on one of his hunting trips. Becca helped to make the bread and the pie. Even little Nate's services were employed. He was given the serious duty of rolling out the leftover pie dough and sprinkling it with cinnamon and sugar.

Outside, the corral stood ready for the stage's arrival. The horses had been fed and watered. They now stood in readiness for the exchange of teams. Each team was harnessed together so all Thad had to do was unhitch the tired horses from the stage and hitch up the fresh teams one team at a time. As far as Beth could see, he had everything done right. But she guessed they would know for sure before long.

They themselves enjoyed a treat for breakfast. Becca and Nate had discovered the nest of a prairie chicken the day before. They brought the eggs to Beth and she prepared some sourdough bread dipped in the eggs with some powdered milk and water. Topped with sorghum, it was a breakfast fit for royalty.

Suddenly, in the distance, they heard the sound of a trumpet.

"Mama, Mama," Nate called excitedly from outside. "The stage is a comin'," he shrieked.

Beth scurried to the table to do whatever last minute things needed to be done. The tin plates and cups were stacked at the end of the table with the silverware. The stew was warming on the back of the cook-stove, and the bread had been sliced and wrapped in a linen towel in a basket.

"It's ready, isn't it Mama?" Becca asked.

"I do believe it is," Beth replied. "I do believe it is."

Having just stated the obvious, Beth went to the door to welcome her first passengers into her home. To say she was nervous would have been an understatement. The meal wasn't the problem. She knew how to cook and had prepared many meals for larger groups on the ranch home she had shared with Jackson. She was just afraid the security they had experienced in the last few months might not last. Her faith and trust in God needed a little adjustment, she supposed. She paused for a moment of silent prayer asking for that very thing.

Thoughts had been flying about in Beth's mind since last evening. She would vacillate from one extreme to another. Would Thad be able to control those big horses? Could he get the exhausted teams unhooked and the fresh teams in their place in time? He was just a boy. Granted, a seventeen-year-old boy now, but would he be able to do the work of a man?

Thad was as tall as his father had been. He had passed her 5 foot 8 inches ages ago. He was strong. He chopped wood, providing for the station's needs, so his muscles were well defined. He was a hunter, providing food for the family and for the station. He was almost a man. *Oh, Lord. He is a fine lad. Help me not to demand too much of him.*

One fellow jumped down from the stage box and opened the door for the passengers. Pulling the steps down, he helped the travelers to disembark. The stage contained seven adults; two women and five men. One of the men had ridden on top of the stage.

The driver also climbed down. He doffed his hat to Beth and introduced himself. "Howdy, Mrs. Eastman. My name is Matthew Cutter. My sidekick here riding shotgun is Tom Harris. I understand that Mr. Eastman has not arrived yet?"

"That is correct, Mr. Cutter. But my son Thad, will be changing the horses," answered Beth.

"Good, good. Tom here will help young Thad then so he can get the lay of the land, so to speak. Any idée when your man will be coming?"

"No, but I'm sure Thad will be able to manage nicely," Beth provided, sidestepping his query. "Come on in folks. Welcome. Help yourselves to clean water and towels," she said pointing to the workbench just outside the door, "and the outhouse is around back."

As the group completed their ablutions and were about to be seated, Beth stopped them by saying, "Please, there is one thing I would always like to do before I serve the meal. Could you all remain standing behind your chairs for a moment while I ask God's blessing?"

Beth noticed a couple of the men looking at one another shyly, but they held their places with their hats in their hands. The two ladies bowed their heads.

"Father in Heaven, we thank Thee for the food Thou hast provided. We thank Thee for the safety of the passengers thus far. We ask for Thy continued care over these people as they continue on their journey. Amen."

Several murmurs of "Amen" were heard as this weary assembly took their seats at the table.

Beth ladled out the rabbit stew into everyone's bowls while Becca passed the breadbasket. Several of them commented on the delicious stew. One of the lady passengers even asked about the unique flavoring of the seasoning. As Beth explained to her it was dried sage, she silently thanked both God and Jackson for the little herb patch that began it all.

As Beth was serving the pie to her guests, Thad and Tom Harris entered the station having just finished with the hitching of the fresh team to the coach. After washing up, they took their seats at the table and Beth served up the stew. She smiled as she watched her oldest son bow his head and offered his silent thanks to God. She was surprised but pleased when she observed Tom follow suit after seeing Thad's bowed head. *My own little missionary,* she thought, *but really not that little.*

"Time to go, folks" Cutter announced. "Settle up with Mrs. Eastman, and I'll see you at the stage in ten minutes."

The passengers returned to the stage and Matthew Cutter and Tom Harris stood on the porch. "Ma'am, if this meal is a sign of what's to come, you got my vote," Matthew praised. "Best meal I've ever had! Isn't that right, Tom?"

"Sure is," Tom agreed. "And Thad here has the makin's of a first-class hostler." He turned to Thad. "You'll be a great help to your dad when he comes."

Beth took note of the large grin on Thad's face that suddenly faded as he was reminded that he was only "filling in" for a dad who would never come. *Sunday - I will set the record straight on Sunday.*

The Eastman family spent the rest of the day doing chores. Beth and Becca washed the dishes, swept and washed the floor and dusted. Beth thought she would never get used to the dust that seeped into their home.

"Why do you suppose we have so much more dust here than we did at the ranch in Texas?" Beth asked when they stopped for a drink of cold water. "It was drier and windier in Texas than it is here."

"The logs need to be re-chinked," was Thad's answer. "Pa kept on top of that pretty good at our ranch in Texas."

"What is that? Do you know how to do it?"

"It's filling in the cracks between the logs with some kind of mud. I don't know how, but I can find out next time we are in town."

Beth nodded. She supposed come next winter, it would be an advantage too. She could just imagine the snow and cold blowing in the cracks instead of dust.

"When will we be going to town again?" Becca asked.

"Sunday for church and then Sunday dinner at the Garrison's," Beth said, mindful of the promise she had made to herself to tell the Garrisons the truth.

Later that night, the outside chores were completed, supper was finished, and they prepared to wash the dishes. Beth dipped the hot water from the reservoir in the cook stove into the basin. Thad took the dishcloth from her and handed a towel to Becca.

"Ma, you go sit down and rest. Becca and I will take care of the supper dishes. You've had a busy day," he offered.

"That's so nice of you. But I can't have you doing this every day that the stage comes in," Beth countered.

"We probably won't do this every time," Thad explained, grinning. "This first time, it was all new, something you weren't used to doing.

Besides preparing a meal for the stage passengers and handlers, you made two meals for our family, washed dishes twice, not to mention the pies you began making before everyone was even out of bed. To my way of thinking, you should be about ready to drop."

"Well, yes, I am a little weary. But I didn't do it all myself, you know. Becca was a wonderful help. And Thad, you yourself took care of the horses. I'm so proud of both of you."

"This first time it wasn't so bad," explained Thad. "Tom helped me with a lot of it. I just want you to know that we appreciated all that you are doing to help our family get by, without being dependent on someone else."

Beth nodded grimly. She knew who the "someone else" was Thad was thinking about.

"I helped too, didn't I Mama?" Nate asked.

"Oh my. You sure did. Helping set the table and passing the basket of bread. What a help you were!"

"So, Thad. Do you think you are able to hitch up the teams to the stage now without Tom's help?" Beth asked her other son.

"Yes, Ma. I had it pretty well under control. I know horses and teams. It helped to have a 6-up on the wagon train, so I can work with three teams now. Tom explained the necessity of having the leader horses in the front team. Then the swing horses are in the middle, and they take the burden off the wheelers. The wheelers steer and keep the coach in the right line. I can have each team hitched up and then hook them to each other."

"My, I didn't realize there was so much to know about the horses. Glad you know what you are doing, Thad."

As Beth lay in her bed next to her sleeping daughter, her mind wandered back to the time they had spent on the trail and how good God had been to provide them warmth and shelter at different times along the way. What a wonderful God they had.

CHAPTER FOURTEEN
JOURNAL ENTRIES

May 1 in the year of our Lord 1876

At long last we finally crossed the South Platte River. It was two miles across, but the water only came up to the axles. We kept the wagons and horses moving though because of the sandy bottom which acted like quicksand. We followed the North Platte on its south side. There was plenty of fresh clean water with no alkali taste to it as we had been used to from the South Platte. The North Platte was faster moving and clearer. We continued along this river until Fort Laramie. I was so glad to leave that dreadful South Platte behind us.

May 3 in the year of our Lord 1876

After negotiating the climb up California Hill, we had 18 miles to go across the high tableland between the South and North Platte rivers. Then we came to a steep hill into the North Platte Valley through Ash Hollow. It was steep but it was the only hill that didn't have rocky ledges.

It was a frightening day. Getting our wagons down the hill was even trickier than going up. The wagons were let down one by one using ropes. The men helped us to lock two of the wagon wheels and hold the wagon back with the ropes. One of the wagons had its ropes break loose and it plummeted to the valley below. I assume the owners were taken in by other travellers. I was thankful our wagon went down without mishap.

At last we made it down and re-hitched the waiting teams to our wagon. When I looked over my shoulder at my oldest son, I saw no fear in Thad's face. On the contrary, he looked like he was downright elated with the whole thing. It seemed it was an adventure to him. The journey west had changed him, matured him perhaps sooner than he should have been, beyond his sixteen years. I guess if truth be known, I was also a little excited about what we are doing. After all, this was a totally different experience for my family.

I breathed a sigh of relief when at last we came to Ash Hollow. The green valley below offered grass for the livestock, pure water for drinking, and wood which had been scarce up until now. The wood was a welcome change after burning buffalo chips. Heading into this valley, I was able to take a deep breath and relax somewhat. Relax. Would I ever again be able to totally relax and not worry about what or who was behind us? Ever-present in my mind was the fear of pursuit.

Ash Hollow was a cool and shady place. The trees were the first we had seen for some 200 miles. There was plenty of green grass for the livestock to enjoy, abundant flowers, grape vines, and currants. It was a Garden of Eden. I even picked some currants to make a sauce for our biscuits.

The wagon master called for camp to be in Ash Hollow where we stayed for two days to be refreshed by the clear water and green grass. I took some cuttings of the grape vines, currants and even the wild roses. This would help to make our new home more like a home, I hoped.

Several of the women, me included, made use of the clear water to do laundry. The muddy water from the South Platte River was so hard on our clothes, and they never looked clean. We had a warm sun to dry them in no time.

When our work was done, several of us women went to a secluded spot to bathe in the river. It felt so good to get the grime of the trail off of me even if the water was icy cold. The men took their turns at bathing later in the day. We were once again a clean group of travellers.

Thad shot a couple of antelope when the men went out on a hunt for game. We shared them with several wagons. The meat was tender and nice. I liked the antelope meat better than deer. Thad was busy tanning the hides. We were told he might be able to sell the hides or barter them for food supplies when we get to Fort Laramie.

Because May 4 was Thad's seventeenth birthday, I planned a birthday supper for him that night. We invited the Wells family to share with us and we all sang many joyful songs to celebrate. Several nearby travelers, catching the joy of our singing, joined in our songs. We sang "Old Dan Tucker," "Pop Goes the Weasel" (for Nate), and "Wait for the Wagon."

Old Dan Tucker was a fine old man
Washed his face with a fryin' pan
Combed his hair with a wagon wheel
And died with a toothache in his heel

Get out the way, Old Dan Tucker
You're too late to get your supper
Get out the way, Old Dan Tucker
You're too late to get your supper

Old Dan Tucker come to town
Riding a billy goat, leading a hound
The hound dog barked and billy goat jumped
And landed old Tucker on a stump

Get out the way, Old Dan Tucker
You're too late to get your supper
Get out the way, Old Dan Tucker
You're too late to get your supper

Get out the way, Old Dan Tucker
You're too late to get your supper
Get out the way, Old Dan Tucker
You're too late to get your supper

Now Old Dan Tucker come to town
Swinging them ladies all round
First to the right an then to the left
Then to the gal that he loved best

Get out the way, Old Dan Tucker
You're too late to get your supper
Get out the way, Old Dan Tucker
You're too late to get your supper

Pop Goes the Weasel
'Round and 'round the cobbler's bench
The monkey chased the weasel,
The monkey thought 'twas all in fun
Pop! Goes the weasel.
A penny for a spool of thread
A penny for a needle,
That's the way the money goes,
Pop! Goes the weasel

Wait for the Wagon
Will you come with me, my Phillis dear,
to yon blue mountain free,
Where the blossoms smell the sweetest,
come rove along with me.
It's ev'ry Sundy morning, when I am by your side,
We'll jump into the wagon, and all take a ride.
Wait for the wagon, Wait for the wagon,
Wait for the wagon and we'll all take a ride.

Wait for the wagon, Wait for the wagon,
Wait for the wagon and we'll all take a ride.

Where the river runs like silver,
and the birds they sing so sweet,
I have a cabin, Phillis, and something good to eat;
Come listen to my story, it will relieve my heart,
So jump into the wagon, and off we will start.

Wait for the wagon, Wait for the wagon,
Wait for the wagon and we'll all take a ride

May 6 in the year of our Lord 1876

After two days at Ash Hollow, we were back on the trail toward Fort Laramie. We encountered some unusual rock formations which were landmarks for those who travelled on the Oregon Trail. The first was called Courthouse Rock. We went to carve our names on it as several wagon train occupants have done before us. The next day and 12 miles farther down the trail, we encountered a tall spire which looked like a stove pipe or chimney. This was even more unusual than Courthouse Rock. I guess that was how it got its name. It would be about 60 miles to Fort Laramie from Chimney Rock, which signified to the travellers that the Rocky Mountains were near. The trail became more steep and rugged from then on. After Chimney Rock, we came to a gigantic formation called Scott's Bluff.

Thad seemed lost in thought as his eyes took in all our surroundings. I noticed that he also kept a watchful eye not only on his younger siblings, but also on the trail behind us. He was becoming so responsible. I wanted to keep him safe from his grandfather, but I knew I must trust God to do that. Please God, Caruthers must never, never mistreat Thad again.

May 9 in the year of our Lord 1876

We passed a series of what Captain Barton called soda lakes. They were shallow lakes often dried up, though some still have water. The rims of the lakes, or the dried-up lake beds, were coated with snow-white alkali. The travellers called the substance saleratus. It was a bicarbonate of soda, essentially baking soda.

Some of it was as light as ash, which blew in the wind and irritated the eyes and nostrils of both people and animals. Captain Barton said that many travellers used saleratus to leaven their bread. He suggested we obtain as much as we could pack away to use for our baking. Sometimes it turned the dough a faint green, but it worked well for baking over high heat—perfect for our campfires.

The odor was strong, but it made good bread and large quantities could be gathered in a short time. We filled pails, cups, and other containers with it. When it was pulverized, it made a light powder good for baking.

May 11 in the year of our Lord 1876

On May 11 we arrived at Fort Laramie. What a welcome sight - the first signs of civilization we had seen in six weeks. They called it the gateway to the Rocky Mountains. Fort Laramie was situated on the fork between the North Platt and Laramie rivers. The Army was in the process of building a Military Shoshone Indians and their wigwams up and down the sides of both rivers. They seemed to be friendly.

Bridge that would span both rivers. But for us, we had to ford our wagons across them. We had seen the Shoshone Indians and their wigwams up and down the sides of both rivers. They seemed to be friendly and liked to trade goods at the Fort Laramie supply store. Still, I made sure that Becca was close by my side even though it wasn't a Shoshone who approached her.

Those who were going on to Oregon were one-third of the way there. Some were so discouraged by breakdowns, illnesses, and the like, they were actually going back. Not us, as we had nothing good to go back to. However, I didn't plan to take my family to Oregon either. If Mr. Garrison gave us an affirmative answer, this was to be our turning-off point. We planned to head north accompanied by the soldiers going north if he did.

Once we rested, we went to the trading post to replenish some of our food supplies. Luckily, my supplies weren't too low as the prices here were extremely high, so I was glad Thad had kept us in meat along the way. Sugar was $1.50 for a cupful. Of course, sugar was what I needed most but I also bought some flour and more coffee. Thad bartered his antelope hides for some dried fruit and vegetables from the Shoshone. He had three of the hides by the time we got to Fort Laramie. He saved some of the more colorful feathers from the sage grouse and gave them freely to the Indian children, making them quite happy, which in turn made their parents happy.

Fort Laramie also had the only reliable post office within 300 miles, and I inquired for any mail for Jack Eastman. I had informed Sam Garrison he could reply to me at Fort Laramie, and I would pick it up upon our arrival. I was excited to find that Sam's letter was waiting for me, addressed to Jack Eastman, and I eagerly opened it.

Jack Eastman,

I have received your letter applying for the position of stagecoach station operator. I am very happy to know of your interest and I accept your application. As soon as you can arrive here, we can proceed with the necessary arrangements and paperwork. I am also pleased to know that your wife will be able to provide meals for the passengers and crew.

> *The Fort Laramie officer in charge will be able to give you directions as to how best to arrive here in Mustang Ridge. Please come to the mercantile which is where I will be. Looking forward to meeting you.*
>
> *Sam Garrison, Supt.*
> *Overland Stage*
> *Division Director*

I believed this news to be God's answer. We had a definite destination, and it wouldn't be long before we got to Mustang Ridge.

Becca ran over to me really excited. She found a place on the fort grounds that offered hot baths for 25 cents. I pondered the cost. We were really grimy and a hot soapy bath would really feel good. If my Boston acquaintances could see me! I decided we would pay for two baths, one for Becca and me, and one for Thad and Nate. Soap and towels were extra but no matter, I had those. Becca and I went to get our towels and soap while Thad waited with Nate. Nate was not excited about a bath as was to be expected. He liked a good dunk in the river better. Becca went first while I watched the tent flap. Then I had my turn. Oh, how good that warm water felt. I washed the grime out of my hair and then soaked awhile. When I came out of the bath tent, I felt like a new woman. Surprising what a little warm water and soap could do for a body. It was so good to have clean hair as well.

I was told by the fort commander that the troop of soldiers going to Fort Baxter north of Deadwood would be leaving in three days' time and if we wanted to wait for them, they would escort us to Mustang Ridge. Of course, we didn't have to think twice about such a decision. To be protected for the rest of our journey as well as shown the way, was a sign to me that God was watching over us. So, we settled into the busy life at Fort Laramie while we waited. Fort Laramie was a large fort and many things were going on. There was a dance that night and my family went to it, along with the Wells family. I hadn't danced for a very long time. Even on the wagon train I didn't participate in the dancing. But this night I did. Several soldiers stood in line to ask me. I didn't let it go to my head as they also asked Sarah and several other ladies from the train. I knew that the soldiers were most of the time without women in the fort, so it was understandable.

The next day the wagon train left the fort to continue their journey to Oregon. We waved goodbye to friends we had made along the trail and wished them well. Several tearful hugs were shared. Two days later we, the Wells family, and a troop of soldiers, left for Mustang Ridge.

CHAPTER FIFTEEN
The Truth Will Have to Wait

The days quickly slipped by and suddenly, it seemed, it was Sunday. The family rose early so that chores could be completed, and once breakfast was out of the way, Thad hitched up the horses to the wagon. They had removed the canvas cover from the wagon." Come on," he called "we'll be late for church."

"Coming," Beth called from inside. She adjusted her bonnet for the third time as she looked in the mirror. *Oh well, that's the best I can do.*

Beth went outside and climbed up beside Thad on the seat and the two younger children got in the back. Thad took the reins. "Hy yup, Lightning. Hy yup, Bullet."

Beth looked at the blue sky with nary a cloud in it. Such a beautiful Lord's day and she wasn't able to really enjoy it because she was so nervous. Not about meeting the townspeople at church. Well, not totally anyway. It was the promise that she had made to tell the truth. As she thought more about it, she wondered that if the Garrisons knew the truth, would her family lose their position at the station? One time wasn't really enough to prove that they could do it without a man. Perhaps she was in too much of a hurry. *I'll just see what today brings. If the opportunity arises, I will confess. If not, we will give it some more time.* Beth took a deep breath. She felt like a burden had been lifted.

"What's wrong, Ma?" Thad asked.

"Oh, you know me too well," she said. "I had thought about confessing my lie today. But now I wonder if it wouldn't be better to have another stage in to prove our mettle so to speak."

Thad nodded, seeming to understand how this deception was affecting his mother. She was normally as honest as the day is long. It must be really hard for her. And yet he agreed that it was too soon to tell all. They needed more time to prove their worth as she had said.

"Change of plans then," Beth said. "I will wait one more week. By then, two more stages will come. Then I must tell the truth."

Becca leaned through the opening of the wagon. "Mama, do you think we are safe from Grandfather out here? I don't want him to find us and take us away from you." There was a catch in Becca's voice as she said this.

"I hope so, Becca, and honey, I will do everything in my power to prevent that from happening."

Beth looked around the church after entering the front door. It was a small structure but she could tell it was cared for with love. The pews were plain wooden benches. There was a large wooden cross which hung behind the podium. It was so good to be back in a real church again. Sure, they had devotions and Bible reading both when they traveled alone and on the wagon train, but Beth always felt like something was lacking. She thought it was probably joining with other believers in worship. *After all, God's Word says we should not forsake the assembling of ourselves together.* Even while they were living in her father-in-law's home, they had to attend his church, a really cold atmosphere for the high society of Boston. Beth knew immediately it would not be the case here.

"Beth, Beth!" It was Martha calling excitedly from the steps. "I'm so glad you made it." She grabbed Beth's arm. "Let me show you around and introduce you to everyone."

As Beth was introduced to all the parishioners, she saw the Wells family. Beth and Sarah saw each other at the same time and rushed to hug each other.

"Beth, it is so good to see you," Sarah said. "How is everything going? I have heard that you are at the stagecoach station now."

"It's wonderful. I feel like we are now home. And you? Has Jacob opened the blacksmith yet?"

"Yes, and he has even had some business. Would you believe Sam Garrison is helping Jacob with setting it up? It seems since Mr. Garrison is an Overland Trail agent, he is in a position to use a blacksmith to do work for the stage line. Isn't it wonderful how God works in our lives? People seem happy that we are here. I even have a dress fitting next week for a new bride. I'm so glad we decided to turn off the trail when you did."

Beth laughed as her friend's excitement finally ran down. "I'm so glad you did too. Come and let me introduce you to Martha Garrison. Her husband, Sam, is the stage line agent and runs the mercantile."

"Oh, yes, I've met him. He is the one who not only helped us to locate our smithy, but to rent a house in town."

"That's wonderful. Where is your house?" Beth inquired.

"It's at the opposite end of this street. It's so nice to have an actual house to settle in instead of a covered wagon."

"I know just what you mean. We will have to get together for a cup of coffee. I will have to come back into town to get supplies for the stage station on Wednesday. Perhaps we could do it then."

"That sounds wonderful, Beth. I will plan on it and come for dinner."

"We will be pleased to."

Beth observed Martha heading their way and called to her. "Martha, I have a friend I'd like for you to meet. Sarah Wells and her family came out on the wagon train with us. They decided to turn off with us and come to Mustang Ridge. Her husband, Jacob, is the new blacksmith."

"Martha, I am delighted to meet you. Your husband has been a great help in getting us settled here," Sarah said.

"So pleased to meet you too, Sarah. Sam told me about you folks. We are so pleased to have you choose Mustang Ridge. I hope you will enjoy our little town."

"I'm sure we will. Thank you, Martha."

Beth was pleased that her two friends were getting on so well. Martha invited the Wells family to supper on a night next week and they parted company saying, "See you next week."

"Come children. The service is about to begin." Beth directed her family to an empty pew and they were seated. Beth was impressed by the young minister, Reverend Prescott, as he opened the service with prayer. He led the people in several hymns of faith. Following his moving sermon on the power of prayer, he closed with the hymn "Sweet Hour of Prayer." Beth thought it an appropriate and fitting end to their time in their new church.

Sweet hour of prayer! sweet hour of prayer!
That calls me from a world of care,
And bids me at my Father's throne
Make all my wants and wishes known.
In seasons of distress and grief,
My soul has often found relief,
And oft escaped the tempter's snare,
By thy return, sweet hour of prayer!

CHAPTER SIXTEEN
Reflection

Today, Beth's thoughts were on her husband. Jackson only dimly recalled his mother. Alice Caruthers had passed away when Jackson was only six years old. However, his memories were of a sweet lady who enjoyed spending time with Jackson. In fact, it was after her death that his father turned into a cruel taskmaster. He sent Jackson away to Russel Military Academy at New Haven, Connecticut rather than put up with him at their home. When Jackson reached the age of sixteen, he ran away from the school and headed to Texas where he later met Elizabeth Blakewell. They were married and eventually purchased a ranch. The two of them were tremendously happy. Jackson was adamant in telling Beth that under no circumstances did he want his father to know of his family or their whereabouts. He knew the elder Caruthers would make his family as miserable as he himself had been as a child.

It was following Thad's revelation of the whippings that Beth made the decision to run away. In addition to the money from the sale of the ranch, she had squirreled away the money from her bank job in her mending basket. She did not say anything to anyone but thought that it would come in handy someday. As far as she was concerned, that someday had come with a vengeance.

Beth held a family conference with her two older children, telling them of the need to run away. They would pack only what was necessary in one bag each. When the time came, they would all be ready to go with only a moment's notice. She had packed Nate's things, having decided not to include him in the plans since he might have let it slip.

Becca was not eager to leave her grandfather's glorious house. His house had been her one pleasure in the whole matter. He didn't allow her to have friends or join in any outside activities, so she was left to find entertainment in the house. She spent a lot of time in the kitchen with the cook.

Beth thought the day would never come and was afraid that Caruthers would see her nervousness and know that something was afoot. But it did come and they made their get-away while Caruthers was traveling to another city. She knew they couldn't go back to Texas; Caruthers would locate them there again in no time. She knew they needed to find another home far away from both Boston and Texas, find a new life, and live inconspicuously in order to be safe. But would they ever really be safe from Caruthers? Beth was simply following the Lord's leading. After reminiscing about the past, Beth decided to put it all behind her and look to the future. With God's leading, she knew He would direct their paths.

CHAPTER SEVENTEEN
Sunday Dinner at the Garrison's

"Martha, you have outdone yourself again with the food," commented Beth as she helped Martha Garrison to set the table and take the food into the dining room.

Martha laughed. "Oh don't you know it. That's what I do. Anyway, Tuck will be here in about two shakes of a rooster's tail, so I just had to have plenty of food with him coming."

"He does seem to have a healthy appetite," Beth agreed.

Sam called from the living room. "Martha, Tuck is coming up the walk. Is dinner ready?"

"It surely is, Sam."

"Howdy there, Tuck. Come on in. Dinner's on the table," he said, taking Tuck's hat and hanging it on the hall tree.

"Sorry, I didn't mean to hold you up. I had to stop at the Sheriff's office to see if anything important had come up."

"You didn't hold us up at all. You are just in time. Let's all gather around the table for the blessing."

Everyone bowed their heads as Sam thanked God for the food and asked for His blessing on both the food and those gathered around the table. Then they took their seats at the table.

"How did it go with the first stage?" Sam asked.

"I think it went well. We had everything ready for them. They all seemed pleased," Beth answered.

"I knew you had it handled. Good to hear they were pleased. So, Tuck, are there any customers in your jail?" Sam asked as he started the platter of fried chicken around.

"No, not right now. Let the last one go this morning before church services. He got a little rambunctious last night. Kept him overnight to cool off."

"Sheriff, do you just police the town, or does your jurisdiction extend out into the country?" Beth asked.

"Oh, I have a large area," answered Tuck. "It is not uncommon that I am gone for days at a time. As the area grows, there are more calls for my assistance. Ranchers are settling into the area and their ranches are several hundred acres."

"Why are the ranches so big?" asked Becca.

"Cows need a lot of grass. And if you have noticed, we don't have a lot of green growing around here."

"I wondered about that," Beth said. "Our ranch in Texas had more grassland than I see around here. Why do ranchers come here when there is a shortage of grass?"

"Good question, Mrs. Eastman. But you will find they will build a ranch just about anywhere," replied Tuck. "Martha, this chicken almost melts in my mouth, it is so good."

Everyone agreed with the Sheriff that Martha's cooking was superb.

"So, Mrs. Eastman. What did you think of our church service?" asked Tuck.

"I thought it was a wonderful service. You have no idea how refreshing it is to attend a service in a building again, and the people are so warm and friendly."

"I agree," Sam said. "We are fortunate indeed that Reverend Prescott decided to settle here. He came out when Martha and I did, so we've known him a while now."

"We all came out on a wagon train too," Martha said, "so we know what wagon-training is like. We had two wagons, so we could bring some supplies for our store."

"That's right. Martha even drove one of the wagons," said Sam with pride in his voice.

"Reverend Prescott had a wagon for him and his wife, Esther. We knew them back east and it just happened that we came out together. The Reverend had a mission to plant a church in the wilderness."

"Yes, he got right busy building a church. And in between, he called on folks and held services under the trees where the church is now. That is until the building was completed," Martha explained.

"How wonderful," Beth responded. "How long have you been here?"

"About seven years," answered Sam.

"And why did you and your family decide to come west?" Tuck asked, turning to Beth.

Beth nearly choked on her potatoes and gravy. "Uh, that's a good question. We were not happy with our lives in Boston and decided to come west."

"I thought you had a ranch in Texas," Tuck commented.

Will this man ever let it be? Beth wondered. *He certainly acts like the law.*

"We did, we did," answered Beth, wiping her mouth with her linen napkin. "But we were forced to sell it and then we moved to Boston, but that didn't work out for us."

"Well, I for one am glad that you came out west," Martha said.

"Thank you, Martha. I am glad too for many reasons."

"So, Martha, bring on the dessert. I still have a small hole that needs to be filled," said Sam, rising from the table. "Let me give you a hand."

"Yes, Sam Garrison. I know just what happens when you "give me a hand." We'll be lucky if there is anything left to bring to the table after you're done sampling," Martha laughed. "See if you can behave yourself this time."

"Are they always like that?" Beth said, smiling as the Garrison's left the room.

"Yep," Tuck replied. "They are a great couple and very fond of each other."

Beth and Tuck continued for a time in their light conversation. Beth had almost forgotten that she and Tuck were not alone. She enjoyed so much talking with this man. Beth wanted to ask Tuck how he came to Mustang Ridge but was afraid he would get on the subject of her husband coming.

As though he had read her mind, Tuck asked, "Have you heard from Mr. Eastman?"

"No, no I haven't." Surprisingly, Tuck dropped the subject. Maybe it was because Martha brought in her apple cake followed by Sam with a bowl of butter sauce with which to top it.

Thank you for your good timing, Martha.

CHAPTER EIGHTEEN
Tuck's Thoughts

Tuck wondered what Beth… Mrs. Eastman… was afraid of. He could see fear in her eyes when he first got there. Yet she held up her end of their conversation at the Garrison's Sunday table. He enjoyed talking with her, and wanted to talk some more, but he knew he needed to remember she is married and her husband will soon be joining her. This was something else that puzzled him. Why did Eastman apply for the position and then not come? What was holding him up? It didn't make sense to him.

Tuck sure enjoyed spending time with the children and he didn't feel guilty doing that. That little Nate is a prize! Nate made him think of what his own baby would have been like had he lived. In fact, Mrs. Eastman reminded him of his Mary. Not that they look anything alike.

They are totally different. Their character and actions are somewhat alike though. Mrs. Eastman is a nice lady. But she is alone out there with those three children. Who knows what kind of trouble could come knocking at her door.

Tuck decided he could check on them every once in a while. After all, he did have to make rounds out that way. He'd just do it more often than he normally did.

In the meantime, maybe he could fill in for the children's father until he arrives. Tuck really liked that little Nate. And he could still spend time with him and be his friend even when his daddy comes. He hoped Jack Eastman knows what a special family he has.

CHAPTER NINETEEN
JOURNAL ENTRIES

May 14 in the year of our Lord 1876

We nearly had our own wagon train as we left Fort Laramie. The troop of soldiers went first, followed by the Wells wagon and then ours. The military chuck wagon was in front of us. The ammunitions wagon brought up the rear. I certainly felt safe with the soldiers riding with us.

We were on our way north to Mustang Ridge where I hoped we would find our future at the stage station and Jacob Wells would open his blacksmith business. According to Lieutenant Rodgers, it was 80-some miles to Mustang Ridge which meant at our rate of 20 miles a day, we should arrive in approximately four days. My excitement, as well as my trepidation continued to grow. Would we be wasting our time? Would they turn us away when they found out I was a widow?

When we stopped for our first camp, Sarah and I prepared supper for our two families. The soldiers took care of their own needs. I made the decision to tell Sarah and Jacob about our secret. I told them the awful story of why we fled from Boston. I told them we had changed our names, but I didn't reveal our true names. I explained the deception I was living to obtain this stagecoach station position, that of pretending to have a husband who would come to work it with his family. I felt it was necessary to let them know since our families had grown close on the trail. I knew they would wonder about the deception and perhaps unintentionally disclose what I didn't want the people of Mustang Ridge to know right away. They were very understanding though and promised they would not give us away.

Sarah hugged me and told me she would always be my friend and would be there for me when I needed her. I was relieved. I don't know what I thought would happen when I told them, but my fears were unfounded. Jacob promised to help in any way he could if anything should happen in the future regarding my father-in-law.

Two more nights and we would finally arrive at our new home at Mustang Ridge. Would I be able to pull off being an operator of the stage station? And was Thad up to handling a man-sized job with the horses?

CHAPTER TWENTY
Making a Home

Beth and her family continued to spend their time getting things more in line with what a stage station look like. Beth and Becca spent their rest time sewing curtains for the windows. Beth had started teaching sewing to her daughter while they were at the Caruthers estate. She had become quite adept at mending and sewing straight items such as the curtains. From stage relay stations she had seen, some were mere shacks. However, this building was nothing like one. She wondered who had been the previous occupant of Deer Creek Ranch and if they had built it. And why did they leave? It sure was much nicer than other stage stations she had seen, for which she was thankful.

Thad spent much of the day mucking out the stalls in the barn, getting rid of the old stuff, and putting in new straw. The straw had been furnished by the stage company and Sam Garrison had hauled it out last week. Beth felt bad for Thad. After all, that is why he was whipped by his grandfather. Not doing it, rather. But he seemed to have a different attitude about doing it here.

Deer Creek ran behind the buildings and when Thad was done with the dusty job in the barn, he took Nate over to it and they swam and bathed. It was a fair-sized creek and Thad wondered if it might have fish in it. It was cold water and Thad remembered Tuck saying it was run-off from snow melting on the nearby mountains.

"Ma, the barn is all done," Thad informed his mother. "I would like to try some fishing out of Deer Creek. There might be some trout in there. Is that all right with you?"

"You surely may. That would taste good right about now. And to think, we had so much trout on the trail, we were getting tired of it. Is Nate going with you?"

"Probably not. I'd like to see if I can actually catch some first," Thad said laughing. "Next time."

So, Beth took the grumbling Nate into the ranch-house and asked him to help hang the curtains.

"That's girls work! Don't want to hang any old curtains." Nate pouted, stomping his foot. "I want to go fishing with Thad."

"Another time, Nate," his mother promised. "You probably don't remember this, but your Papa used to help me hang curtains. He didn't think it was girls work. He just wanted to help out."

"I guess it's okay then if Papa helped you."

So, Nate helped his Mama to hang the curtains, though he actually caused more work for Beth than he did help. He dropped them on the floor and one time actually stepped on one. But that was satisfactory with Beth. He had to start somewhere in doing responsible jobs. After all, he was only six years old. Later, when she saw the string of fish which Thad brought in from the creek, it made it all that much better.

"Looks like we will be having trout for supper tonight," Becca commented.

"Yes, those three fine specimens should be just right for the four of us," said Beth.

"I'll get them cleaned out back," Thad offered. "What do you want me to do with the innards?"

"Bury them in the garden. It will be good fertilizer. It's a good thing someone had it planted earlier. That should help fertilize what is growing there now. Becca," Beth continued, "could you get out the cornmeal and flour and put some bacon grease in the fry pan? Then we'll be ready to coat them in a mixture of flour and cornmeal when Thad brings in the cleaned fish. We'll make some Johnnycake to go with the trout."

While Becca placed bacon grease in the fry pan, Beth took some warm water from the reservoir in the iron stove and mixed it with cornmeal. Patting the dough into individual cakes she fried them in another skillet. Beth was so thankful for the cast iron stove. She was perfectly capable of cooking over a hearth or even a campfire on the trail, but this was so much better.

As the family enjoyed the fresh trout for their supper, Beth thanked Thad for catching them. "They tasted so good, Thad. Next time you go fishing, please let Nate help you. I think he will be able to help you without causing you problems, won't you Nate?"

"Yes, Mama. I caught lots of fish when we were traveling, remember? I like to fish better than hanging curtains."

After everyone enjoyed a good laugh with Nate, Beth said, "Children, when our chores are done Wednesday morning, we will take the wagon into town and get some food supplies at the mercantile. But first we will stop at the Wells' and visit with our friends."

Nate was excited. "Can I get some lemon drops at the mercantile, Mama?"

"If you are a good boy and help with the chores. Lemon drops are for children who do their chores."

"I will. I will."

CHAPTER TWENTY-ONE
JOURNAL ENTRIES

May 16 in the year of our Lord 1876

At last we had reached our destination. We had come through a pass of the Mustang Mountains and below us was the town of Mustang Ridge. I assumed the peaks rising above the canyon to the east must be Mustang Buttes. The Wells family opted to set up camp on the outskirts along Deer Creek so as to allow us to take care of our business first. They would come into town the next day and get settled. We waved goodbye to both the Wells family and the soldiers. After thanking Lieutenant Rogers for accompanying us, we continued into town, while the soldiers continued to Deadwood.

Thad tied Buck to the back of our wagon. He had taken over the duty of driving while I sat with him. Becca and Nate rode in the back of the wagon. Normally they would be walking, but I didn't want them to be on foot when we came into our future home. I didn't think it was seemly, so we made room for them in the wagon.

Mustang Ridge was a very small town. Nothing the size of Boston, of course. Even Fort Laramie was larger than this with all its buildings, but it was a western town just getting its start and hopefully we would be a part of its growth.

So, we entered town, driving along the main street until we came to Mustang Ridge Mercantile. This was the place the flier as well as Mr. Garrison's letter said we were to go. We were here! Thad helped me down from the wagon and we entered the store. I was surprised at the size of the building and the many goods contained there. For a town of this size, it was quite a going concern. It was indeed a growing community.

CHAPTER TWENTY-TWO
Stocking Up on Supplies

"Horses are hitched up to the wagon, Ma," Thad called. He had hitched only Lightning and Bullet as lead horses and Star and Blackie next to the wagon for this trip. Beth wanted to see about buying another lighter wagon. In that case they would need another team. He had his horse, Buck, also ready to go.

"Coming. Nate, Becca, go out and get into the wagon. Time to go into town."

They both complied while Thad mounted Buck. "Giddy-up," urged Beth.

Beth was excited to talk to her friend since she didn't have much time to talk on Sunday. She wanted to know more about Jacob's blacksmith, Sarah's dress-maker business, and how their children were doing.

They pulled up in front of the Wells' house. "Whoa," called Beth to the horses. Thad jumped down from Buck and was helping his mother down from the wagon as Sarah came running out the front door of their house.

"Beth, I'm so glad you came. Come in, come in," Sarah said, vigorously hugging her friend.

Beth returned Sarah's hug. "I thank God every day that you folks decided to settle in Mustang Ridge too. I didn't feel quite so alone when we said goodbye to the wagon train,"

"I felt the same way."

A she opened the front door and the Eastmans filed into her home, Sarah said, "Children, would you like to go out back where Ben and Isabelle are? They are working on a rock garden."

"A rock garden?" Beth had never heard of such a thing.

"Yes, they plant flowers and cacti in and around the rocks. It's really quite pretty."

Beth's children complied and went outside. Beth looked around. "Sarah, your place is lovely. You've made it so homey."

"Thank you. We may be able to buy it after Jacob has worked a while. Jacob will be coming home for dinner soon. Won't you stay and eat with us? I have plenty. It is a big roast."

"We'd love to, Sarah."

"Good. Let's sit a spell. The roast and potatoes are in the oven, so there's not much to do until dinner time. I can't tell you how happy I am to see you.

"I know just what you mean, Sarah. Are the children happy with being here in Mustang Ridge?"

"At first they both were. Anything to not be walking next to a wagon on a dusty trail. I can sure understand that, but Izzy is at loose ends. She misses Becca."

Beth nodded. "Yes, Becca has been pretty busy but now that things have settled down, I think she is feeling the same way."

"I wish we had a school here in Mustang Ridge. I take care of their schooling at home, but they need friends to play with."

"Yes, I school my children at home too. Are there enough children for a school?" Beth inquired of her friend.

"Probably not yet, but Mustang Ridge is a quickly growing town. Why just last week, a lawyer hung out his shingle and they are trying to get a doctor to come to town. And I hear tell there are plans to open a bank. Professional business people keep moving in."

"If you were to open a school, you would have to hire a teacher, which might take a while," said Beth.

"Funny thing that. I have my teaching certificate," Sarah said with a smile.

"Oh, that is wonderful," Beth said. "How many students would you need to start? I would see that Becca and Nate got here, but Thad at seventeen would be too old."

"That would help. I would have to talk to the town leaders before doing anything further, but I want to get my family more settled before proceeding."

"I understand. Count Becca and Nate in when you are ready."

"Sure will. I see that it is time to get lunch on the table," Sarah said.

"I'll help. What can I do?"

Sarah showed Beth where she kept the plates and cups while she plated up the steaming hot food. At that moment, Jacob came through the door and hung up his hat. He welcomed Beth. Going to his wife and giving her a hug and a kiss, he asked, "Is it time to call the children?"

"Yes, dear. They are out back with Beth's children."

Beth heard Jacob call out the back door to the children that it was time to eat. Then he quickly ducked out of the way as five hungry children of various sizes stampeded into the kitchen. She laughed at the sight. "You must wash up first," she reminded her children as well as the Wells children.

After Jacob gave thanks and plates were filled, things quieted down. Jacob cleared his throat. "Thad, how goes it at the stagecoach station?"

"Fine, sir. I really like working with the teams. The driver says I have a real knack with horses," Thad said with enthusiasm. "I think I'd like to work with horses in some way when I am older."

"You mean, like a stagecoach driver?" Sarah asked.

"No, ma'am. Not that. The driver works more with the stage than with horses. No, I think like a hostler or something like that. Or maybe have a horse ranch of my own."

Beth had not heard of Thad's desires, but she did know he enjoyed working with horses with his dad. It seemed reasonable that he would want to work with them when he was older.

"Like a veterinarian?" Izzy asked. "I think you'd make a good horse doctor, Thad."

"Don't think I haven't thought of it," Thad replied, nodding to her. "It would require schooling. I would need to go away for that. But plenty of time before that kind of decision needs to be made."

My, he sounds more mature than 17 years. It is evident he has been thinking on these things. Give him wisdom, Lord.

"Mama, can I make a rock garden like Izzy has?" asked Becca. "It really looks pretty and we have plenty of rocks out at the ranch."

"That sounds like a good idea, Becca. I'll have to take a closer look at it before we go."

"Any problems with the powers that be concerning the operation of the station?" Jacob inquired of Beth. She knew Jacob was being vague because his own children were not aware of Beth's deception.

"No, Jacob. Things are working out well. They like the meals I have prepared for them, and they are happy with the work Thad is doing. We have another stage coming through this week, and then I shall have to talk to Sam."

"Good to hear. Good to hear."

Beth knew Jacob was concerned about her deception. He felt the same way she did and would be glad when the truth was revealed. He and Sarah had promised to stand by her when she did with whatever happened.

"Jacob, I would like to get a smaller wagon. One that we can use for our family transportation but would not need two teams to pull it. Our covered wagon is way too large for us now. Do you know of anyone in town who might have one to sell?"

"If I were you, I would stop in and see Pete Ballard down at the livery stable. He might be

able to sell you one. Are you going to get rid of the covered wagon?"

"Thanks, Jacob. No, I want to keep it for a little while yet in case I have a need for it, and it comes in handy for hauling things."

Jacob nodded and excusing himself from the table, he said his goodbyes then and left to go to his blacksmith shop.

"Becca, let's help Sarah clean up and wash the dishes. Then we need to get going and take care of our errands. I want to stop at the livery along with the mercantile before we head back."

"Thank you, I appreciate the help," Sarah said. "Beth, I wonder if you would like to get together to make some soap. I have been saving up my wood ash and leaching it in small quantities. But if we did it together, we could make a larger batch."

"What a wonderful idea. Like a quilting bee, only with soap," laughed Beth. "When we first moved into the stagecoach station, I asked Thad to make a leaching barrel so that would make quite a lot for us. Maybe we could ask Martha to join us too."

"I think that is a wonderful idea. I can ask her if she has been saving wood ash, though I'm sure she has."

"Yes, we will have to get our lye water made. Perhaps everyone could bring their wood ashes out to the station and I can get the lye water made for all of us. That will take about three or four weeks to make depending on how much we have."

"Would you like to take my wood ashes with you now?" Sarah offered. "That would save me a trip out there."

"Yes, I can do that," Beth agreed.

Sarah brought her bucket of ashes out to Beth's wagon with Thad's help. "What will you do with the ashes you save for now?" Beth asked.

"Oh, I have another bucket for them. Don't worry."

As the Eastman family thanked Sarah for a delicious dinner, they climbed into the wagon, they drove through town to the livery. Pete was out front working on a wagon wheel when they pulled up.

Beth had met Pete and his wife, Jenny, at the church service the Sunday before. He remembered her and spoke, "Afternoon, Mrs. Eastman. What can I do for you today?"

"Good afternoon, Mr. Ballard. I'm in the market for a smaller wagon, one that would seat the four of us. Do you have anything like that?"

"Well, this one I am working on. It just has the one bench seat, but I have another bench seat inside which I could put in for you. I think it would work for you once the second seat is added."

"Oh, that would be great, Mr. Ballard." After discussing the cost, Beth asked, "How long would it be to do that?" Beth asked, hoping they would not have to make another trip into town to get the wagon.

"Oh, it won't take long at all. About an hour. If you've got other errands to do, stop back in an hour, and it will be ready for you."

Beth was elated to hear it. "I have to get supplies at the mercantile and talk to Sam about the station, so we will come after that."

Beth and her children went on to the Mercantile for the needed supplies. She had two lists. One was for the food needed for meals at the stagecoach station and the other for her family's personal needs.

"Hello there, Mrs. Eastman," Sam Garrison greeted her from behind his counter. "Nice to see you and the children today. Need some supplies?"

"Yes, Mr. Garrison. Here is the list of things I need for the station. Then I have a list of things I need for us."

"Sounds good. I'll work on getting this together for you. You can have a look around and what you can't reach, I'll get for you after bit."

"Thanks, Mr. Garrison."

While Becca watched Nate out on the sidewalk in front of the store, Beth looked at the dry goods rack. She saw a bolt of blue and white gingham. It would make such a pretty dress for Becca, and the red and gray would make a nice dress for herself. In fact she should get some material for shirts for the boys too and Nate's jeans were getting too short for him. Beth guessed this trip would be more about clothing needs than food. Well, maybe they would have to get both. She was really dipping into her savings on this day, what with the purchasing of the wagon also. It was a good thing she would receive payment from the stagecoach line at the end of the month, which was two weeks away.

Beth wondered at the wisdom of spending so much of her savings not knowing if they would be allowed to stay or not. Although she had not thought it through completely, she did have a plan to fall back on. She could open a place that served meals. The only place in Mustang Ridge which served meals was the saloon, not a family-type establishment. perhaps she could open a boarding house and serve meals from there. Either one would require a building, so it would be something to mull over and pray about.

"Mrs. Eastman, I have your order for the station filled. If Thad can help George load it into your wagon, I can get started on your personal items," Sam said.

"Thank you. I want to get some material." She told him what she needed and how much of each.

"Let's all go into my office and talk about the station," Sam suggested, loading the last of the packages into their wagon. Beth paid Sam for the family portion of the bill and they went to his office.

"I've heard some good reports from stage passengers regarding the two meals which you served them. Several say it was almost worth riding on such uncomfortable transportation just to get your meals,"

"Thanks, Mr. Garrison. That is good to hear."

"I've also received reports back concerning the excellent job Thad did with the horses."

"Oh, that is good to know, isn't it, Thad?" Thad was obviously pleased with that report if the wide smile on his face was any indication.

"Mr. Garrison, could you give me some information on how to re-chink the logs in the station? The dust really seeps through. I know my dad did it at the ranch, but I don't remember what he did it with," Thad asked.

"Oh, that is something the Overland Company will supply. We can come out and help you get that done."

"Thanks, Mr. Garrison."

Once the supplies were loaded into the covered wagon, Beth drove down to the livery stable. Pete was just finishing his work on their new wagon. He looked up and waved to Beth.

"Mrs. Eastman, you're just in time," Pete called. "I just finished tightening the extra seat. It's all ready for you to go."

Beth climbed down from the covered wagon and Thad pulled it up closer to their new wagon. He unloaded half of their supplies and put them in the new wagon. Since they would be dividing the teams of horses and the covered wagon was a much heavier wagon, this was necessary. He then unharnessed Lightning and Bullet and hooked them up to the new wagon. Once the harnesses and riggings were all taken care of, Thad tied Buck to the back of the wagon and prepared to drive the big wagon back to the stage station with Nate beside him. Beth settled the payment with Pete, and she and Becca drove the wagon back to Deer Creek Ranch.

When Beth arrived there, she saw Thad was backing the big wagon into the barn. They would not be using it for riding to town now that they had the new wagon.

"What are you planning for lunch for the stagecoach passengers tomorrow?" Thad asked.

"I'm making a stew out of the beef I bought at the mercantile today. I have fresh potatoes and carrots and will use dried vegetables for the rest of it," Beth answered. "Why do you ask?"

"I want to go fishing today and see if I can catch some more trout. I thought maybe I'd build a smoker into the hill back of the station. We could smoke some of those and that would taste pretty good, don't you think?"

"Makes my mouth water to talk of it," Beth replied. "Do you think it would be ready for next Tuesday?"

"Providing I catch some fish," Thad grinned. "I'll go get started on the smoker first. Nate, want to come and help me?"

"No, I want to fish."

"Of course," said Thad. "That's how you will help me. Go get your pole."

CHAPTER TWENTY-THREE
JOURNAL ENTRY

May 26 in the year of our Lord 1876

I have not been able to make any entries in my journal since arriving at Mustang Ridge. So much has taken place and so much work needed to be done.

First, we were given the opportunity to open the stagecoach station at Deer Creek Ranch and to be ready for the first stage in a week and a half. This was done by Sam Garrison with the belief that Jackson would soon be arriving. I hope to tell the truth after we have proved our worth. I have all confidence that Thad will prove to be a worthy hostler, and I know my abilities in the kitchen will pass.

Sam Garrison was the Division Agent or Superintendent for this part of the Overland Route. He was in charge of purchasing equipment and supplies, hiring drivers, blacksmiths, and station keepers.

On the first day we met the sheriff of Mustang Ridge. Sheriff Tucker is a friend of the Garrisons and frequents their table often. The sheriff works with Sam on maintaining the station. He evidently has some sort of vested interest in the station.

The first stage has come and gone. We did an excellent job in providing the services required as the stage driver complimented me on my food and Thad on his skill with the horses.

Apparently, some of the town leaders had planted wheat and corn in the field next to the barn and even vegetables in the garden. They were anticipating having the station open and knew those crops would be needed for the livestock. I have my suspicions that those leaders included Mr. Garrison and the sheriff.

I am hopeful that we will be able to show what we can accomplish. In the meantime, we went to church services in Mustang Ridge and then to the Garrisons for Sunday dinner. Of course, Sheriff Tucker was there. I only took a deep breath when we were able to leave. Not because of the Garrisons. They are wonderful people. No, it's because of Sheriff Tucker. The thing is I like him. He is a nice person and has been very welcoming to my family. My children have taken to him. Will he understand once he learns the truth? I want to count him as a friend like the Garrisons, but he is the law, and the law could notify Caruthers. Still, I will have to let him know as well.

I find myself wishing I was not living this lie when I am around him. Tuck is a kind and gentle man. He cares about my children. I see that he enjoys spending time with them. But I need to be careful as everyone around believes me to be married, and I don't need to start a scandal. It would not be fair to Tuck.

CHAPTER TWENTY-FOUR
Another Stage Run

Beth was up at the crack of dawn preparing a spice cake for the noon meal. Once it was baking in the iron stove, she woke the children and their busy day commenced. Becca made flapjacks for breakfast while Thad and Nate saw to the chores. The chores included feeding and watering the horses, bringing in wood for the stove, and replenishing the water, both for inside the station as well as for the passengers to wash up at the side of the building.

While her family went about their respective chores, Beth prepared the beef stew by chopping carrots and potatoes and braising the chunks of beef in her cast iron Dutch oven. By that time, the sun had begun to peak over the horizon, so Beth went outside behind the building where her herb patch was starting to grow. She picked some sage and oregano and took them inside.

While the stew simmered, Beth made the dough for biscuits to pop into the oven just before the stage was due to arrive. She added the herbs to the simmering stew. *Mmm. That smells so good.*

Beth could hear hungry boys coming back to the house after finishing the chores. Becca set a platter of warm flapjacks and sorghum on the table. As they sat at the table and bowed their heads, Beth prayed.

"Father, we give Thee thanks for the food Thou hast provided. Bless it for the use of our bodies. Help us to be mindful always of Thy loving kindness. Father, I thank Thee for my family and the love we share. Amen."

As the family ate breakfast, they talked about various things that needed doing around the station and inside. Beth didn't know what to call it: the station, ranch-house, or home. They all decided it was time to call it home.

"I have an idea," Becca suggested. "Do you think we could get some chickens?"

"Oh, I'd love some chickens so we can have fresh eggs," Beth commented. She also liked the idea of having fried chicken.

"Can we get a rooster too?" Nate implored.

"Yes, of course," Beth answered. "We would need a rooster for the hens."

Thad agreed with the idea, saying, "I could build a cage for them in the barn with a way to go outside too. How many do you think we will have?"

"I'm not sure. I will talk to Sam and see where we can get them and what he thinks."

"I'll wait then till we know how many we will have. The size of the chicken house will depend on how many chickens we will have."

"Mama, did we have chickens on the ranch?" asked Nate.

"Yes, we did Nate. We had a good-sized flock. Since our ranch was so far from town, we had to be self-sufficient in many ways."

Beth and Becca cleared the breakfast dishes and washed them. When they were done, Becca stacked the tin plates and tin cups at one end of the table. Beth put spoons, knives, and forks in a tin canister and set it next to the plates. The eating utensils were ready, the spice cake was done, and the beef stew continued to simmer on the back of the iron stove. The blue and white enamel coffee pot was warming on the back of the stove also. The baking pan with the biscuits was ready for the oven as soon as she heard the trumpet sound announcing the arrival of the stagecoach.

"I hear it! I hear it!" Nate exclaimed jumping up and down. "The stage is coming!"

"Did you hear it Mama?"

"I did, Nate," Beth said as she slipped the biscuits into the heated stove. "We are ready for them."

Beth left the station and stood on the porch, waiting for the stage to pull up. She wondered how many passengers would be on the stage today. A slight breeze blew a wisp of hair into her face and she pulled it back. *It's such a nice warm day. Good for working in the yard. I guess I'll do that after the stage leaves.*

As the passengers exited the stage, she saw Thad unhitching the three teams and leading them to the corral. She knew he would take fresh horses and hitch them to the stage. She noted that Tom Harris did not help him this time. After all, his job was to ride shotgun, not work with the horses. Beth gave a last proud look to her son and turned to great her guests.

"Howdy, Mrs. Eastman. I've got five hungry passengers, not to mention myself and Tom," Matt greeted her.

Beth noted that the passengers washing up outside were all men. She was glad she had planned for more. She was sure that hungry men could put away a lot of stew. Becca removed the biscuits from the stove and the aroma of them and the stew filled the room.

As the passengers finished washing up and came to the table, she was pleased to note that Mr. Cutter and Mr. Harris stood behind their chairs waiting. The passengers followed suit. They either knew Beth gave thanks before a meal or Cutter had warned them ahead of time. Either way, it warmed her heart.

Soon Thad came in after washing up outside. He had completed the job of hitching up the teams and was ready to eat himself. There was some pleasant bantering between Thad and Cutter and Harris during the passing of the stew and biscuits. The passengers joined them in-between mouthfuls. It was clear they were enjoying the meal. Beth served up the cake amidst shouts of pleasure. One passenger said the cake was the best he had ever eaten. Beth was pleased that her cooking seemed to pass the muster.

Beth saw Cutter look at his watch. "Break's about over gents," he said. "I'll let you boys settle up with Mrs. Eastman for the meal, and I will see you out at the stage in ten minutes."

After the stage left, Beth took the $5.00 she had received from the passengers for the meal and placed it in the clay jar with a lid. It joined the money she had received from the passengers from the first two stages last week. In two weeks, she would receive her pay from the Overland Company. Things were looking up, financially anyway.

That afternoon, Beth kept her promise to herself and worked in the yard. She took the rose cuttings she had obtained at Ash Hollow and planted them in front of the ranch house. She moved to behind the ranch house and planted the grape vine cuttings and currant bushes.

# # #

The fourth stagecoach arrived on Thursday and the Eastman family went about the business of providing a meal for nine passengers. Thad changed out the horses in record time. Beth served the smoked fish Thad had prepared. It really tasted delicious and the travelers seemed to enjoy it too.

Tom issued more praises to Thad and this time even mentioned that he could run his own stage station. Of course, Beth noticed the pride in her son's walk after such worthy compliments from one who knows. Beth stowed the $9.00 away in the clay jar.

CHAPTER TWENTY-FIVE
Re-chinking the Ranch-House

Thad and Nate had just finished the morning barn chores when they heard horses riding into the ranch-house area. Looking up, Thad saw Sam Garrison and Sheriff Tucker riding in.

Nate began to jump up and down with excitement. "It's, Sheriff Tuck and Mr. Garrison" he shouted.

"Go tell Mama they are here," Thad instructed.

"Mama! Mama! Sheriff Tuck and Mr. Garrison are here," he shouted, bursting into the ranch-house.

"My goodness, Nate. Slow down and breathe."

Sam had his canvas carrier with his tools tied behind his saddle. He dismounted, untied the carrier, and dropped it to the ground. Then he went to Tuck and took the large bundle he was carrying in front of his saddle. Dismounting, Tuck took the bundle from Sam and squatted down in front of Nate.

"Nate, come see what I have for you." Tuck uncovered the wriggling bundle to reveal a half-grown puppy.

Nate shouted with glee. "A puppy for me?"

"Yes," Tuck said. "If it's acceptable with you, Mrs. Eastman? I know I should have asked first, but Sam and I agreed that the stage station needs a dog out here."

"That's perfectly fine, Sheriff. It will be good for Nate to have a responsibility all his own. And as you say, the station will need a dog's protection. What kind is it?" Beth asked, eyeing the struggling mass of black and white fur in Nate's arms.

"I don't know that it is any one kind," Tuck answered her with a grin. "He appears to be a little of everything."

"Where did you get him?" Nate asked Tuck.

"While I was traveling around on one of my inspection trips, I came upon a small camp of Shoshone Indians. They traded me the pup for tobacco and jerky."

"So, Nate, what will you name him?" Tuck asked.

"I don't know yet. A name is pretty important, so I need to ponder it a while before I saddle him with something that won't fit," Nate answered, sounding so grown-up.

"A wise decision," Tuck agreed, hiding a grin. "Say Sam, we better get to work chinking those logs."

"That's right, Tuck," Sam answered him. Turning to Beth, he asked, "Will that be all right with you, Mrs. Eastman?"

"Of course," Beth replied. "And Thad can help you. If Becca and I can be of any help, we will be glad to also."

"Ma, did you see where my hat went to?" Thad inquired of his mother.

"It's up on the porch, Thad," Becca pointed out.

"Wonder how it got there," Thad mumbled.

"What we will need is a good supply of sand, dirt, and water. There is a large wooden box in the back of the barn that was originally used to mix the chinking cement in," Tuck directed. "I'll get that out."

Sam filled the water bucket at the well and brought it up onto the porch while Tuck carried the wooden box from the barn. Beth wondered how Tuck knew the box was there. On move in day, he and Thad had worked in the barn, so he must have seen it then.

"I've misplaced my trowel," Sam said searching the yard. "Anyone seen it?"

"Yup. There it goes," Thad laughed, pointing at the puppy.

The new little puppy was carrying Sam's trowel up to the porch where Thad's hat had been found. They also found a few other things that could be attributed to the thieving puppy. Becca's hair ribbon, a bone of unclear origin, and the trowel were some of the things they found,

"Why you little bandit!" Beth exclaimed.

"Nate, I think you have a name for your puppy now," Tuck laughed.

"Yeah, come here, Bandit," Nate called. "Here, Bandit."

Beth and Becca had gone to the creek to fill buckets of sand and Nate gathered dried grass. Thad brought a bucket of soil. They were ready to mix it. Breaking up the dried grass and adding the sand and soil, the men then slowly added water. Stirring it with a board until it was thick and pasty, they began to spread or daub it over the old chinking. The job of daubing took most of the day with all of them helping. Beth served left-over stew that she had simmering on the stove.

It was late afternoon before all four of the exterior walls of the ranch-house had been completed. It was a good job done. Beth thanked Sam and Tuck for helping them do the daubing as the men prepared to leave.

"Mr. Garrison, before you go, I wanted to ask your advice about chickens. We wanted to get some so we won't be reliant on sage grouse for eggs. Can we order some through the mercantile?" Beth inquired.

"Yes, I can order some to be freighted in, Sam replied. "Do you know how many you want?"

"Thanks. Maybe 25 to start with, if you think that would work."

"I'd order 30 then because there might be some loss during the shipping," Sam said.

"Oh, I never thought about that," Beth said. "It will sure be nice to have our own eggs and an occasional chicken to eat."

"And of course, you'll need some roosters," Sam added. "I'll go ahead and order them when I get back to the store if you want. You can settle with me when they come in."

"Wonderful. Thank you. Fresh eggs of our own. Now all we need is milk."

"Got an answer for that. How about a nanny goat?" Tuck offered.

"That would be great. Where would you get one?"

"Same place I got Bandit," Tuck answered. "I can get one next time I'm out their way."

"That is just great!" Beth exclaimed, clapping her hands together. "It will make cooking so much easier with eggs and milk. Thanks, Tuck."

CHAPTER TWENTY-SIX
Tuck

Tuck was anticipating daubing the Deer Creek Ranch house. Not because he loved doing it, but because he had the puppy for Nate. The Shoshone family he visited when he made his rounds was a friendly group. A small family, they seemed to be separate from the other Shoshone further north. Tuck tried to convince Grey Wolf to trade at Sam's mercantile, but so far, he just did his trading through Tuck. They were not quite ready to come into the white man's town, although they had at Fort Laramie.

Tuck was looking forward to seeing Nate's reaction. He always thought a little boy should have a dog. He wasn't disappointed. Nate and Bandit were fast friends by the time he left.

He was glad he had thought of getting a nanny goat for Mrs. Eastman. Tuck would go out to Grey Wolf's again soon to get it for her. He liked being able to help out the Shoshone family, too. He thought if he gave them cash money for the goat, they would reconsider about coming to Sam's for their trading.

Sam and Tuck were getting the Eastman's settled in pretty good. Sometimes though, he forgot that there was a Mr. Eastman, and he would be coming soon. Tuck kept wondering about that. Mrs. Eastman doesn't talk about him at all. For that matter, none of the children do either. Thad does, but mostly in talking about what he learned from his father on the Texas ranch. It's definitely confusing. Don't they have a good relationship with this feller?

And Tuck just thought of something. She'd called him Tuck instead of Sheriff Tucker. He thought, *she likes me. Aw, Tuck. What are you getting yourself into? Better pull back on the reins.*

CHAPTER TWENTY-SEVEN
Berry Harvest

On Monday, after the family had eaten their breakfast and the chores were done, Beth asked Thad, "If you would hitch up the team to the two-seater, we can all go berry picking up on the mountain. Becca, help me gather some baskets and pails."

"Can Bandit come too?" Nate inquired.

Beth looked at Thad who nodded. "Yes, Nate, but you need to make sure he doesn't run off."

Nate picked Bandit up in his arms and climbed unto the wagon. Thad drove the wagon up to the foothills where the chokecherries were thickest. They all got down from the wagon and retrieved baskets for the berries. Thad also took his rifle.

"What do you need that for?" Becca asked.

"We need to stay close together because bears also like berries. I need the rifle in case we get too close to one," Thad replied.

"Bears!" Nate's look of terror was nearly comical. He clutched Bandit even tighter in his arms.

"Just stick close to me, little brother. I'll keep the bears away from you," Thad said.

Beth wasn't so sure she even wanted to pick berries if there was the slightest chance of seeing a bear. She couldn't help but recall the fright they had from the bear when they were traveling, and apparently they were much bigger here in the west.

"Thad, do you think we might see a bear?" Beth asked.

"No, Ma. But I do think it is best to be prepared,"

"Thanks, Thad. For taking care of us."

The Eastman family enjoyed a bear-free morning of picking chokecherries. When they had all their containers filled, they loaded them into the wagon and made their way back to Deer Creek Ranch.

That night while the family sat around the fire just resting and enjoying the solitude, Beth removed a small box from her trunk and brought it out by the light.

"What do you have there, Mama?" Becca asked.

"It's the box of recipes given to me on my wedding day by your grandmother, my mother," Beth answered. "It is a tradition in my family that when a daughter marries, her mother gives her the recipes that she used during her marriage."

"May I look at them?" Becca asked.

"Certainly. Here, set beside me while we both look."

"Are these in Grandmother's handwriting?" Becca asked.

"Yes, they are. She had fine handwriting, didn't she?" Beth said. "One day when you get married, these will be yours."

"Ma, I think Nate needs to go to bed. Look at him," Thad pointed out. His eyes closed, Nate was curled up on the rug in front of the fireplace.

"Poor little guy. He worked as hard as any of us today. Thad, can you take him up to the loft?"

"Sure. I think I'll turn in too," Thad said.

"Yes, we all should."

As Beth prepared for bed in her room, she began to make plans for the truth-telling she would need to do the following Sunday. She had spent a lot of time thinking on how she should do it.

They had once again been invited to Sunday dinner at the Garrison's home, and Beth surmised this was the time and place to unburden herself of her lies. *Lord, please give me Thy strength to do this.*

CHAPTER TWENTY-EIGHT
Another Week of Work

Two stages came through during the week. There were six passengers on Tuesday, and Thursday brought seven. Beth added the $13 to the clay jar with the other income. It was gratifying to be able to put this money aside.

On Tuesday, Beth made a sauce with some of the chokecherries to pour over biscuits. She served this for dessert to the passengers. She and Becca put up the rest of the berries on Wednesday by making jam.

While Beth and Becca made the jam, Thad helped Nate with his schooling. Beth had never stopped teaching her children even as they traveled. She knew knowledge was important for them to grow into fine upstanding adults and encouraged the older children to help Nate.

Beth talked about treaties and agreements between the Indians and the whites. She had taught them a little about the Indians when the brave had tried to trade his pony for Becca near Fort Laramie. Now she talked about how the whites had failed to honor their promises in the treaty simply because of their greed for the gold discovered in the Black Hills where the Sioux lived.

Beth thought this to be a timely subject to study because of word about Indian attacks near the Black Hills. She secretly worried about the safety of the stagecoach and their passengers and handlers. She prayed God would protect them as they traveled in the Deadwood area.

# # #

Tuck had brought them the nanny goat as he had promised. However, he also brought something else – her two kids, or baby goats. After some humorous attempts to milk the poor thing, they finally got the hang of it. Beth debated over who would be responsible for milking her and for caring for the kids, but decided on Becca. Becca wanted to and begged to be in charge of the goats. Becca named the little nanny goat Buttercup. The kids she named Hansel and Gretel.

CHAPTER TWENTY-NINE
Chores

Thad rose early to attend to the livestock chores. Becca was in the barn already milking the nanny goat.

"It's about time one of you sleepy heads came out to do your chores," Becca taunted them. "I've been up and fed my little goat family, and I just finished milking Buttercup. Now I will go to the ranch house and help Mama get breakfast ready and then help with the meal for the stage passengers." Becca rose from her stool with the pail of fresh milk.

Thad grinned. "That's good. I enjoy fresh milk, but don't forget who allows the stages to come through and get fresh horses that are already hitched, ready to trade off with the tired teams. I know you couldn't handle the horses."

Nate entered the barn to lend a hand to his brother as he fed the horses. "Mornin', ya all," he drawled.

"Nate you are so funny. You are starting to talk like an honest-to-goodness westerner," remarked Becca laughing.

"Well, I just came out to tell you that Mama has breakfast ready and is wondering where that milk is. She wants to make a custard with it for dinner."

"Oh right. I'm taking it in right now," Becca hurried out the barn door with the pail.

"Thad, when are we going to get my chickens?" Nate inquired.

"It will take a while. They have to come out on the freight wagons from St Jo, where we started on our wagon train. They come on the same trail as our wagons did," Thad explained.

"That took forever!" Nate exclaimed.

"But it won't take as long for the freight wagons," Thad explained. "They don't go with the covered wagons. They can go faster than the covered wagons. You should ask Mr. Garrison about it the next time you see him. He can tell you when he expects the next shipment and more about the wagons."

"I'm going to be in charge of the chickens," Nate boasted. "You better hurry up and finish building that chicken house."

"I only have the door to put on it," Thad assured him, "but how do you know you are going to be in charge of the chickens?" Thad asked. "Did Ma say so?"

"I guess she didn't say for sure when I asked her about it. But it makes sense that it'd be me because you and Becca have the horses and goats. Don't you see, now it's my turn?" Nate offered.

"Yes," Thad agreed, "but maybe since you are younger, Ma will have you be in charge with one of us to help you."

"I wish I wasn't younger," Nate grumbled. "I wish I was older."

"It'll come, it'll come." Thad patted his brother's back. "Now let's go inside, so we can get fed too."

All three of her children were seated at the table for breakfast. Beth had already started the rabbit browning in the Dutch oven on the cast iron stove. Thad could smell the biscuits as she removed them from the oven. He knew she would be cooking more biscuits later to go with the rabbit, but for now, they would enjoy some with chokecherry jam. Nate reached for a biscuit and was stopped mid-reach as Thad beat him to it and took the biscuit he was aiming for.

"Mama! Thad took my biscuit," Nate whined.

"There's more Nate!" Beth snapped. "What is wrong with you boys?"

Becca looked up from her plate. "Mama, are you feeling all right?"

Beth suddenly sat down in her chair and held her head in her hands. "I am so sorry," she apologized. "I have no excuse. I guess I am just tired. Its nerves. And thinking about telling the Garrisons the truth is wearing on my soul. Please forgive me."

"I'm sorry too, Ma, for snatching the biscuit from Nate," Thad said.

"Me too," Nate murmured.

CHAPTER THIRTY
Sunday at Garrison's – Time for Truth

Sunday morning came and Beth and her family were seated in their same spot in the little church. The opening hymn was "Amazing Grace." Beth's heart swelled as she sang the words of the hymn.

> Amazing grace, how sweet the sound
> That saved a wretch like me!
> I once was lost, but now am found,
> Was blind but now I see.

Yes, Lord. I thank Thee for saving me, Beth thought.

> 'Twas grace that taught my heart to fear,
> And grace my fears relieved;
> How precious did that grace appear
> The hour I first believed

Lord, I thank Thee for Thy grace.

> Through many dangers, toils, and snares,
> I have already come;
> 'Tis grace hath brought me safe thus far,
> And grace will lead me home

Oh, Lord, I feel as though this verse was written just for me. Thou hast brought us through so many dangers. Your grace is sufficient.

Later, they greeted Reverend Prescott at the church door, Sam said to him, "Say, Martha and I want to have you over today for dinner if you are able."

Reverend Prescott looked uncertainly to his wife. Esther nodded and Prescott said, "Of course. We will be there as soon as we close up."

"Fine. Take your time. Tuck will have to check on the jail before he comes, and the Eastman and Wells families will also be in attendance," Sam said. "Martha is excited about having such a big houseful of company for Sunday dinner. She has already hurried home to attend to the food."

Beth felt like her heart had dropped to her stomach. The day she was to reveal her lie, Reverend Prescott would also be there, as well as Tuck. But she didn't see any way around this. The Lord had given her definite direction that she was to reveal all today. Maybe confession with a man of God present would be good for her soul. Yes, get it all over with at once.

"Sam, I think we will head over to your place, so I can help Martha with the preparations," Beth informed him.

"Mama, can I go with Tuck?" Nate asked eagerly.

Beth looked to Tuck. "If it's agreeable with Sheriff Tucker," she said.

"Sure. Nate, you will have to come help me check on things at the jail first though. Think you can do that before you eat?"

"Sure, Tuck. You know I can."

"All right then, Beth said. "I'll see you later at the Garrisons. Bye Nate, Tu..er... Sheriff Tucker."

When Beth knocked on the Garrison's front door, she opened it and poked her head inside. "Yoo-hoo, Martha. It's Beth."

"Come on in, Beth. I'm back in the kitchen," Martha called.

Beth entered along with her two oldest children. She went back to the kitchen with Becca, and the two of them began to help Martha with the dinner preparations.

"You certainly are going to have a houseful of company for dinner, Martha."

"The dining room table pulls out so I think all the adults can be seated there. The children can set at the table here in the kitchen," Martha explained.

"Just tell us what to do and we can help, Martha. Oh, here comes the Wells family now."

Sam had just walked up to the house and opened the door for their family. Sarah and Izzy came into the kitchen and began helping. Sam took Thad and Jacob into the parlor. Jacob shook hands with Thad. "How's it going at the way station?" he asked Thad.

"It's working out great, Mr. Wells. And your blacksmith business? Is that keeping you busy?"

"Yes, it's surprising how much work is coming my way. I am thankful for that," answered Jacob. "Sam thanks to you for helping my family to get this start here."

"Not a problem, Jacob. Good to have your business here. I think you will find the good people of Mustang Ridge and the surrounding country will continue to use your services even more," Sam responded, "not to mention the business from the stage company. Always a wagon wheel needing to be repaired."

A knock sounded at the front door and Tuck entered with Nate at his side. "Come on in the parlor, Tuck," Sam called out. "Isabelle and Ben are out on the back porch, Nate."

Nate looked as though he were torn between the children or Tuck. Thad saw the indecision in his little brother and said, "Come on, Nate. I'll go out with you."

The two of them went through the kitchen to the back porch, and Becca joined them. Jenny Prescott had just arrived in the kitchen, so Becca was no longer needed and could spend time with the other children.

It was a full kitchen of women. They chattered away as they helped Martha prepare the food and set the two tables.

"Beth, will Thad set at the adult table or in the kitchen?" Martha asked.

"I'm not sure," Beth replied. "I'll let him make that decision."

"Yes, it's hard for him, I can tell. He's at that stage of not being sure if he is a man or a boy."

"The last few months he has become more of a man, I believe," Beth said wistfully.

Sarah nodded knowingly. She understood what Thad had accomplished of late and how his lifestyle had changed for him.

"I think the food is ready to serve. I'll let Sam know," Martha said. "Sam, dinner is ready. Let's gather the troops."

The menfolk poured into the dining room, followed by the children.

"The children will be eating in the kitchen, but stay here while we ask the Lord's blessing on the food," Martha directed. "Reverend, would you ask the blessing?"

Following the blessing, Martha directed her guests to their seats. "Thad, there is a spot for you here with the adults or a spot in the kitchen. Where would you like to be?"

Thad looked at his mother, noting her nervousness and flushed cheeks. He knew she was going to tell her story today. He decided he didn't want to be there when she did. Perhaps she would do better without him in attendance.

"I'll eat in the kitchen," he replied. "They'll need someone older to make sure they behave."

Beth was surprised at Thad's decision but on second thought, she understood why he didn't want to be present when she made her confession. She didn't even want to be present herself.

CHAPTER THIRTY-ONE
The Truth Shall Set You Free

As the Garrisons and their guests finished their meal with one of Martha's scrumptious desserts, Sam was about to rise from the table, but Beth stopped him.

"Before you men leave the table, I would like to say something that concerns everyone here, if that is acceptable with you, Mr. Garrison?" Beth asked.

"Certainly. Go right ahead."

"First of all, my family and I want to thank you all for the help you have given us in getting settled here at Mustang Ridge, and for trusting us to take on the stagecoach station." Beth paused.

"However, I need to come clean about a deceit I have been engaged in. The truth is that my husband, Jackson, was killed by a fall from his horse on our Texas ranch three years ago." Beth heard the intake of breathes around the table.

"What happened to the ranch?" Reverend Prescott inquired.

"I was forced to sell it. A mother alone with young children just couldn't cope with a ranch that size. I tried for a time, but felt God was leading me to sell it. We moved into town and I took a position at the bank. It was at the bank that a man who was a banker from Boston came to visit. When he realized my name was the same as his, he investigated and found my children were his grandchildren."

She continued with the story. "Even though Jackson had warned me to never have anything to do with his father back in Boston, I was rendered helpless when he arrived in Texas and discovered us. Like a Texas tornado, he immediately prepared to take the children back to Boston with him. He told me I could come too, but if I interfered, he would charge me as an unfit mother. He was a very influential man and used to getting his way. So, I did what he demanded, thinking that my children would get the things in life that they needed and I could be with them. We went on this way for a year."

"What changed?" Martha asked.

"I discovered that he had been whipping Thad." Another collective intake of breath around the table.

"After that, I made plans for our family to run away at the first possible moment. The sale of our ranch had afforded me a sizable nest egg which I had secretly taken with me. We took a stage, rode horses, followed by a covered wagon to eventually reach Mustang Ridge. We changed our last names to Eastman, which was my father's middle name. I wanted to get my family as far away as possible from Boston. I thought that the wilderness would provide a quiet safety for my family." By this time, the tears were streaming down Beth's face.

"I have been overcome with guilt about this lie I have lived. I wanted to confess it before, but I also wanted to prove to you, Mr. Garrison, and to the Overland Company, that we were capable of running a stagecoach station properly. I believe that we have, but if you want us to leave, I will understand," Beth finished.

Martha jumped up from the table and ran around to hug Beth. "Beth, you poor dear. How awful for you and the children. Of course, we don't want you to leave, right Sam?"

"Of course not, Beth. You have proved your worth, both in the kitchen and Thad with the horses. I think Matt and Tom would mutiny if I didn't keep you on," Sam added with a chuckle.

One by one the guests rose from the table and came to Beth. The women hugged her. The men all shook her hand. Except for one man, that is. Tuck sat with his head down. He didn't get up to shake her hand. In fact, he avoided her eyes as she searched his face for some hint of what was going on with him.

"Sam, I need to get back to the jail. I'll talk to you later," Tucker said. He slowly rose from his chair and looked at Beth. He turned, and retrieving his hat from the hall tree, he left.

There was an uncomfortable silence following the sheriff's retreat. It did not go unnoticed that he had not responded to Beth. Beth felt sick to her stomach. It was what she had feared. Tuck hated her. Oh, why did she feel so bad? And why couldn't he understand like Sam and the others? It was the hardest part for her, Tuck turning away. Why did it rip at her heart so?

CHAPTER THIRTY-TWO
Tuck

Tuck couldn't stay there at the table after Beth dropped the staggering news on them. He felt like he had been punched in his stomach. He couldn't catch his breath. He didn't know what to say. He didn't know how to feel. And still didn't. The more Tuck thought about it, the more he was irritated with her for her lie. She lied to him as well as to Sam. Sam! Tuck couldn't believe Sam was in agreement with this. And Martha, rushing to her side. He felt like his good friends had stabbed him in the back. How can they be okay with this? Even the Reverend forgave her.

Sam even tried to talk to Tuck later that day. He came by the Sheriff's office to ask him about his reaction, to win him over to his way of thinking. He thought Tuck was wrong in the way he was taking it. Surely Tuck could understand the position that Beth had been placed in because of her father-in-law, he pointed out. She was merely thinking of the safety of her children. Yes, Tuck admitted, that did get to him for a time. The thought that someone in their own family treated those children the way he did, really made Tuck feel anger toward him.

However, Tuck's thoughts soon began to move in a different direction. Beth had lied about this; how could he know if this was really the truth? He didn't. This could also be a lie. Deep down Tuck knew he didn't believe this was a lie, but his destroyed ego wouldn't accept it.

Tuck guessed it was the guilt he was having because he was starting to really like her and because it was wrong, thinking she was married. Now knowing she wasn't married; his emotions were all turned upside down.

Tuck guessed he'd better get back to business. He needed to make rounds to the north. He had gotten word about the Sioux attacking ranches. They were angry with the whites because the treaty was not being observed. Once the settlers discovered gold in the Black Hills, the white man no longer respected the treaty made with the Sioux. In fact, a lot of whites didn't even believe the Indians were human. *Must not do much reading of the Scriptures to believe that,* he thought.

Tuck's thoughts lit on the Scriptures for a moment and about what they may say about his unforgiving attitude toward Beth, but he pushed them away and went about his business.

He filled his saddle bags with extra shells, loaded his long gun and his side arm. He rolled clean clothes inside his bedroll and tied it behind his saddle. Tuck filled one side of his saddle bag with dried food and filled up his canteen. He was ready to go warn the settlers of the Indian attacks. Tuck wanted to stop at the Shoshone camp on his way back, too. They could be caught in the middle between the Sioux and the ranchers. He wished he could convince them to move their small camp closer to Mustang Ridge, but that's not likely.

CHAPTER THIRTY-THREE
Stagecoach in Danger

"Ma, the stage is coming in at a dead run. No trumpet sounded!" Thad yelled from the yard. Bandit was also frantically barking.

Beth ceased what she had been doing and drew in a frightened breath. She wiped her hands on her apron and hurried to the door. Thad was right. It was obvious that the stage was in trouble. She had never seen it run so fast. Matt had told her they don't normally run fast as it would wear out the horses too quickly. As it approached the yard where Thad waited, she could see that Matt was not driving. It was Tom. As Tom called to the teams to stop, Thad ran up to the lead and grabbed a hold to slow them down.

"Thad, be careful!" Beth gasped at the recklessness of her son. She could see however, that his action had aided Tom in getting the teams to come to a stop. It was then that she saw Matt lying back against the seat with an arrow protruding from his left shoulder, blood seeping from his wound. That explained why Tom was driving.

Beth hurried to the stage. "Tom, are you injured? How is Matt?"

"I'm fine, Mrs. Eastman. But Matt has an arrow in his shoulder. Thad, can you help me get him down and into the ranch-house?"

"Take him into my room, Thad. Becca heat some water. Nate, help the folks out of the stage and bring them in. You know the routine." Beth was all seriousness as she directed those around her to do her bidding.

Beth had learned much about repairing wounds, but this was the first arrow for her. Because there was not yet a doctor at Mustang Ridge, Beth would have to do her best.

"Tom, the first thing we need to do is get that arrow out of his shoulder so I can work on the wound. Can you help me with that?" Beth asked.

"Sure, Mrs. Eastman. I've had to do this before, though not on a friend."

Between the two of them, they were able to extract the arrow. Beth was thankful that Matt was unconscious during this as she had nothing to give him for the pain. She washed out the wound and sewed it closed using her needle and household thread. She spread an ointment on it which she had obtained at Fort Laramie from the Indians. Wrapping Matt's shoulder with a bandage, she pronounced him ready to be left alone. Closing the door to her room, she went to see to the needs of the passengers.

Beth was pleased that Nate and Becca had given instructions to the passengers on where to wash up and were helping them get seated at the table. Becca was dishing up the hot food. There were only five men riding inside the coach. Beth thought it was probably a good thing there had been no women on board during the attack.

"Folks, welcome to Deer Creek Ranch Stagecoach Station," Beth said. "I'm so sorry you had to experience this. I see Becca is getting you started on your meal. Were any of you injured?"

Beth was assured they were not. They told her that the excitement of the race to the ranch had only intensified their hunger.

"It's a good thing then that I have enough for seconds," Beth assured them with a smile.

Beth took a cup of soup into Matt. He had awakened and was attempting to sit up. He smiled at her. "Thanks, Mrs. Eastman. Tom told me you stitched me up."

"Yes, Matt. I'm so glad you weren't hurt any worse than you were. I brought you some soup. Do you think you can handle some?"

"I think so, thank you kindly."

"Tom, you and Thad go out and get something to eat before the others eat it all up," Beth directed.

"Matt, I don't know what your plans are, but I don't think you should be on the stage. That bouncing around will only open up your wound. You are bleeding through the bandage now as it is. Do you think you could manage to stay here for a few days while you heal?" Beth asked.

"I guess I don't have much of a choice, if you don't mind that is" Matt answered. "Tom can drive the stage. That is no problem. Maybe one of the passengers would be willing to ride shotgun. Tom is going to talk to them."

"It would be best if you did remain here," Beth said. "Is that all you want to eat?"

"Yes, thanks. I'm worn out. Think I'll sleep some." Matt was becoming weaker.

Beth helped Matt to lie back down and taking the soup cup, she went out of the room. The passengers had finished their meal and were getting up from the table. They made their $1 payments for the meal to Beth and prepared to leave. Tom told Beth one of the passengers would ride shotgun.

"Folks, we will be leaving shortly. I just want to tell Matt to behave himself," Tom said with a grin.

As the stage took off with Tom driving and a passenger filling in for shotgun, Beth turned to her children saying, "Whew. That was a bit of excitement we don't need to have repeated. Thank you all for taking over while I worked on Mr. Cutter. Nate even did his best. Speaking of, where is Nate?"

Becca laughed. "He is reading a story to Matt."

"What! Matt was sleeping."

"Not anymore. But in all fairness to Nate, he did look in the door first to make sure he was awake."

Beth went into her room and took out some of her things and moved them to Becca's room. She was proud of her son, hearing him reading to Matt.

"Guess I'll be bunking with you for a while, Becca."

"That's fine, Mama. I hope Mr. Cutter will be fine."

"I'm sure he will be. We will have to pray for him as well as Tom tonight," Beth said.

In the days which followed when Beth was in between chores, she would sit with Matt and talk with him. She asked him about the Indian attack on the stage.

"Did the Indians attacked because the whites broke the treaty?" Beth asked.

"Probably. The United States government signed a treaty in 1868 with the Sioux Indians at Fort Laramie. It gave the Sioux the Black Hills forever. Some of the land north of here was for hunting ground. But the discovery of gold in the Black Hills this year changed that." Matt told her.

"Are we in danger here at Deer Creek Ranch?" Beth asked, worried.

"I don't think so," answered Matt. "It was in the south part of their hunting ground where they attacked us. Still it is best to be on the lookout and be prepared."

Beth nodded. She would keep her children close to the ranch-house. She would close the shutters on the windows at night to double ensure their security. And she would pray for their safety and for the Indians.

"Time for you to get some rest, Matt," Beth said.

"Thank you, Mrs. Eastman," Matt said shyly. "I really appreciate you caring for me and giving up your bed for me."

"Not to worry about that, Matt," Beth said. "I am used to bunking with Becca, and we certainly couldn't turn you away when you were in need. And you can call me Beth."

Tom had told Beth that Matt didn't have a home. He would bunk at Deadwood and Cheyenne. But no real home, so Beth did not have a problem in offering her home to help him convalesce.

CHAPTER THIRTY-FOUR
Matt's Convalescence

As Matt's wound healed, he was able to come out and sit by the fire for short periods of time. Thad and Beth helped him to walk out from her bedroom and usually he ate his meal sitting there. Before long, he was able to walk out to the great room on his own with his arm in a sling. Matt had been pretty weak due to the bouncing in the stagecoach and the blood loss. Tom had hurried, wanting to get him to Deer Creek Ranch so Beth could fix him up. Apparently. Tom's idea was a good one as Matt was now healing.

When Tom drove the stage back from Cheyenne, he found that Matt had improved but not well enough to ride on the stage. Tom had picked up another driver, William Barnett, in Cheyenne so he could get back to riding shotgun. Barnett would be the driver until Matt was back on the job.

Matt was sitting at the table when the stage came in and shared the meal with them. "Glad you're up and taking nourishment, Matt. You had me kinda worried when you got shot," Tom shared with him.

"You were worried!" Matt exclaimed. "I was real afeared for my life too. Real glad you got me into the station here so Mrs. Eastman could fix me up."

"I'm glad too, Matt. And glad that I could help you. Tom is the one who helped take the arrow out of you. I had doctored bullet wounds but never an arrow wound."

"What! You let Tom work on me? I'm lucky to be alive," Matt exclaimed.

"Matt! That's not nice." Beth scolded him.

"I'm just joshin' him." Matt seemed a little chagrined. "Serious though. Thank you both for what you did to help me."

CHAPTER THIRTY-FIVE
Soap Day

On Sunday at church, Beth had discussed with Martha and Sarah the possibility of making soap as soon as possible. They all decided it would be a good idea to get it done given the Indian scare. Before it got any worse, they would meet at Deer Creek Ranch for a day of soap-making.

Sarah came with her children and Martha in their covered wagon. They also brought the lye water they had been preparing for this day. Beth also had been making good use of the leaching barrel Thad had built. She had used her ashes and the ashes supplied by Martha and Sarah which she would pick up whenever she was in Mustang Ridge. They also brought their fat drippings, which would be boiled with the lye water from the leaching barrel.

It was a beautiful day to be outside. Sarah's and Beth's children enjoyed some time outdoors. Thad took Ben and Nate fishing in Deer Creek.

They were excited to bring back a stringer of trout. Thad cleaned the fish and set aside Ben's share to take home with him and the rest he would send with Martha. Izzy and Becca sat with their embroidery hoops, working on dishtowels.

As the sun began to spread its warmth on them, Beth asked Thad to help Matt out onto a wicker chair on the porch. With a blanket over his lap, he sat and watched the goings on with the soap making. Beth noted Matt was beginning to show more color in his face as his convalescence progressed. She was happy with his improvement.

"Sure wish I could help you ladies carry some of those pails," Matt said. "I feel pretty helpless here."

"Well, you are not sufficiently healed to be doing such a thing," Beth said. "Just you wait. You'll soon be back on the stage driving those horses."

The ladies added bones since lime from the bones improved the quality of the soap. They boiled down the bones and added the lime to each barrel of ashes to neutralize salts which lowered the quality of the soap. Sarah and Martha added the lime to the grease mixture and set it aside to harden. While that was happening, they took a break to feed their children, Matt, and themselves. When the soap had hardened, they broke it into small pieces and divided them amongst the three of them. A hard day's work had been completed and Sarah and her children and Martha left for Mustang Ridge. All three women were glad to have this job done. They would have a good supply of soap to get them through until next spring.

Beth was thankful that someone had thought to plant the garden before she arrived. Beth cut some of the herbs and hung them in bouquets from the rafters. She stood back and breathed in the aroma of the sages and mints. Her thoughts turned to the ranch-house she and Jackson had shared in Texas, but this time her sadness did not take over. Instead, it brought a pleasant memory. *I must be moving on,* she thought.

CHAPTER THIRTY-SIX
Matt Returns to Work

Sam came out to Deer Creek Ranch a couple of weeks later to see how Matt was doing. Beth had pronounced him well and that traveling by stage and driving the stage wouldn't affect his shoulder.

"That is good news to hear," Sam commented. "Will Barnett will drive the next stage up from Cheyenne this Thursday and Matt, you can take over driving. Then I'll have Will ride along to Deadwood. He will stay on as a substitute driver for this and other routes."

"Sounds good, Sam. I'm anxious to get back to work." Then as an after--thought, -he added "Not that you folks haven't been good to me, Beth."

"I understand perfectly, Matt," Beth laughed.

"Say, Mr. Garrison. There are a couple of horses that need to be replaced," Thad informed Sam "They are just plain worn out, I guess."

"Okay, Thad I'll see that you get some more horses this week," Sam said.

"Sure, Mr. Garrison. Any time," Thad responded.

"I believe we will do it in the next day or two. I'll see when it will work out with Tuck," Sam said. "See you then. Oh, and Thad, you can call me Sam."

"Okay, Sam," Thad grinned.

# # #

Thursday came along with the stage from Cheyenne. By now, the routine of switching to fresh teams and getting the passengers fed was accomplished with ease. Matt made ready to take on his job of driver, or Whip, as they had learned the driver was sometimes called. Beth could see Matt was anxious to get back to work.

"Matt, we will miss you around here, but we will continue to look for you on your stage runs. God bless you," Beth told him.

"Thank you, Beth. You and the children have been good to me," Matt said, clasping Beth's hand.

As Beth waved goodbye from the porch, she said a prayer for the safety of the stage and its occupants as they headed north once again into Sioux territory.

With the $7 from today's passengers, Beth now had $136 just from the meals in the jar. The reactions from her friends, except for Tuck, showed that she would keep this job and this home. She felt so blessed. *Father, I thank Thee for these blessings.*

One downside, however, kept niggling at her. Tuck had made himself scarce after that day at the Garrison's. She found that she missed him. His sense of humor, his hearty laughter, the way he befriended Nate. Even Nate wondered why they had not seen Tuck.

Tuck had not even come to church and that hurt Beth deeply. To think that her deceit had been a reason for Tuck to stop coming to church was hard for her to bear. Perhaps she would see him when he and Sam brought out the additional horses. She hoped so.

# # #

The day after Matt had left on the stage, Beth heard Nate calling, "Horses comin'. Mama! Thad! Horses!"

"Yes, Nate. We hear you," Beth laughed. She dried her hands on her apron and took it off. She laid it on the back of a chair and hurried out to the corral, watching for Tuck. Thad had the corral gate open for the newly arrived horses.

Sam and Tuck each led three horses by their reins and took them into the corral. Thad closed the gate and helped Sam and Tuck as they removed the bridles of the six new horses.

"Hello Sam, hello Tuck," called Beth. Sam waved to her. Tuck touched the brim of his hat and turned away.

Nate climbed up onto the corral and called, "Tuck. Howdy Tuck. Will you ride me on Irish?"

"Sorry, Nate. Don't have the time. I've got to get back to the office."

Beth's heart hurt for her little boy as she watched the disappointment wash across his face. His shoulders slumped as he trudged back to the ranch-house. *Can't Tuck see how his actions are hurting Nate?*

Later, Beth sat at the table in the great room with paper and pencil while Thad and Nate worked in the barn and Becca swept the floor. Beth was sketching a design for a dress for Becca's birthday but she would need the time to sew. It was hard to keep it from Becca's curious eyes.

"What are you writing there, Mama?" Becca inquired as she swept closer to the table.

"Nothing. My you sure are kicking up dust," Beth complained, picking up the paper preventing Becca from seeing it. "I'm going out on the porch until you are done."

Becca leaned on her broom wondering what that was all about. Her Mama sure had been acting strange lately. Becca supposed it had something to do with Tuck.

Now that she was away from Becca's prying eyes, Beth could continue with the dress pattern. She planned to make a dress for Becca out of the blue and white checked gingham she had purchased from Sam a while back.

Once Beth was done with the pattern, she would cut it out from the brown wrapping paper Sam had given her. It was so hard to do this with Becca always observing what she was doing. She would have to figure out a way to get her out of the ranch-house for a day. Perhaps she could talk to Sarah about Becca going to town to stay with Izzy, maybe overnight. The girls would like that.

In the meantime, she could cut out the material for a shirt for one of the boys. Perhaps she could get the dress cut out while Becca thought she was still working on the shirt. Becca had become a fair seamstress and wanted to help with the shirts. So, Beth gave her one of the shirts to hem and sew on the buttons. My, it was hard to keep a secret. She also wanted to invite some of their new friends in Mustang Ridge to share a birthday celebration for Becca. Her birthday was on a Friday, so there would not be a stage.

CHAPTER THIRTY-SEVEN
Becca Stays with Izzy

Beth and her family took the two-seater into Mustang Ridge. Becca had packed a bag, as she would stay with Izzy until Sunday so Beth could get her dress sewn. It was afternoon when they stopped at the Wells' home. After they had been there for a while, Beth spoke to Sarah about how Tuck was responding to her family.

"I'm so sorry, Beth," Sarah empathized. "I know how important Tuck has become to you."

"I didn't realize how much I like him until he began pulling away."

"Just give it time. He'll come around."

"Yes, but what will Nate do about Tuck ignoring him in the meantime?" Beth mused. "He doesn't understand what is going on."

After a short visit, Beth said, "Well it's time for us to get going. I want to run into the mercantile before we head back to the ranch." She went to the back door and called the children to come to the wagon. "Goodbye, Becca. We will see you on Sunday. Be a good girl now, won't you?"

"Yes, Mama, I will." Becca kissed her mother goodbye. "Thanks for letting me stay with Izzy."

As they climbed into the wagon, Beth noticed Nate was not there. "Where is Nate?" Beth asked Thad.

"He already took off down the street," Thad answered her. Beth shrugged. He would be all right; the mercantile was only three blocks away. She and Thad went in to do some shopping. Beth bought some fresh beef which Sam had hanging. She wanted a roast or two for the next couple of stages coming.

Beth took advantage of Becca's absence to talk to Sam about Becca's birthday. She gave him the invitations for the party for her daughter and asked him to see that they were delivered.

"What are you planning, Beth?"

"A surprise birthday party for Becca, Sam. So keep it under your hat, so to speak." Beth eyed Sam's hatless head. "I plan to make a cake for her and have some party games. You and Martha are invited, too, of course. It will be next Friday. Can you come?"

"We'll be there. George can run the store in my absence."

"Good. Your invitation is in that pile I gave you. Be sure to give it to Martha when you…"

Beth stopped talking as Becca and Izzy came into the store. "If everything is in the wagon, we can get the bill settled and head back."

"Got the bill right here, Beth."

"What about Nate?" Thad asked. "Where is he?"

"I saw him walk down to the Sheriff's office," Sam said. "Maybe you should let him be for a while. It might be that Nate can speak some words of wisdom to Tuck."

"Hmmm. Well, maybe I should let him be for a while," Beth said as she watched Becca and Izzy picking out some sweets.

CHAPTER THIRTY-EIGHT
Tuck and Nate

Tuck was seated at his desk in the office when he heard the door open. He looked up and groaned inwardly when he discovered that his visitor was none other than Nate Eastman, or whatever his name really was. He didn't want to deal with Nate now, or any of his family for that matter. Why couldn't Nate just leave him be?

Brushing Nate off the other day when they delivered the horses made him feel bad in a way. Tuck had seen the look of hurt on Nate's face as Tuck whipped his horse around to ride back to Mustang Ridge. He would have to have been a really bad person not to feel a little guilt over his actions.

Tuck thought Nate would be so dejected he would not want to have anything to do with him after that. But no, here he was in the office. What to do now?

"Tuck?" Nate asked in a small, quiet voice.

"Yes, Nate. What is it?"

"Are you mad at me?"

There it was. The question that even Tuck couldn't really answer. He should have been prepared for such a time. He should have known Nate would pursue this, knowing Nate like he did. But here it was, the clear question of why Tuck was treating the Eastmans the way he was. And he didn't have a clear answer. Tuck rose from his chair and went over to where Nate was standing by the door, waiting for an answer from his friend the sheriff.

"Nate, come sit with me," Tuck said leading Nate to the bench.

"No, I'm not mad at you, Nate. I don't know what to say or how to explain it to you."

"Well, why don't you just start at why you stopped talking to us and even coming to church," Nate prompted him.

Tuck was almost tempted to smile at Nate's simple response. How could he explain this mess to such a young child like Nate?

"Okay. I'll try," he answered. "I don't really understand it myself, but when your mother shared the story about your grandfather and that your father was not alive, I guess I took it too personal. I felt like she had lied to only me and it really hurt here." Tuck put his hand over his heart.

"Tuck, it's all right. That's why Mama was afraid to tell everyone the truth. She was only doing it to protect us. She didn't mean to hurt you, Tuck. Mama wouldn't want to hurt you on purpose. She really likes you." Nate's small hand patted Tuck's arm.

The sheriff's emotions were raw. He placed his hand on Nate's. "Nate, how did you get to be so wise? Will you forgive me?"

"Sure. I will, Tuck. That's what friends do, and I will always be your friend."

There were tears and not just from the little guy. Tuck wiped some moisture from his own eyes also and not a moment too soon, as the door opened again and there stood Beth. It was at that moment Tuck knew why he had been reacting the way he had. Sheriff Adam Tucker had feelings for Beth Eastman. And he knew he had been fighting these feelings because she was married and he had felt so guilty about it, knowing it was wrong. So wrong. But now, he felt like the air had been punched out of him. He couldn't breathe or speak.

"Nate. Thad is at the mercantile. Would you go tell him I will be there shortly," Beth said quietly. "I want to talk to Tuck."

"Sure, Mama. See you later, Tuck."

As the door closed behind Nate, Tuck turned and looked at Beth. Neither of them spoke for a while. Then both Beth and Tuck spoke at the same time, uttering the very same words, "I'm sorry."

"Tuck."

"Beth, let me try to explain," he said, stepping closer to her. "It was such a shock."

"I can understand that, Tuck, in a way. But you stopped talking to Nate – just a little boy –and you even turned away from church. Why stop going to church?" Beth asked.

Tuck bowed his head and tried to explain. "When my Mary died, it was in childbirth. I lost both my wife and my little boy all in one horrible day. I blamed God for taking them from me. It was a long time before I was able to return to my faith. Sam and Martha helped with that. When I met you and your family, I took to little Nate right off because I believed my son would have been like him. It happened six years ago. My little boy would have been Nate's age. I guess that's why I felt so close to him."

"Oh, Tuck. I am so very sorry for your loss. In a way, I can identify with your sorrow having lost my husband, too. And then almost losing my children to their grandfather," Beth said. "It can be very daunting."

"I'm glad for your understanding, Beth. I didn't understand myself until Nate came and asked if I was mad at him. That sweet little boy. I could never be mad at him," Tuck stated.

"Are you mad at me then?" Beth asked quietly.

"No," was his one-word response.

"I'm so glad, Tuck, I'm so glad," Beth said, taking his hand in hers. "Will we see you in church next Sunday then?" Her hand felt warm and comforting in Tuck's hand. He wanted to hold it more.

"Yes, I'll be there, and you can tell Nate I'll save a seat for him."

Beth opened the door to go out, then turned and smiled at him. Tuck thought he would melt on the spot from the radiance in that smile. He sighed. All was well in his world once again.

CHAPTER THIRTY-NINE
JOURNAL ENTRY

June 14 in the year of our Lord 1876

This is the last page in my journal. It seems fitting that now that Tuck and I have aired our differences, I will end this journal, this journal which has detailed our travels from Boston to Mustang Ridge - from being terrified and running away to the joys of new friends and operating our stagecoach station.

I am happy that once again my family and Tuck are on a good footing because I really don't want him out of my life. I hope we can become better friends, maybe more than friends. But I will leave that to God. He alone knows what is best for us.

We have gone through a lot this past year with our traveling here to begin the stagecoach station. We have made some dear friends in the Wells and Garrisons. I don't know what the future holds, but as it says in Joshua 24, "as for me and my house, we will serve the LORD."

Well, I'm down to the last line on the last page. I thank Thee Lord for Thy protection throughout this journey.

CHAPTER FORTY
Tuck Returns to Church

Sunday morning found Beth and her boys on their way to Mustang Ridge to attend church. Thad was driving their two-seater, so Beth was spending the ride in deep thought. She hoped Tuck would be in church as he had said he would. She had not said anything to Nate, not wanting to get his hopes up. She knew, however, that Nate was hoping he would see Tuck after having his talk with him.

"You're sure quiet, Ma," Thad noted. "Something on your mind?"

"I guess you could say that," Beth admitted. "I was thinking about how our life has played out. We have been given the opportunity to continue running the station even though I lied to get it. I feel such a relief my deceit is over and I have been forgiven."

Beth lowered her voice so Nate would not hear. "And Tuck has even come around so that he is speaking to us again. He promised he would be in church today."

"It does have a good ending, doesn't it?" Thad said.

"Indeed, but I am hoping that my deception has not taught you children that a lie will always benefit you. That has been the hardest part of this," Beth confessed, "and I guess I'm a bit concerned about how we will be received by the people of Mustang Ridge."

"I understand, Ma. It was hard on all of us keeping it secret and living a lie. If I've learned anything from this, it is the pain of telling a lie."

Beth patted her son's arm. "Well, here we are." She pulled the yellow bonnet off her head and let it drop to her back by the ribbons. She climbed down the side of the wagon with Thad's help. Straightening her yellow print dress, she took Thad's arm and they mounted the steps to the church.

"Good morning, Mrs. Eastman." Reverend Prescott greeted her. "Good to see you and your family."

"Thank you. Glad to be here." Beth shook his hand.

"Beth, Beth," Martha called from behind. She came up to Beth and vigorously hugged her.

"Now, let's go find our pew and sit down. Not sure about the people of Mustang Ridge – how they will react to you this morning. I guess your news has spread throughout the town, so best start out with a friend."

"Thank you, Martha. You're quite a friend indeed."

Beth was pleased to see Becca coming into the church. "Mama, good morning." She hugged Beth. "I put my bag in the wagon."

"Did you have a good time visiting Izzy?" *It gave me ample time to sew your dress,* Beth thought.

"Yes, I did. We talked about her coming out to the ranch to stay for my birthday. Do you think that would be acceptable?"

"I will talk with Sarah and Jacob to see what we can arrange."

The congregation was on their second song and Beth had still not seen any sign of Tuck. All sorts of questions ran through her head about why he had not come as he had promised. She was glad she had not said anything to Nate about Tuck's promise to save him a seat. Nate would just have been hurt again.

As the song was closing, Beth felt rather than saw him as Tuck slid quietly into the seat between her and Nate. "I'm sorry," Tuck whispered. "I got held up at the jail." He patted Nate's knee.

Beth smiled at him. He had kept his promise after all.

As Reverend Prescott closed the service, he said he had an announcement. "Folks, Independence Day is a few weeks away, but I wanted to let you know that we as a church will have a picnic following the service the Sunday before Independence Day. Everybody in and around Mustang Ridge is invited."

Prescott paused and smiled at his congregation. "That means we will need to have lots of people bring lots of food. God has blessed us with a great country, with good friends, and with a good year. This is a way to celebrate our nation's birthday with our friends and neighbors and even people we don't know. And if any in town are unable to supply food, don't worry. There will be plenty here."

Sarah and her family approached Beth. "Good morning, Beth. How are you this morning?"

"I'm doing well, thank you. I am …"

Beth was interrupted by a group of women approaching her. *Oh, no. This may not end well. Lead me, Lord.*

Grace Norby greeted her. "Mrs. Eastman, I wanted to make a point to say hello to you and your family. My husband, Paul, and I want to tell you we are happy you are here as the stagecoach station operator. What you and your family have been through is just terrible, but we are so glad you have come through this as you have."

"Thank you, Mrs. Norby. I appreciate your support."

By the time the Eastman family had left the church, most of the people in the congregation had stopped to tell Beth that she had their support. Beth was nearly overwhelmed by the outpouring of Christian love from the people of Mustang Ridge. *Thank you, Father. I needed this.*

Tuck took Beth's arm as they left the church following the service. Nate was excited to see that his friend had been in attendance. He settled in beside Tuck on his other side as Tuck walked them to their wagon.

"Oh, I can hardly wait until the picnic," Becca squealed with excitement. "I'll bake some of my cookies. What will you bring, Mama?"

"I don't know yet, Becca. I'll have to think about it. After all, we have plenty of time." Beth laughed and hugged her daughter.

CHAPTER FORTY-ONE
Tuck Visits the Shoshone Camp

Weaving his way through the dry washes and the looming rock ledges of the Mustang Mountains, Tuck made his way to the small Shoshone camp. He enjoyed the family there. To him, they seemed alone, yet they are happy. Tuck wondered how a family could live away from the tribe this way. Did they miss their brothers and sisters? He wondered too, why they had left.

As Tuck pointed Irish along the stream to the Shoshone camp, he thought about the people of Mustang Ridge. Weren't they the same? They had left family behind to come West on the wagon trains, just as Tuck's parents had. He guessed he could understand somewhat how they felt leaving home and family behind. But they had a different culture, so it maybe it wasn't the same.

Tuck was happy living in Mustang Ridge. Even losing Mary and the baby didn't take that away. He had made some good friends in the town. Yes, he would always feel a sadness that Mary died in childbirth, but time had dulled some of the pain and he was no longer angry with God about it.

It was Tuck's belief that the Eastman family had been a major part of his attitude adjustment, and to think he almost let his feelings about Beth's masquerading as a married woman instead of a widow cloud his acceptance of her and her family. Why did he react the way he did? He should have been jumping for joy.

Irish snorted recognition to the Indian camp as they approached. Tuck patted his neck. "Yes, Irish, old boy. You know where we are, don't you?"

The Shoshone family had set up a camp backed up to the towering cliffs of the Mustang Mountains to the north. It would be a good protection from the bitter north winds this winter. However, Grey Wolf wanted to build his family something warmer. He had learned from other tribes and from the whites at Fort Laramie and was intent on building something similar for his family. Tuck had promised he would help Grey Wolf when he was ready. He was particularly interested in building a combination of hogan and a long house. He would build it by using poles and covering the surface with branches, leaves, and mud. It would have poles from ceiling to floor to support the roof. The soil in his area would make the mud more of a type of clay and therefore, his home would be somewhat adobe.

White Eagle ran up to Tuck and Irish. He judged the Indian boy to be about ten years old. It was evident that the boy was pleased to see both him and his horse.

The Shoshone family had learned a smattering of English while they lived outside Fort Laramie. Because of that, Tuck was able to communicate with them in basics. Grey Wolf had moved his family away from the other Shoshones in the south. They were ostracized by the Shoshones because he had taken a squaw outside of their tribe. Prairie Flower belonged to the Blackfoot tribe, an enemy of the Shoshone. However, she was only half Blackfoot. Her father had been white.

Wondering where White Eagle's father was, Tuck both signed and asked. The boy pointed to the corral where his father was roping one of the wild horses they had captured. He would break these horses and then take them to Fort Laramie to trade or sell.

Tuck rode up to the corral and dismounted from Irish and signed a greeting to Grey Wolf. He tied Irish to the corral and looked at the horses inside. Tuck told him that the horses looked good and asked if they were all ready to sell. He shook his head no and pointed at the horse he had just put a rope on.

Tuck asked the Shoshone once again if he would like to sell the horses in Mustang Ridge instead of traveling with them all the way to Fort Laramie. This time, Tuck thought he detected a certain amount of hesitancy when Grey Wolf shook his head no. Perhaps he would reconsider.

Tuck heard a woman's voice calling from outside the family teepee. Grey Wolf turned to Tuck. "Come, we eat."

Tuck nodded and followed Grey Wolf to where the rest of the family was seated around the fire. Prairie Flower was Grey Wolf's wife. White Eagle and his grandfather, He-Who-Is-Wise, were already eating. His older sister, Singing Butterfly, was helping her mother.

No one spoke as they ate the food prepared for them by the Indian women. Tuck knew it was their way, and he was careful not to break that custom. When all had finished eating, Grey Wolf stood and motioned for Tuck to accompany him. He had the poles put together for his adobe hogan.

Tuck spent the rest of the day helping the Indian construct the new home. Prairie Flower brought sticks into the structure once it was complete. She laid a fire in the center. This would help the mud to dry faster. The smoke would go up and out a hole at the top of the hogan.

As the sun drew lower in the sky, Tuck prepared to bid his Indian friends goodbye but not before he had issued a special invitation for the family to attend the church picnic. Tuck explained that it was following the service where they worshiped their God. It would be outside in the church yard when the sun is straight up in the sky. Everyone in Mustang Ridge and the surrounding area was invited. Tuck hoped they would come. It would be an opportunity for both sides to show friendship to one another, but he would have to wait and see. He knew they had attended church services at Fort Laramie. Once again, Tuck talked to Grey Wolf about trading at Sam's Mercantile. He told him that he would introduce him to Sam at the picnic.

Tuck asked Prairie Flower if he could buy one of her bags she made out of tanned antelope hide. She had tanned it to a soft material. She sewed brightly colored beads on the outside and made a drawstring closing. He thought it would be a good birthday gift for Becca.

CHAPTER FORTY-TWO
Becca's birthday Party

Jacob brought Izzy out to the ranch Thursday morning to stay with Becca for a few days. Becca wanted to have her friend here on her birthday which was Friday. Little did Becca know that more people would come to celebrate her birthday. She also wanted Izzy to see what it was like when the stage came in.

Becca ran to hug Izzy. "I'm so glad you came. You are just in time to help me with the potatoes for dinner."

Izzy was excited too and put on her apron she had brought along. "When does the stage get here?"

"Around noon. They let us know by blowing a trumpet when they are nearing the ranch. Bandit also runs around barking, not to mention Nate yelling that the stage is here." Becca rolled her eyes.

"Sounds like quite a commotion," laughed Izzy.

Later when the food was ready except for the biscuits, Izzy jumped up from her chair. "I hear the trumpet!" she yelled. Then she laughed when she heard Nate yell that the stage was coming, and Bandit began barking.

Izzy sure thought it was exciting to have a stage stop at the ranch. When seven passengers disembarked from the stage, she happily went to take the biscuits out of the oven. Beth went out on the porch and took charge as was her custom when the stage came. Soon they were fed, made their payments, and were on their way once again with fresh horses.

All in all, the girls had a great day. They went to the barn and Izzy helped Becca feed the goats. Izzy even took a try at milking Buttercup. She looked at all the stage line horses – at a distance.

After bringing the milk to the ranch-house, the girls took a walk down by the creek. "Nate and Thad catch trout in the creek," Becca said. "Thad even smokes the fish they catch."

When supper was over and the girls had helped with the dishes, they went to Becca's room and played games in their night clothes. The end to a happy day. Becca didn't know that the next day would bring even more fun, although Izzy did, as she had received an invitation for a surprise party.

Beth had not told Nate about the party. Nothing remained a surprise when he knew about it. He did, however, know it was Becca's birthday, so when she was not around, he spent his time cutting up paper and pasting together a card with the flour paste Beth made for him.

#

Friday arrived. Becca was now 12 years old and Beth smiled at her excited daughter. The girls helped with the dishes when everyone was done with breakfast. Since it was a nice warm day, Beth asked Thad to take them fishing on Deer Creek. Of course, Nate went too. This gave Beth some time to bake a Sugar Plum Spice cake for Becca's birthday cake. While the cake was baking, she had fried some chicken and when the cake was cooling, she packed the chicken and some lemonade and took it out to the creek for the children.

"Happy birthday, Becca. I made a surprise picnic for you children to enjoy while you are fishing."

"Thank you, Mama," said Becca hugging Beth.

"Thank you, Mrs. Eastman," said Izzy.

"You are welcome."

The party was scheduled for 1:00, so Beth whispered to Thad that he should have them all come in to change out of their fishing clothes a few minutes before that. She would hang a towel in the back window, so he would know when fishing time was up.

Beth went back to the ranch-house and began her decorating. She unfurled a paper banner she had cut up and hung it from the loft floor. She made a sweet syrup to pour on the spice cake. By then, it was time to change clothes, so she hung a towel in the back window. Then she went to the water reservoir and dipped warm water into a pitcher and took it to Becca's room for the girls to wash up. She did the same in her room where the boys could wash up.

Soon they trouped in, laughing and having a good time.

"There is warm water in your room for you to clean up," Beth told her daughter. "Did you catch any fish?"

"Yes, Thad left the stringer in the creek until we can clean them," Becca answered.

When the girls came out of Becca's room all fresh and in clean clothes, Becca noticed the banner hanging from the loft for the first time. "Thank you," she squealed with delight. But her attention was directed to the yard where buggies were entering. "What's going on?"

"Let's go see," said her mother with a tiny grin, and they all went outdoors.

"Happy birthday, Becca!" was shouted from each buggy as the visitors drew near to the porch. "Surprise," others called.

Becca was indeed surprised. She saw Tuck, Sam and Martha, Sarah and Jacob and Ben, Pete and Jenny Ballard, and Reverend and Esther Prescott. Everyone was invited into the ranch-house where the cake was served topped with the sweet syrup. Following the cake, some birthday games were played with even some of the adults participating. Then Becca opened her presents from the guests as well as those from her family. Her eyes got big when she opened Beth's gift, the blue and white gingham dress. Tuck gave her the beaded Indian bag he got from Prairie Flower. From the Garrisons she received a book titled "Little Women." The Wells family gave her several pretty ribbons for her hair.

As the guests prepared to leave for their homes in town, goodbyes and more birthday wishes were called from buggies. Tuck was one of the last ones to leave and that was because Nate didn't want him to go yet.

"Time for me to go, Nate. I'll see you Sunday."

"Bye, Tuck."

Later in the evening, they were sitting in front of the fireplace. "Mama, you really surprised me. Thank you for a wonderful birthday," Becca said. "The dress is beautiful. I can hardly wait to wear it. And the hair ribbons are the same color as my dress. Did they know about the dress?" Becca asked her mother.

"Yes, I showed Sarah a swatch of the material. The bag from Tuck will go nicely with it too. He told me he bought it from Prairie Flower for you. She is the wife of Grey Wolf where Tuck obtained your goats."

"That's nice. I'm glad he came."

"Happy twelfth birthday, Becca."

"Thank you. Now I'm as old as Izzy, for a while anyway."

CHAPTER FORTY-THREE
Chickens

The freight wagons were due to come in and since no stage was due, Beth and the family went into Mustang Ridge and stopped at the mercantile. Sam greeted Beth as she and her family entered.

"Are my chickens here yet, Mr. Sam?" Nate was excited find out. "Are they, huh?"

Sam laughed as he greeted Nate. "So those chickens are yours. Is that right?" Sam looked at Beth for verification.

Beth nodded and said, "Apparently so, Sam."

"Well, have they come in yet?" Nate was getting antsy wanting to know if the wagons had arrived yet.

"Nate," cautioned his mother. "That's not nice."

"I'm sorry, Mr. Sam," Nate said chagrinned.

"Yes, yes. They are here now." Sam smiled at the reaction he got from Nate. "In fact, they are unloading out back right now. You can go back there and watch if you want…"

Nate didn't hear the last part of what Sam said; he was already tearing through the back of the store. No chicken farmer had ever been this excited to receive new chickens. Nate skidded to a halt at the back door. He watched the teamsters unloading the wagons, his excitement building.

When he observed one of the teamsters bring a wooden crate and he heard the distinctive chirping of chickens, his eagerness knew no bounds.

From inside the store, Beth heard Nate yelling, "There they are! I see them! I see them!"

Beth hurried to the back of the store. She found she was nearly as excited as Nate, though she wasn't jumping up and down like he was. She stood aside as Sam held the door for the teamster. Sam directed him, "Bring the crate through here. You can just load it on Mrs. Eastman's wagon out front."

Beth noticed that the chickens appeared to be full-grown. "Sam, I thought they would be chicks."

"No, they would not have survived the trip on the freight wagons all the way from St. Jo. They are big enough that they should start laying once they become used to their new home."

"So, these chickens are Nate's, huh?" Sam asked with a smile.

"They sure are, Mr. Sam." Both Sam and Beth turned to see that Nate had returned to the store.

"Nate, would you let me help you sometimes? I really miss the chickens we had in Texas." Beth asked her son.

"If I let you help sometimes, they would still be my chickens though, wouldn't they?"

"They surely would, Nate. They surely would."

Thad walked up to the counter. "Ma, could I get some beef? I want to try making some pemmican," Thad inquired. "The Indians at Fort Laramie showed me how to make it. With the dried current we have left from the wagon train, I just need some beef to dry. They made it with buffalo meat but told me I could do it with any kind of meat, like beef."

"I've made that before" Sam said, taking Thad to the cold room where the beef hung. "Here, let me slice off some scraps that you can use. This will be easier to trim off the fat, so you can use that for your liquid."

"Thanks, Mr. Garrison." Thad said helping Sam with the strips while Beth looked on.

"Why would you want to make pemmican?" Beth asked.

"I've been wanting to ever since they told me how. It is a good source of food to have on hand for emergencies or to carry in your saddlebags," Thad explained.

"And it lasts a really long time," Sam added.

"I could help you," Becca offered.

"Sure," Thad agreed. "That would be great."

"Well, now that we have that settled, let's get the rest of our order and head for home," Beth told her family.

Beth removed the money from her purse and handed the payment to Sam. "Thank you, Sam. I appreciate your help with chickens. We'd best get them back to the ranch and introduce them to their new home, right, Nate?"

Beth had to chuckle to herself at Nate's actions. He kept looking behind the wagon seat to make sure his chickens were riding safely on the way back to the ranch.

"Thad, did you get the chicken coop all done?" Nate questioned his brother.

"Yes, Nate. I told you it was done two days ago." Thad hid his grin from Nate.

"Just wanted to make sure."

Later when they reached the ranch, the whole family helped put the chickens into their coop. They wanted them to get used to their new home before they were allowed to roam outside. "What will the chickens eat?" All Nate saw was a water dish for them.

"Chickens eat bugs, dried alfalfa leaves, ground up corn – that sort of things" Thad answered him. "That's why we'll let them out once they are used to the chicken coop."

"Thad, I think you did a fine job building the coop," Beth told him.

"Thanks, Ma. There are little cages inside for them to sit and lay their eggs."

"I see that."

"But don't forget – they are my chickens!" Nate just wasn't about to relinquish any of his responsibility for his flock. As the last one was put in their new home, he closed the door. Thad had constructed the outside coop on legs to keep the chickens safe from weasels, foxes, and other predators. The chickens could enter it by using a ramp into their home – when the door was open. In bad weather they could go into the barn.

"I'm going to go milk Buttercup," Becca announced.

"It is chore time. Guess I'll see that the horses have feed and water."

Thad took Nate's hand. "Come with me and I'll give you some ground corn to give to the chickens. In the morning you can turn them out so they can feed themselves. Then at evening chore time, you will have to get them back in the coop for the night and give them some more ground corn."

Thad paused and turned to his sister. "Becca, want to help me make some pemmican later?"

"Yeah, that's sounds fun. Tell me what to do."

"Yes, and I need to go start our supper." Beth walked into the ranch-house, removed her cloak, and hung it on the hook behind the door. She donned her apron and set about preparing the family meal.

One day I won't have all my children at home for meals. They will soon grow up and leave home. Thad is almost at that crossroad now. It will be a while before my other two are ready to leave, and that is probably a good thing for me.

CHAPTER FORTY-FOUR
Thad and Becca Make Pemmican

"First we have to cut the fat off of the meat and then we will melt it down later. For now, we need to dry the meat until it is almost crisp. Then we pound it down with stones until it's like a powder. We can start the meat drying tonight," Thad explained. "I'm not too sure how long it will take to dry. The Indians told me they do it in the hot sun or over a fire. Since it's not very hot out there, I think we will have to do it inside."

"Thad, maybe you could put it in the oven to dry," Beth interjected. "Even when I'm not baking, it is warm inside the oven."

"Good idea, Ma. Thanks."

Becca helped Thad lay the strips of meat which Sam had furnished on a grate to lay in the oven.

"Seems like a lot of meat," Becca remarked.

"It won't be once we pound it down," Thad replied.

When the two of them had all the meat in the oven to dry, they cleaned up the table and went to bed. They hoped the meat would be dry enough to work on in the morning. Either way, it would need to be removed from the oven as Beth needed to heat the stove up for cooking. If need be, they could finish the drying over the fireplace.

The next day Thad checked the meat and found it crisp, ready to pound. He removed it from the oven and added wood to the stove for his mother to cook with. After chores were done and breakfast had been finished, Thad started getting the supplies ready to make the pemmican.

Together Thad and Becca pounded the meat with stones until it was a powder. Nate even came and asked to help for a while. Thad took the fat and put it in pan over the stove to melt it down. When it was melted, they poured it into the powdered meat until it was moist.

"Now what do we do?" Becca asked.

"It can either be rolled into balls or into strips, but let's make balls. Sometimes they add nuts or dried fruits."

"Let's use some of the dried currants you got in trade from the Indians. Is that okay Mama?" Becca asked.

"I guess that would be okay," Beth answered. "How much will you need?"

"I would think a half cup would be plenty," Thad said. "We will just use them in some of the mixture. We may not like it with the currants."

"I'll go down and get some," said Becca taking a tin cup and heading to the root cellar.

When Becca returned with the dried currants, she and Thad added them to the meat and slowly poured a little more of the melted fat into the mixture to help it hold together.

"If we had some wild bergamot we could add that for flavor," Thad said. "We need to add some salt. The Indians told me salt would help it keep even longer."

"How long does it keep?" Becca asked.

"Evidently for years. Up to ten years, according to Mr. Garrison," Thad answered her.

When the mixture was of a nice consistency to form, they made the balls and set them aside.

"How did the Indians store the pemmican?" Becca asked.

"In leather bags, sealed up tight."

"Sometimes, the pemmican was made into rubbaboo. The pemmican was made into a kind of soup by boiling it in water. Flour was added if they had it."

"Thanks for helping me, Becca."

"Sure, it was fun."

CHAPTER FORTY-FIVE
Matt Returns to Driving Stage

It was Thursday morning and the Eastman family was once again involved in preparation for the southbound stage from Deadwood. Beth had the provisions for the noon meal well in hand. Thad had the horses fed and watered. They were ready to be hitched up. Becca brought in the milk she had just obtained from Buttercup.

Nate entered the ranch-house with a whoop and a shout. "Lookee here, Mama! Three eggs! My chickens just laid three eggs!"

Of course, everyone in the family had to stop what they were doing and come to see the first eggs from Nate's chickens. He was really proud of them. You would have thought he had something to do with laying them. In reality, maybe he did. After the evening meal last night, Beth had discovered Nate sitting on the ramp of the chicken coop softly singing to the chickens. She stood and watched for a while and discovered that it seemed to settle them down for the night. *I wonder if he will do that every night.*

"Here, Nate. I'll take the eggs." Beth held out her cupped hands for the eggs and took them to the counter. "What shall I make with them?"

Nate thought a while. "How many eggs does it take to make egg dumplings?"

"Just two eggs, Nate. Then you would have one egg left over for breakfast tomorrow."

"That sounds great, Mama. Can you make some egg dumplings for the stage dinner? I want Matt to be able to taste them."

"That's right. Matt will return to work." Beth pulled out a bowl and a pan from the cupboard. "It doesn't take long to make egg dumplings, so I will have them ready for dinner. You can go wash your hands and come help me grate the nutmeg to put on them."

Nate was excited to do his mother's bidding. He washed his hands in a hurry, but when he saw his mother watching, he went back and did a better job of washing. Beth grinned.

Nate had just finished grating the nutmeg when he heard the trumpet sounding. "The stage! It's here, it's here." He ran to the door and watched as the stage rounded the bend. He saw that Matt was indeed driving. Nate bounced up and down on the porch, waiting for the stage to pull into the ranch yard. He saw that Thad had the teams of horses ready. He looked back in the ranch-house and saw that his mother was bringing the pot with the stew in it to the table. He saw that the utensils were on the end of the table ready to go. *Good,* he thought.

Six passengers this time – all men. Beth went to the porch and greeted them and showed them where to wash up. After giving a word of thanks for the food, Beth asked them to be seated. "Mama, can I pass the egg dumplings? Nate asked.

"You surely may. And be sure to tell them where the eggs and milk came from to make them, won't you?"

Beth knew she didn't need to remind him, but it would open the way for him to tell them. She handed him the serving dish with the steaming hot egg dumplings topped with butter and grated nutmeg.

The passengers complimented Nate on the dumplings made with eggs from his chickens and Becca's milk from Buttercup. Nate fairly glowed with the praise, but especially so when he served them to Matt. Matt had gotten to know little Nate quite well during his convalescence at Deer Creek Ranch following the Indian attack. He put Nate on his knee and thanked him for taking such good care of him both then and now.

As the passengers settled with Beth over the dinner costs, she inquired as to how Matt was doing. "This is your first full run," she said. "How is it going now?"

"No pain anymore. Just a mite stiff at first. Suppose I will really feel it tonight, but thanks for asking."

"I'm glad, Matt. That could have been so much worse."

"Don't I know it?" Matt turned to the passengers. "All right folks, time to get on the road again. Thank you, Mrs. Eastman." Beth nodded. She noticed that Matt was no longer addressing her by her first name as he had done when he was a patient in their home. She supposed he was being respectful of her in front of the paying customers.

"Adios, Mrs. Eastman." Matt tipped his hat to Beth as he climbed atop the stage.

"Goodbye, Matt. Take care."

CHAPTER FORTY-SIX
Running Bear

Friday night, Beth followed Thad and Nate out to the barn for the evening chores. She watched Nate give some ground corn to the chickens, then he gathered the eggs. Becca had already fed her goats and milked Buttercup and had taken the milk to the house. Thad tossed loose hay into the horses' feed boxes, then went out to the corral and brought them into their stalls.

As he put the last horse into his stall, he saw straw fall down from the haymow. He nodded to Beth and motioned for her to look up towards the haymow.

"Bullet, get over there. That's a good horse. You need some more straw for your bed? I'll go up and throw some more down for you." Beth watched as Thad took hold of the pitchfork and began to slowly climb the ladder to the loft. Once he was up there, he stood and looked at the spot where the straw had fallen through. He was certain something was under the straw.

"All right, come on out of there before I start poking the straw with this pitchfork."

The straw began to move and Thad soon discovered the figure of an Indian boy clad in buckskin breaches and shirt. He carried a bedroll and had a leather bag on his shoulder. Thad put the pitchfork down. "Don't worry. I won't hurt you."

The boy slowly got up. Beth could tell he was scared. She was too, although she could tell by his dress that he was from a different tribe than the one who wanted to trade for Becca. He was also dirty, maybe hungry too.

"Do you speak any English?" Thad asked.

The boy nodded and gave the sign for a small amount.

"My name is Thad. This is my mother, Beth. What is your name?"

"Running Bear."

"Nice to meet you, Running Bear. Are you hungry?"

When the boy nodded, Beth said, "Come. I'll get you some food."

The Indian boy followed them, not sure if he should trust Thad and Beth or not. When Thad led him up to the porch of the ranch-house, the boy held back. "It's all right, Running Bear. My mother will get us something to eat."

Becca was putting the milk away and looked up as the door opened to reveal Thad with an Indian boy. Beth got a plate of food for him and pointed to the chair as she set the plate on the table. She studied the boy. He was perhaps twelve years old and stood ramrod straight. He wore a blue bandana around his head, holding back his medium length black hair. On his back he carried a bedroll and on his shoulder was a fringed leather bag with colorful beading. Also, on his back was a bow case and quiver of arrows. He removed them and set them on the floor as he prepared to sit on the chair.

"Who do you have there, Thad?" Becca asked. Beth noted a look of apprehension in her daughter's eyes.

"His name is Running Bear and he's hungry," Beth said. "You boys have a seat. Running Bear, you come and have a seat too. I'll help Becca dish up the food."

Nate entered the house and set his basket of eggs by the door. He washed his hands and came to the table.

"Come sit, Nate. Running Bear, this is my daughter Becca and my youngest son, Nate. You've already met my oldest son, Thad." Beth began serving the pieces of fried rabbit unto plates.

"Where is your home?" Beth asked.

"No home, parents die of sickness. Tribe burn teepee, run away."

"Oh, how awful for you. Where did you come from?" Becca's curiosity was stronger than her fear of an Indian. Even though Beth had attempted to keep her hidden from the sight of Indians on the wagon train, here was a young Indian boy at their very table.

"Fort Laramie."

"Goodness, that's a long way. Did you ride or walk?" Beth inquired.

"Walk. No horse."

"Well, no wonder you were hungry. That's a fair piece to travel on foot," Becca observed. Running Bear shrugged his shoulders.

"How old are you, Running Bear?" Beth asked him.

"I have seen thirteen summers," he responded with pride.

"What are you doing all the way up here?"

"Look for Grey Wolf. Want to stay with him. He is of my family."

"That's the name of the head of the Shoshone family that Tuck has been visiting, Ma. He can show Running Bear how to get there," Thad said.

"That's a great idea, Thad. Running Bear, my son could take you tomorrow to this man that knows where your people are. Would you mind staying here with us until he can take you in the morning?"

"Good," the Indian boy grunted.

They had finished the evening meal and the dishes were washed and food put away. Beth watched the Indian boy. It was obvious he was used to white people and his grasp of the English language was not too bad. She noticed that he sat cross-legged on the chair. He was probably more comfortable sitting on the floor.

"Thad, would you show Running Bear where he can spread his pallet in the loft."

"Sure. Come with me," he said, leading the way to the ladder. Running Bear picked up his fringed shoulder bag and bedroll and followed Thad up to the loft. "Goodnight, Ma," Thad called.

Later when Beth retired to her bedroom, she thought of the young Indian boy who had walked so far to find someone who could accept him, and thanked God for bringing him safely to them.

Father, I pray for Thy leading in this boy's life. Help him as Thou hast helped my family. And thank Thee for Thy favor on us. And I am so thankful that Tuck has been able to work through his hurt and anger with Thy help,

The next morning, Beth prepared flapjacks for breakfast. Running Bear rolled his up and dipped it in the sorghum. She thought it was a good thing she had fixed rabbit last night. Soup would not have worked very well. Nate thought it was a good way to eat flapjacks, so he followed suit.

Thad asked Running Bear to help him with his chores. Thad was surprised when Running Bear picked up his spear which he had hidden in the barn. It was probably a good thing that the boy had not brought it to the ranch-house. It might have upset his mother and sister. Then Thad saddled Buck and got another horse for Running Bear. He wanted to ride bare-back, so no saddle was needed. Telling Beth they were heading into Mustang Ridge, the two of them left for town.

CHAPTER FORTY-SEVEN
Tuck and Running Bear

When the door to the sheriff's office opened, Tuck was surprised to see Thad with a young Indian boy. "Hello, Thad. Can I help you?"

"Yes, this is Running Bear. He came up from Fort Laramie to find his family, Grey Wolf. We were wondering if you could take him."

"Running Bear, good to meet you. I'm the sheriff here. You can call me Tuck. I can take you out there if you like. I have been to their camp several times. Grey Wolf and I have become friends. We can leave now if that is okay."

Running Bear nodded and Tuck buckled his gun belt to his waist and grabbed his jacket.

"Okay, ready then?"

Running Bear motioned for Thad to come too. Tuck saw that and asked, "Thad, would you like to come with us?"

"Sure."

So, the three of them mounted their horses and headed out of town. A few towns-people saw them, but Indians were not rare in the territory so they went back to their business without further thought.

Tuck was interested in talking with young Running Bear. He was more proficient with English than Grey Wolf, so he could communicate easier. He could see that Running Bear was indeed used to being around white people.

When they neared Grey Wolf's camp, White Eagle came running up to them. He was excited to see Tuck, but when he saw Running Bear with them, he whooped for joy. The rest of the family came to greet him also. Tuck could see that the warm welcome their young relative received meant a lot to him. He watched as Running Bear explained the death of his family and loss of his home. Apparently, from what Tuck could gather, Running Bear was a cousin to Grey Wolf.

Prairie Flower showed their cousin where he could put his bedroll and other things. The guys went to the corral and Grey Wolf showed Tuck his herd of twenty mustangs ready to be sold. He also asked Tuck some more about Mustang Ridge and he could tell he almost had him convinced.

"The church picnic is seven days from tomorrow. Come join in and I will help you meet the men who will buy your horses. Two men for sure: Sam Garrison at the mercantile and Pete Ballard at the Livery."

Finally, Grey Wolf nodded. "We come."

"The horses look good, Grey Wolf. You will have no trouble selling them in Mustang Ridge," Tuck told him. Grey Wolf nodded: whether in agreement or acknowledgment, Tuck was not sure.

They began their journey back to Mustang Ridge with Thad leading his second horse which Running Bear had ridden. Even though it was close to mid-day, they didn't stay to eat with the family. They had not been asked, and Tuck didn't want to presume upon their hospitality any more than necessary. Tuck had asked them to be his guests at the church picnic.

The fact that they had dealt quite a bit with the whites at Fort Laramie was probably the reason they had not refused his invitation right off. Tuck hoped it would work out all right for them. He thought he knew the folks of Mustang Ridge and how they would receive the Indian family, but he would still give a few of them a heads up.

Thad shared his pemmican with Tuck which he now carried in his saddle bag. Tuck pronounced it very good.

They parted ways outside of Mustang Ridge, Thad heading on back to Deer Creek Ranch and the sheriff on into town. Tuck pulled up in front of the mercantile and tied Irish to the railing. He went in and found Sam at the counter.

"Howdy, Tuck. I heard you went out to the Shoshone camp with Thad and an Indian boy."

"Word sure does get around, doesn't it?" he laughed. "Thad found him in the barn last night so they kept him overnight and brought him in to me this morning. Seems his only family left is Grey Wolf, so he was traveling by foot up from Fort Laramie looking for his camp."

"Amazing. Was Grey Wolf open to taking him in?" Sam asked.

"He was. Family is important to Grey Wolf, though his tribe more or less shunned him because he married a Blackfoot woman whose father was white. Blackfoot and Shoshone are enemies, so Grey Wolf's tribe didn't accept her."

"That's too bad," Sam replied. "Families are important in any culture."

"The Shoshone go off by themselves in family groups. He-Who-Is-Wise, the grandfather, is with them."

"Anyway, reason I stopped was to let you know I invited Grey Wolf and his family to come to the church picnic. He finally agreed this morning and said that they would come."

Sam's eyes opened wide. "Really!"

"Grey Wolf has about twenty mustangs he is ready to sell or trade. He has been making the long trip to Fort Laramie with them, but I convinced him to bring them here to Mustang Ridge instead."

"Great idea, Tuck. I could take several off his hands."

"That's what I told him, and maybe Pete down at the Livery could take the rest. I told him if he came to the church picnic, I could introduce him to those who would be interested."

"Sounds like a good idea, but do you think he will be comfortable with everyone?" Sam inquired.

"Yes, I think so. They are used to the whites and their ways from living by Fort Laramie."

"Tuck, did you invite them to the church service before the dinner?"

"No, I guess the thought didn't occur to me. Though I'm sure they attended services at the fort while they were there. Guess I should have." Tuck felt bad about the omission. "I guess one step at a time."

After leaving the mercantile, Tuck went down to the Livery and told Pete the same thing. He was receptive to the idea and promised to talk with Grey Wolf about his horses at the picnic.

"Are they coming to the church service too?" Pete asked.

"You and Sam both asked me that. Fact is, I never even thought to ask them," Tuck said with chagrin. "Don't know why I didn't think of that."

Pete laughed. "Well, see you Sunday"

As he left the Livery, Tuck thought of Pete's parting call. *I better go talk to Reverend Prescott and let him know about Grey Wolf's family coming for the dinner.*

CHAPTER FORTY-EIGHT
Church Picnic

Beth had risen early in the morning to fry a chicken which Thad butchered for her. The pies and bread had been baked the day before. Those and Becca's cookies filled a big basket. Thad helped them by loading the prepared foods into the wagon while Becca and Beth got dressed for church. The boys had changed clothes after the chores were done. Thad took care of Becca's goats, also doing the milking to enable his sister to finish with the food. They were ready to go.

"Do you think Grey Wolf and his family will come to the dinner?" Beth asked Thad once they were on the way to Mustang Ridge.

"Hope so. Grey Wolf said they'd come. I think his word is true," Thad said.

"Will Running Bear come too?" Nate asked.

"Well, all I can say is when Grey Wolf said, "we come" he meant all of them."

As they pulled up to the church, they were surprised to see the Shoshone family outside the church. They were the first ones to arrive, coming even before Reverend Prescott. The Eastmans and Tuck were the next ones to arrive. Grey Wolf rose to greet Tuck as he dismounted from Irish.

"We come to hear stories of Tam Apo, the Great Spirit," Grey Wolf explained.

"That's great," Tuck exclaimed. "Here are some people I'd like you to know. This is Beth Eastman who is Thad's mother, her daughter, Becca, and other son, Nate." He then introduced each of Grey Wolf's family to Beth and her family.

On the wagon train, Beth had been fearful of the Indians and their close proximity to them. Unfortunately, she realized her resistance to them was not helping her daughter accept them as people. She saw how Becca was fearful when Running Bear came to the ranch, but she also saw how Becca warmed up to the Indian boy. Once she realized that these Shoshones were a family and not like the Indians along the wagon train, she had no problem. *Help me, Father to right this wrong.*

Tuck took Grey Wolf to meet Sam and Pete while other families were arriving. There was a great deal of excited chatter going on as the church members anticipated the picnic following the service, not to mention the fact that an Indian family was in their midst. Fires had been built outside the church to keep the hot foods warm until time to serve them.

Beth took Prairie Flower by the hand and led her to the pew where she and her family sat. "Prairie Flower," she said. "You and your family can sit by my family. Come."

Beth saw Sarah come down the aisle with her family and Beth waved her over. She introduced Prairie Flower to the Wells family who then sat down behind them. Several other families came forward to meet the Indian family, including Martha. Although she was aware that some parishioners would be skeptical, Beth was pleased with the response to the Shoshones. She understood that Grey Wolf and especially Prairie Flower might be fearful of how they would be received given how the tribe had treated him because he had married her.

As Beth tried to concentrate on the words spoken by Reverend Prescott, her mind kept straying to Grey Wolf's family. How wonderful it was that they not only came for the picnic, but for the service as well. And she had observed soft wicker baskets slung over Prairie Flower's horse, which were their contribution to the dinner. *I thank Thee, Father that Thou hast brought this family here to worship with us. Help us to be good friends to them in the future.* Reverend Prescott closed the Sunday service with prayer, thanking God for His provision and care. A few women left to fill the waiting tables with the food brought from many homes as the congregation closed the service with the hymn, "Blessed Be the Tie That Binds." After the Amen, the pastor directed the congregation to file out to the tables laden with an abundance of various food items. As Beth descended the church steps, she saw that her fried chicken was on the serving table with steam rising from it.

Beth saw that Martha was evidently in charge of the women who had been getting the food ready. "Martha, is there anything I can do to help?"

"No, dear. It's all ready for the hungry crowd. You just go and get in line with your family and new friends."

Beth turned to look for Prairie Flower and saw that she had gone to get the baskets from her horse. The Indian woman took the baskets to Martha. She had furnished pemmican and a wide array of dried nuts and fruits. Beth couldn't hear what they said, but Martha took the baskets and gave Prairie Flower a hug.

Tuck took Beth's arm. "Shall we join the others in line? Grey Wolf, you and your family join us. We would be happy to share our table with you."

Beth was pleased that Tuck was thinking of her as well as Grey Wolf and his family.

The Shoshone nodded. Beth could see that all these people were probably overwhelming him. She should have known Tuck would be able to see it too and was already making moves to help Grey Wolf. Prairie Flower apparently felt at home around tables of food. She had no problem taking a plate and handing one to each of her children, including Running Bear.

This is as it should be. It is the sharing of our food with those who have taught us so much about the country.

Soon they all had plates with food piled high, especially Tuck. Everyone in Mustang Ridge knew how much Tuck liked to eat. As Beth glanced around at all the people eating, she

noticed that many of the men had plates resembling Tuck's. She was thrilled that there

was so much food for everyone. There were breads of all kinds. Many different soups were available, as well as pie, cookies, and cakes. Her

own children were busy eating and visiting with Running Bear, White Eagle, and Singing Butterfly. *Children never seem to have a problem communicating with each other.*

"Prairie Flower, Tuck said he had helped with the building of your hogan. Is it all finished?"

"Finish?" Prairie Flower signified with her hands that she didn't understand.

"Completed, all done," supplied Beth.

"Oh, yes. All done. We sleeping there now. Tuck good to help Grey Wolf build home. Tuck good friend."

"Yes, I've found that to be true too. He makes a good sheriff because he helps so many people."

"What's this? Did I hear someone say my name?" Tuck asked with a grin.

Prairie Flower and Beth both giggled. *I love this. I have another good friend in Prairie Flower.*

As the afternoon's festivities of games for the children came to a close and the families started making ready to leave by packing up their food, Prairie Flower took Beth's hand.

"I thank you," she placed Beth's hand over her heart. "You are good friend to me, like Tuck is to my husband. Tuck help Grey Wolf to sell mustangs. Grey Wolf, he talk to two mans about it selling horses."

"Prairie Flower, I'm so glad, and you are a good friend to me too."

CHAPTER FORTY-NINE
Independence Day at Deer Creek

Independence Day fell on a Tuesday, which meant the stage was on its return trip from Cheyenne. As Beth prepared the meal for the stage passengers, her thoughts wandered to the picnic Sunday. What a wonderful time with friends and with new friends. She finished cutting out the biscuits and sent the pan aside, waiting for the trumpet to sound. The trumpet had become a routine part of their time at the stagecoach station. Except for the time when Matt was injured following the Indian attack further north. Tom couldn't blow the trumpet because he was driving the stage.

Beth shuddered thinking about how close they came to losing Matt on that trip. As he had spent time at Deer Creek Ranch while he recuperated, Matt very nearly became a member of their family while Beth nursed him back to good health. She was thankful God provided protection for the rest of them and for Matt's healing. Now she waited once more to hear that trumpet.

Beth had invited Tuck to share their table with them as well as the stage occupants. She heard him outside as he greeted Nate and Bandit. When he entered the ranch-house, he hung his hat on the peg and turned to greet Beth. He didn't have time to say anything other than hello because at that moment the trumpet sounded, Bandit barked, and Nate called, "Stage is here!"

Beth served fried chicken in keeping with the festive fare. Matt, Tom and the five passengers enjoyed the meal and when well sated, boarded the stage for their ride to Deadwood.

Tuck hung around enjoying the time with Beth and her children. They went outside and sat on the porch, hoping for some cool air. Beth's cheeks were quite rosy from working over a hot stove. As the afternoon wore on the heat outside became nearly as oppressive as her stove. It was then that Tuck noticed the sky turning dark with roiling clouds moving in.

"Looks like a storm coming," he said, "Maybe I better head back to town."

"Tuck, I think you should stay until it passes over. It wouldn't be good to get caught on the road if the storm is to be intense."

"Okay, Beth. Thanks. Why don't I help with the chores and we won't have to worry about doing them in the storm?"

Tuck joined the children as they tended to their livestock. Thad thought they should put the horses inside too so they would be protected. Nate shooed his chickens inside and closed their door. While the menfolk fed and watered the livestock, Becca milked Buttercup.

When Becca and Nate returned to the ranch-house with milk and eggs, Beth asked, "Where are Tuck and Thad.

"Oh, still out in the barn talking about the horses," Becca answered. "I think Buttercup knows a storm is coming. She wouldn't let down her milk until I sang to her."

"Maybe she just likes your singing," Beth laughed.

It was getting dark enough in the ranch-house that Beth lit the kerosene lamp on the table and the one on the end table next to her rocking chair.

"Mama," Becca said. "I'm going to do some sewing while I still have some light."

"That's fine." Beth said, "I will start supper."

Becca finished stitching and came over to mix some biscuit dough. She placed them on the pan ready to pop them in the oven. They waited for Thad and Tuck to come in from the barn.

"What's that noise?" Becca asked alarmed.

Both Becca and Beth rushed to the window to see what was going on outside. The sky was filled with black clouds. The wind had increased in intensity. Beth saw Tuck and Thad bent over and hurrying to the ranch-house. She opened the door to let them enter.

"Mama, I'm scared." Nate's fear was evident on his face. "What is that noise?"

"It's hail," Tuck said. "Beth, we need to go to the root cellar. There's a tornado coming."

Beth's eyes grew big with alarm, but she felt calmed by Tuck's take-charge attitude.

"Children, we need to go to the root cellar. Tuck says there is a tornado coming." Beth turned down the kerosene lamps and moved the food to the rear of the stove.

All eyes turned toward Tuck. "Take your coats; it will be cool down there. And grab something that is important or means a lot to you. You don't know if it will be here or not when this passes."

They all took their coats off the hooks and donned them. Beth took her sewing basket, as that is where she kept the money both from the sale of the Texas ranch and from the stage passengers. Thad took his rifle and hunting knife, as well as his whittling knife. Nate grabbed his flute which Thad had made for him on the wagon train. Becca didn't know what to take so she just grabbed some candles and ran to the trap door and opened it.

"Bandit, come on," called Nate as he descended the steps after his sister.

Tuck grabbed his gun belt along with his coat and brought up the rear of those going down the stairs. He no sooner closed the trap door than the roar of the wind outside began to violently shake the ranch-house.

Once they were huddled in the cellar, Tuck lit one of the candles Becca had brought with her. "Thanks for bringing these, Becca. I didn't even think about the need for light," Tuck said. "We'll just light one at a time. No telling how long we will be down here."

"Sure glad we put all the livestock in the barn," Thad shared. "Hopefully, the barn will be okay."

"Poor Buttercup. No wonder she didn't want to give her milk," said Becca. "She must have known."

"Yes," agreed Tuck. "Animals have an uncanny ability to sense when the weather is going to turn."

"I hope my chickens won't be scared," Nate voiced his fear for their safety.

Thad laughed. "Chickens are always scared. That's why I told you not to burst into the barn like you do sometimes, but they are inside the barn like the rest of the livestock."

"Just listen to that!" Becca exclaimed. "What a noise!"

CHAPTER FIFTY
After the Storm!

"It's quieted down," Beth remarked. "Do you suppose the storm has passed?"

"I'll go check. Everyone stay here until I say it's safe." Tuck opened the trap door and slowly peered into the interior of the ranch-house. "Everything is still in place. You can come up now."

They all started up the steps behind Tuck. Beth could tell from the sound that the wind had passed. They went to the window and looked out while Tuck opened the door and went out onto the porch.

"There is debris all over the yard. Looks like there is damage to the barn and some to the porch of the ranch-house," he announced. One corner of the porch was hanging down. "Thad, let's you and I check on the damage."

Thad followed Tuck out to the barn while Beth put some more logs in the fireplace. "The wind must have sucked out the flames," she said. Then she went outdoors to pick up things in the yard with Becca and Nate's help.

When Thad and Tuck entered the barn, they saw that the wall where the horses were penned had a gaping hole in it. Two of the stage line's horses were lying on the barn floor, dead. Thad counted three horses missing. One of Becca's goats lay dead on the floor. Nate's chickens had not all survived either. Two lay dead and the rest were frightened. The horses which were in stalls were all safe.

Tuck helped Thad pull the dead animals out of the barn with another horse. Then they erected a temporary fence against the hole in the wall of the barn. Thad took the two chickens up to the ranch house for his mother to dress, then returned to the barn and dressed out the dead goat. He hung it from the rafter with Tuck's help. They told Becca and Nate about the demise of their animals. They were both upset over the news.

"Thad, let's saddle up and go look for the missing horses," Tuck said. He went to the stall where Irish was standing and hefted his saddle onto his back. Thad did the same with Buck.

"We better stop back at the ranch-house and let your Ma know what we are doing."

Thad nodded, and leading the saddled Buck to the ranch-house, he poked his head in the door saying, "Ma, Tuck and I are going out to find the three missing horses."

Beth handed them some biscuits with jelly to take with them since they didn't take the time to eat supper. "Stay safe," she called.

CHAPTER FIFTY-ONE
Tuck

When Tuck arrived at Deer Creek Ranch, on Independence Day, he tied Irish to the hitching rail. Bandit was running around barking furiously. He could hear Nate announcing with gusto that Tuck had arrived. He chuckled. *That boy sure gets excited.*

He entered the ranch-house as Nate opened the door to him. The aromas of cooking filling the inside of the house made his stomach rumble with anticipation. Beth looked at him smiling, and then she greeted him, saying she was glad he had come.

When Nate yelled that the stage was coming, Tuck laughed. He really didn't need to announce it because they all heard the trumpet, not to mention the horses galloping into the yard, and of course, Bandit barking.

Later, when the stage arrived, Tuck greeted Matt and Tom and opened the stage door for the passengers. There were five men among the passengers. Tuck directed them to the privy and the whereabouts of the wash basin. Tom helped Thad unhitch the spent teams and turn them into the corral. They hitched the fresh teams up to the stage. Then they headed into the ranch-house.

Tuck thought Beth was really something for sharing her family Independence Day dinner with the stage passengers and Matt and Tom. He was happy he had been invited as well.

Beth and her daughter served up some mighty good grub. *Though 'grub' really doesn't do it justice. Both of them are good cooks.* He could tell the passengers were happy that they were included in Beth's family dinner.

After the stage left, Tuck helped Beth clear the table. Then Nate asked him to come and see his chickens, so they went outside. The main part of the coop was in the barn, but Thad had utilized a small door in the wall of the barn to let the chickens run outside. The coop outside was enclosed with chicken wire to keep them safe from predators. Thad did a good job of constructing the chicken coop.

They were some dandy looking chickens and Tuck asked if Nate fed them. Nate said he sure did and watered them, too. And he gathered the eggs every day. He even wondered about ordering some more. But Tuck said it was getting kind of late in the year to be ordering them on the freight wagons. The heat might be kind of hard on them. Anyway, his hens could hatch some of the eggs. That's why Sam had included roosters in the order.

Tuck told Nate he had done a good job with them and asked who took care of the goats. He said Becca. She fed them and milked the nanny. Tuck noticed Buttercup's kids had sure grown since he brought them out here.

Nate and Tuck went back to the ranch-house and played checkers on the porch. Tuck glanced over at Beth sitting in her rocking chair sewing. *She is really a beautiful woman.* He had to tell himself to stop staring at her.

When he noticed the weather was getting bad outside, he said he would help them do the chores early. They asked Tuck to stay the night because the weather was so bad. He said he would help with the chores and they all went outside except for Beth.

They brought all the animals into the barn, including Irish because the sky was beginning to look pretty bad. Tuck put Irish into one of the stalls next to Buck. He and Thad stood around talking about horses. Thad had a dream to breed horses and was wondering what Tuck thought about it and if he would be able to do it on the stage line ranch. Tuck told Thad he didn't think that would be a problem, but they could talk more with Sam about it.

Looking back Tuck guessed he should have paid more attention to what was going on outside. They headed out of the barn and to the ranch-house. It was then he saw how bad the sky looked now with a funnel cloud heading their way. Time to take cover!

After surveying the damage, Tuck and Thad went out in search of the horses which had run off in the storm. They didn't have to go very far. Just down the valley road, they found them winded. They were able to dismount and walk up to them with bridles and eventually bring them back to the ranch.

Tuck was saddened by the extensive damage to the barn and the loss of animals. He knew they needed to get to work right away on the hole in the barn.

They dug holes to bury the dead horses and then went to the ranch-house for a late supper.

CHAPTER FIFTY-TWO
Plans to Rebuild the Barn

Beth was watching out the window when Tuck and Thad returned with the missing horses. She breathed a prayer of thanks to God for their reappearance. They returned them to the barn and then came to the ranch-house.

Beth served a late supper to everyone when they were all back in the house. While they were eating, Tuck took a piece of paper and was writing on it while Beth poured hot coffee.

"What are you writing?" Beth asked him.

"I'm making a list of materials we will need to repair the barn," Tuck answered. "Thad and I will take the big wagon into Mustang Ridge tomorrow morning and get the building materials for repairing the barn."

#

The next morning after breakfast, Tuck and Thad hitched up two teams to the large wagon.

That wagon would hold the materials they needed to repair the barn, plus fencing supplies.

Beth waved goodbye as Thad clicked to the two teams of horses, Bullet and Lightning, Blaze and Copper. Tuck sat next to Thad.

When they returned later in the afternoon with a wagon loaded down with building materials, Beth went to the barn to greet them. Thad told her that Sam had provided it all through the stage line, so there was no cost to them. Beth was thankful, as she had been concerned about how much it would cost, and had mentally recalled how much she had in their dwindling savings.

Tuck said Sam and two men from town would be out tomorrow morning to repair the barn. It was close to the supper hour, and Thad asked if Tuck would stay again the night to be available in the morning. Tuck said he would. Nate and Becca joined Thad and Tuck in doing the evening chores.

Nate found that his still frightened chickens had not laid any eggs during the day. Becca, saddened that Gretel had been killed in the storm, consoled Buttercup in the loss of her kid.

Buttercup finally let down her milk, and Becca milked her while humming softly to her. The horses, chickens, and goats were fed and watered, in addition to milking Buttercup. Chores completed for another day.

Later in the ranch-house as they were seated around the table partaking of the evening meal, which consisted of one of the chickens that had died in the storm, Tuck told about his and Sam's idea to enlarge the barn, and to eventually fence off a larger part of the grassy area to the north for raising horses. Thad told his mother his plan was to raise horses as his father had done in Texas.

"Does the stage line agree to this?" Beth wanted to know.

"Yes, Tuck talked to Sam about it and he agreed. Although I think I should pay for the extra fencing," Thad said.

"Well, that is commendable, but the larger pasture area will benefit the stage line horses as well," Tuck offered, "and the owner also benefits. I don't see a problem with going on as planned."

"I like that your plans for the barn will include a larger enclosed area for the teams to keep them out of the harsh weather," Thad said. "And it gives a larger area for Becca's goat herd to increase."

"Yes," Tuck added. "I will have to visit with Grey Wolf and see if he has anymore goats for Becca. He will be herding his horses into Mustang Ridge sometime next week. I'll ask him then."

Beth saw that Becca was excited about more goats. She never thought she'd see the day when her daughter would become a goat girl. *God, Thy blessings never fail to amaze me.*

Those in the ranch-house spent the evening playing games, mending, and whittling. Then they all retired for the night, ready to take on a busy day at dawn.

Thad had butchered the goat in the barn so his sister would not have to see it. He brought the cuts to the house for Beth to store in the root cellar. Beth took one cut and chopped it up in small pieces to make a stew since goat meat can be tough. She wanted to make a dish where it could cook long and slow. She would call it beef stew.

CHAPTER FIFTY-THREE
Half a Barn Raising

First thing Thursday morning, Paul Norby and Gerald Walters came out from Mustang Ridge after chores had been completed. They told Thad that Jacob Wells would be out a little later to help also. These men had helped many ranchers with new barns, and even though this was simply repairing the structure, they jokingly called it a half a barn raising.

Jacob came to the ranch a couple of hours later. He also had experience in barn raising. Actually, just about any man in the Territory had this type of experience. It's what a man did for his neighbors.

The men worked continuously except for a break at mid-day when they went into the ranch-house for dinner before the stage came in. Thad changed out the horses, then joined the men working on the barn. Fortunately, they had nice weather to do the work. The storm had cooled the weather off. Good weather for working outdoors.

By the end of the day, the addition and repair to the barn had been completed. The men planned to return the next day to repair the porch and work on the fencing.

Beth thanked them all for their help. "Paul, tell Grace 'Hello' for me. I haven't had a chance to talk to her for a while."

"Will do, Miss Beth."

Beth waved to the rest of the men, expressing her appreciation for their help. Thad shook their hands, thanking them as well. "See everyone tomorrow," Thad said.

CHAPTER FORTY- FOUR
Matt is Back on the Box But for How Long?

Several weeks later, Becca and Nate entered the ranch-house, Becca with the pail of milk she had just obtained and Nate with a small basket of eggs. Beth watched her two younger children as they completed their chores. They were growing more responsible now that they each had their own animals to care for. Thad was still out at the corral where he was hitching up the teams for when the stage came in. He would hitch each team up and when it was time to switch out the horses, he would hook the wheelers, in front of the stage, then the middle team, the swingers, and finally in front, the leaders.

"There it is! The stage is coming." Nate shouted. Bandit barked.

"We heard. Must you shout it out every time the stage comes?" Becca was exasperated with her younger brother. "Between you yelling and Bandit barking, it's too much."

"Easy, Becca," Beth said with a hand on her daughter's arm.

"Sorry, Mama."

"I'm not the one you should be sorry to," Beth said nodding at Nate.

Becca nodded. "Sorry, Nate."

Matt pulled the stage to a halt in front of the ranch house and climbed down from his seat. He opened the door and let the passengers out.

"Folks, this here's Deer Creek Ranch Stage Stop. We'll be stopping here for mid-day meal. Mrs. Eastman is the manager, and she will feed you," Matt instructed. "She's a mighty good cook, so enjoy."

Meanwhile, Tom climbed down and started to help Thad unhitch the teams. "Howdy, Thad."

"Afternoon, Tom. How was the trip this time?" Thad inquired of the shotgun messenger.

"Really starting to settle down as far as Indian attacks go. Sure hope it keeps on that way. I heard the railroad had planned to put in a line from Cheyenne to Deadwood, but it was put aside because of the Indian uprising."

"Say, Tom, go on into the ranch- house and eat," Thad urged him. "I've got it down to fifteen minutes now. I've got this."

"Yeah, I guess you do. Thanks, Thad."

Beth had been watching Tom and her son from the window. She was so proud of Thad. He hardly looked like the same sixteen-year-old boy who revealed his whippings to her over a year ago. Now at seventeen, his slender body had filled in with muscles. He had grown tan from the spending so many hours is the sun. He indeed looked like a man.

Beth turned back to the task at hand. The passengers had washed up and were coming to the table. She approached and signaled that she would ask the blessing over the food. When she was done, Becca passed the platter of beef around. Nate followed with the basket of hot biscuits fresh from the oven. Of the eight passengers, three of them were women who were traveling with their husbands. They complimented Beth on the tasty food. Everyone was pleasantly surprised by the squash pie she had made.

Once the meal was finished, Matt made the usual call for paying for their meals and to load up. Beth left Becca to take the payments while she went to speak with Matt on the porch.

"Matt, how has your shoulder been feeling?" she asked. "Is it giving you any trouble?"

"It has healed just fine," Matt replied, "but it gets to aching pretty bad by the time I get to the end of the line. I'm thinking of resigning from the stage line."

"Oh, Matt. I'm sorry to hear that. Did you see a doctor?"

"Yep. The stage line urged me to see one when I got back to Deadwood after I left here. He said I would always have the aching and should maybe try to find different work. Trouble is- I don't know what I could do."

"Matt, I'm sure God has a plan for you, and He will reveal it to you in due time," Beth encouraged him. "I promise you, I will pray for that to be done." She patted his arm.

"Thanks, Beth. I appreciate it." Matt then called, "All right folks, time to get on the road."

"Bye, Matt." Beth wondered about Matt. She couldn't imagine the stage line without him. What else could God have in mind for him?

CHAPTER FIFTY-FIVE
End of Summer

On a trip to Sam's to buys supplies, Beth noticed two crates with large white birds in the back of the store. "Sam what are these? Are they turkeys?"

"Yes, they are. I ordered several of them. They are domestic turkeys. I wanted to have some for families who want to have a roast turkey for Thanksgiving," Sam explained. "Funny that there are no wild turkeys in the Wyoming Territory.

"What a grand idea. I think I should like to buy one for our family." Beth and Sam discussed the price and Sam added it to her bill. Beth walked back to the counter where Sam was filling her order.

"Sam, I have an idea for the stage that will stop on Thanksgiving Day. Do you suppose it will be possible to allow extra time so the passengers and Matt and Tom can share our family dinner table like they did for Independence Day?" Beth asked him.

"That sounds like a great idea. I'll make it happen. "

CHAPTER FIFTY-SIX
Harvest at Deer Creek Ranch

The Deer Creek Ranch occupants spent the next week finishing harvesting and taking in two stage stops. By this time, Becca had obtained three more goats and Thad had turned them out onto the field from which they had harvested the straw. Thad wanted to plant some winter wheat there. The goats not only ate what was left of the grain, but their hooves tore up the ground enough that Thad said they practically plowed the small field. He prepared the field by hitching Bullet to a small harrow which had been in the barn, no doubt provided by Sam for the stage station. He tilled the soil and then spread the wheat seed from a canvas shoulder bag with a hand crank whose gears spread the seeds over the ground. He then took the harrow over the field a second time to cover the seed to protect it from the wind and birds. This way, they would have a fresh harvest of wheat come spring.

Beth and Becca were busy as well harvesting the vegetables from the garden. Potatoes, carrots, and squash were placed in the root cellar. More herbs were hung to dry. Beans were dried in plentiful supply to be reconstituted and used in stews and soups during the long winter months. Nate was busy at the creek fishing for trout which Thad would smoke then store away in the root cellar.

Thad's most recent hunting trip provided deer and antelope meat which was salted down, smoked, and hung in the root cellar. Thad who by now had become and expert at tanning the hides, provided additional bed covers out of them.

Thad also had the job of storing winter food for the livestock. Hay and straw were forked into the barn. Corn was picked and dried on the cob, then stored in the barn. He hoped that between the small amounts he had been able to harvest and that which was provided by the stage company through Sam, that there would be enough to get through the winter. Next year he planned to plant more crops that could be used as feed for his livestock. His dream was to purchase a plow and a planter. He certainly had the horse power for it.

Thad observed the prairie grass back of the barn. "Ma, the hot summer sun has really dried that prairie grass. I think we can put it up for bedding for the horses."

"I think that is a good idea, we don't want to waste anything. I'll get some lunch ready for us, and we can take care of that this afternoon."

"Mama, do we have to do it today? I'm worn out," Becca groaned.

"I think we should do it today. We have a stage coming in tomorrow and can't do it then," Beth answered her.

"Can't we do it the next day?" Becca urged her mother.

"No, Becca. We will do it today. No sense it putting it off if we can do it today."

After lunch was out of the way, the four of them went out back of the ranch buildings to the prairie grass. Thad used a scythe to cut the grass while the rest of them followed behind tying the dried grass into bundles using the grass itself.

Thad hitched up the team to the big wagon, and they began throwing bundles of the dried grass into the back. When they had hauled it back to the barn, they carried the bundles into the barn.

All in all, Thad was contented with his life here and his dream to have a horse ranch someday continued to resurface every so often. Beth was at peace with her life at Deer Creek Ranch, feeling confident with her position as operator of the stagecoach station. Becca and Nate also appeared to enjoy being at the ranch. It had been a long, sometimes grueling journey to arrive at this point, but all seemed contented now.

CHAPTER FIFTY-SEVEN
November 26, 1876
Thanksgiving at Deer Creek Ranch

The members of the Eastman family were excited and rushing around getting food ready for the celebration of Thanksgiving at the ranch. Beth was thrilled that Tuck would be coming to share their meal once again.

Beth barely rested the night before. She had to get up really early in the morning but then so did Thad. He rose early to kill the turkey. After plunging it in hot water in a big pot over a fire outside, the turkey was ready to pluck. Thad helped Beth to pluck the feathers from the big Tom turkey. The feathers would be used in mattress ticking. When that was done, Thad returned to his mat in the loft to get some more sleep before he had to get up for early chores.

The thing about celebrating a holiday on a Thursday is that it didn't preempt the stage from coming. So, however many passengers would be coming in on the stage, they would be sharing their Thanksgiving table. Sam, in his position as the stage division director, had already made arrangements for a longer stopover for the stage after Beth's urging.

Martha, knowing that Beth would have her hands full, had invited the Wells family to their house. Beth hoped that Sarah didn't feel bad about not being asked to her home. Martha had told Sarah about Beth's full house, so Sarah understood. Sarah asked Beth and family to come to Sunday dinner after church the following Sunday.

The turkey was roasting, the potatoes were tender, and the pumpkin pies were stored in the pie safe. Beth looked over the food to see if there was anything she had forgotten. Becca had the table set with all the plates and silverware.

"Tuck's here! Tuck's here!" Of course, Bandit was barking too.

"Howdy there, Nate," Tuck said swinging Nate in the air. "And Bandit. I can't forget you, can I? Not when you are lapping me up with your wet tongue."

As Tuck walked further into the ranch-house, Beth looked up at him. She caught her breath as their eyes met. Neither of them moved for a moment. Beth was brought back to the moment by the sound of a trumpet, Nate yelling "the stage is here," and Bandit was outside running around barking wildly.

"It's so good to see you, Tuck. I'm glad you could come. You have just witnessed what happens every time the stage comes in," Beth laughed.

"Thank you, Beth. I wouldn't miss this day for anything. I'll go out and help with the passengers," Tuck offered. Beth watched him walk out to the stage and felt a yearning inside that confused her. *What is it about this man?*

"Matt, Tom, good to see you men," Tuck called to the stage driver and his shotgun.

"You too, Tuck."

Matt climbed down from the stage and opened the stage door while Tom helped Thad to unhook the three teams and turn them into the corral. Then they both headed up to the ranch-house.

As the five weary passengers climbed out of the stagecoach, Tuck directed them to the privy around back. As the days had gotten cooler, Beth had moved the bench with the wash basin just inside the ranch-house door. She directed them where to wash up. When they all came to the table ready to eat, Beth said, "Happy Thanksgiving everyone. Before we are seated, let's hold hands while we have the blessing."

Tuck was standing next to Beth and when she took his hand, she felt a tingling jolt. She was encouraged by the warmth of his hand but mystified by the accompanying emotions which left her speechless. Tuck, apparently intuitive, gave a Thanksgiving blessing and ended with "amen" as he gave Beth's hand a final squeeze.

Beth brought the roasted turkey to the table. She handed the carving knife to Matt and asked, "Matt, would you be a dear and carve the turkey for us? Becca, bring the potatoes and gravy please. I already scooped the stuffing out of the turkey."

Matt looked as proud as he could be that Beth had asked him to carve the turkey. While the happy chatter at the table continued, Beth filled the cups with coffee and gave the children milk.

"Mrs. Eastman, what is stuffing? I don't think I've ever had it before," asked Matt. Several others nodded and murmured they also wondered.

"Well, it's made with bread, onion, dried herbs like sage and thyme, egg, and water. At least that's how I made this one. You can also use cornbread, nuts, and dried fruits. Then you stuff it into the turkey to cook," Beth explained.

"Sure is good," commented one of the passengers. "Glad I got to try it."

"Thank you very kindly," Beth responded.

When they were all finished stuffing themselves, Beth brought out the pies and Becca brought the bowl of freshly whipped cream. Beth explained that the whipped cream for the top of the pies was made from the separated cream from Becca's nanny goat. Becca smiled at the collective ahs from those seated at the table. She had whipped the cream until she thought her arm would fall off. So, it made it all worthwhile to hear the response.

The guests had finished their dessert and some were visiting the privy before heading out on a bouncing stage. One of the passengers, Horace Martin took Beth's hand and said, "Mrs. Eastman, I want to thank you so much for sharing your Thanksgiving table with us. I don't have a family and this made me feel like I had one. And the food was superb. Bless you, my dear."

"You are quite welcome, Mr. Martin. I'm glad you enjoyed it," Beth replied.

Later, as the passengers finished their meal and had left the table, Beth saw Matt and Mr. Martin off by themselves talking. She wondered what it was about as they appeared to be earnestly engaged in conversation.

The passengers finished making their payments to Beth as Matt called, "All aboard."

"Matt," said Beth taking him aside. "I am praying for your comfort on the stage runs with   your shoulder. And I'm also praying for that other matter."

"Thank you kindly, Beth. I appreciate it," Matt answered as he swung up into the box. "See you next trip."

As the stage pulled away from the station, Beth waved to them all. She went back inside and began clearing the dishes. She was surprised when Tuck joined her in clearing the dirty dishes.

"Tuck, you don't have to do that."

"I know, but I want to. I'm pretty sure you got up pretty early to get started on this meal, so the least I can do is help clean up. Besides, it was a first-rate dinner."

Beth beamed at Tuck's praise of her cooking.

As they finished the dishes, Nate called, "Tuck, how about a game of checkers?"

"All right-ee." They set up the board in front of the fireplace. Thad took up his knife and a piece of whittling wood. Beth sat in her rocking chair near the fireplace and knitted.

Beth watched Tuck as he interacted with Nate. *It's too bad his baby didn't live. He would have been such a good father.*

CHAPTER FIFTY-EIGHT
Tuck Spends Thanksgiving at Deer Creek Ranch

Once again Tuck had been invited to Deer Creek Ranch to partake of her family's dinner with the stage passengers and handlers. As he entered the ranch-house, he called, "Happy Thanksgiving."

"Just in time, Tuck. There is the trumpet now," Beth greeted him. He heard Bandit and Nate also announcing its arrival.

Tuck went to the door and greeted the stage occupants, showing them where to go. He noted that several of them were struck with the wonderful smells emanating from Beth's kitchen.

Before long, they were all standing at the table, ready for Beth's prayer. Tuck's seat was next to Beth and when she took his hand, he felt a tingle go up his arm. He knew she felt it, too, as she wasn't able to deliver the prayer. He was somewhat speechless himself, but did the best he could with a simple prayer of thanks.

There was one guy who was a banker from Texas, who was on his way back to Texas from a trip up north. It seems he had bought a horse ranch a few years back, and was now involved in both the banking business and raising horses. Tuck heard the conversation between him and Beth after the meal and wondered too what he and Matt were talking about. He wondered if Beth knew that Martin was a banker from Texas. He probably should say something to her later.

CHAPTER FIFTY-NINE
Beth Meets Mattie

Sunday brought continued warm weather. Just before the service was to start, Jennie Ballard came up to Beth and said, "Beth, I'd like you to meet Pete's sister, Mattie McLeod. She has come out to stay with us. Her husband died last year, and she has no family left back east so she has moved out here. Mattie, this is Beth Eastman. She and her children operate the stagecoach station."

"Mattie, I'm so pleased to meet you. I'm sorry about your husband."

"Thank you, Beth. I've heard a lot about you. In fact, it was Pete's letters to me about you that gave me the courage to come out west."

"Land sakes! Did you come out on the wagon train by yourself?" Beth was astonished that she had been the impetus for this sweet young woman to come west alone.

"Yes, I did, but not alone. I hired a driver. That way I could have my own wagon and bring a good amount of my belongings."

"Well, I'm happy that you are here safely settled in Mustang Ridge," Beth said.

Beth left her with Jennie and Grace Norby and went to talk to Sarah and Martha. The two of them looked like they were planning something.

"Beth, we are talking about the women coming out to Deer Creek Ranch on a day that the stage comes in, "Martha explained. " We women want to have a part in service to you, our friend, just as our men did."

"Yes," agreed Sarah. "Now don't say no. I can see in your eyes you are about to say no. Just hear us out."

"Reverend Prescott has been talking about service to others in his Sunday messages and this is one way we women can do it, and we can help you to cook and serve the noon meal to the passengers," Martha said.

"But ladies, I have to start the meal quite early in the morning," Beth argued. "You would have to leave Mustang Ridge pretty early."

Martha and Sarah did seem to hesitate, but only for a moment. "No matter," Martha said firmly after a nod from Sarah. "It will be that much better. Service isn't always easy."

Sarah followed Martha's lead. "We can have a Bible study after the noon meal is out of the way. On service."

Martha took Sarah's arm. "Come, Sarah we need to talk to the other women."

Beth heard Sarah telling Martha they could ask the new lady to join them as they walked away from her. *Oh my,* she thought. *Welcome to Mustang Ridge, Mattie.*

As Beth turned to go into the church, she heard Reverend Prescott say, "Grey Wolf, it is so good to see you and your family here. Welcome."

Beth was pleasantly surprised. She had not expected to see the Shoshone family again at church, but there they were. She went to Prairie Flower and welcomed her. Everyone had met her and Grey Wolf when they were there last so many came up and greeted them. Mattie McLeod had not been there, so when she saw them, Beth could see she was a little leery.

"Come, Prairie Flower. Come and meet a new lady to our town. Mattie McLeod just came in last week on the wagon train to Fort Laramie. Her brother is Pete Ballard, who runs the Livery Stable."

"Pleased to meet you, Prairie Flower." Mattie offered her hand to the Indian woman.

"Hello." Prairie Flower was timid; as if fearful her grasp of English would not be good.

Beth was pleased that the church women and Mattie were accepting of Prairie Flower. With the Indian attacks up near Deadwood, it was understandable that they would not be. However, Beth found that these women were God-fearing women who tried to live their lives as their Heavenly Father directed. Once again she was thankful He had led them to this town.

Beth found it hard to concentrate on the sermon. Her mind was going off in all directions. She would have to plan a menu that would take many hands to make, one that would keep them all busy. She had to admit though; it would be nice to have the ladies in her home, and to have a Bible study. Yes, maybe it would turn out to be a good thing after all.

Following the church service, Beth and her family drove to the Wells' home for Sunday dinner. It was good to all be together again.

CHAPTER SIXTY
Women of Service

The following week the women of the church came out to Deer Creek Ranch to do their acts of service. Martha had arranged with several of the women to come out early to get the meal started. Esther Prescott would lead them in a Bible study after dinner. Sarah said she would bring Izzy and Ben. Izzy and Becca could have play time with Ben and Nate. Becca always worked, so this would give her time away as well as Beth. Martha also arranged for the women to bring the food supplies to cook for the stage passengers.

Early Thursday morning the women came out in wagons. Martha drove her wagon with Jenny Ballard, Grace Norby, and Mattie McLeod. Sarah in her wagon brought Esther Prescott, Rachel Walters, Izzy, and Ben.

This time of service seemed to be a fun outing for the women. Could service still be service if it was so enjoyable?

The two wagons contained supplies for cooking, cleaning, and extra chairs. Martha had thought of everything. Beth had found her to be a take-charge kind of woman in the past, and she was no different today. Martha directed everyone to the chores they would do. Beth started to help but was told by Martha to just sit and rest.

Becca and Nate still had their chores to do, so Izzy and Ben went with them to help. When they returned to the ranch-house laughing and talking about how much fun it was to milk a goat and gather eggs, Beth laughed with them. Who would have thought work could be so much fun? Becca took the children into her room and they spent the rest of the morning in there. Beth wasn't sure what they were doing, but she heard lots of giggling.

Beth heard the trumpet sound and told the women that meant the stagecoach was coming in. Bandit ran around barking, although he pretty much had not stopped barking since the women came. He surely didn't know what to make of everything going on.

Beth pulled her shawl around her shoulders and went out on the porch to greet the stage, its handlers, and those riding. She opened the stage door to greet each person. Matt swung down from the box and helped the others down from on top.

"Morning, Beth," Matt greeted her.

Once the passengers were all out, Thad unhitched the horses and took them to the corral and Beth instructed the passengers as to the where-a-bouts of the privy and the wash basin. There were nine passengers today; two couples and five men. Beth was glad there had been all the help in cooking.

Martha continued her leadership role saying, "Ladies and gentlemen. We women of Mustang Ridge are preforming a service as part of our church there. We have taken over the preparing of your meal for Beth here, but she will tell you how she wants you to be served."

"Thank you, Martha. Folks, just take a seat anywhere, but before you are seated, I ask you to join us as I lead us in a prayer of thanks for this food."

The passengers stood behind their chairs and bowed their heads with the church women and Beth as she prayed.

"Our Father in Heaven, we thank Thee for providing this food today. We thank Thee for bringing these kind women to prepare the food. We thank Thee also for the safety and comfort of the passengers of the stagecoach and for the expertise of Matt and Tom in bringing the stage safely here. Bless this food, and bless each one here today. Amen."

As Beth raised her eyes, she heard several voices repeat *Amen*. The church women began to serve the passengers one by one. Mattie had a bowl from which she spooned mashed potatoes to each of the passengers and stage hands. Jenny followed her with the meat platter, Martha with the gravy, Sarah with the green beans, and Grace with the biscuits. This was not the way Beth usually served the food, but then again, she was only one person.

Beth had to smile when she saw Mattie serve Matt his potatoes. She could almost see the sparks as Matt looked up into Mattie's eyes. *Is it possible that these two young people might be attracted to each other?*

Beth imagined that Matt and Mattie would make a great couple. Their names were so much alike, it was just meant to be. She would have to wait upon the Lord to provide the way. The Lord still had not shown her what Matt could do in place of driving the stage. *Please, dear Father, provide an alternative for him.*

After the passengers had finished their pie, Matt rose from the table and said, "Folks, we will be leaving in ten minutes. Make your payments for the meal and any last-minute trips to the privy."

The passengers began to make their payments to Beth. She announced that since the church women had done the cooking today, she would donate the money to the church. The passengers nodded their approval and thanked the women for serving them. They went out onto the porch. Tom was already out there. Matt had not left yet. Beth saw him glancing at Mattie. Beth took the bull by the horns. "Mattie, would you come here a moment? I'd like you to meet a good friend and the best stagecoach driver I know," She chuckled at this. "Matthew Cutter, this is Mattie McLeod. She is Pete Ballard's sister. Pete runs the Livery in town."

Matt reached his hand out to Mattie. "Pleased to make your acquaintance, ma'am."

"I'm pleased to meet you too, Matthew. How long have you been driving the stagecoach?" Mattie asked.

"Oh, just since they started the Cheyenne to Deadwood run. Before that I was a ranch hand," answered Matt. "Come out and I will give you a close up of my stagecoach. This is my…"

Beth didn't hear anymore as they went out the door onto the porch. She turned to the ladies taking the dirty dishes off the table. Now that the passengers were gone, it would be time for the women and the children to eat and Beth was hungry. She called the children to come, have a seat and eat some dinner. This time the church women took a seat at the table, and everyone served themselves.

Matt called, "Stage is leaving, all aboard."

Beth looked up when Mattie entered the ranch-house. She had remained on the porch until the stage left and waved goodbye to Matt. "Mattie, come fill a plate and have a seat," she invited.

The seats were all taken at the table, so Beth led the way to the living area in front of the fireplace. This is where the extra chairs were set up for the Bible study afterwards. Grace and Jenny also joined them.

Mattie sat next to Beth. She leaned toward Beth and whispered, "Beth, I would like to speak to you in private before we leave if it can be arranged." Beth nodded. She wondered what this could be about.

"Ladies, if you are finished eating, we should get started washing all these dirty dishes," Martha announced. Beth removed the dishpan from its nail and another pan to rinse the dishes. The water had been heating in the reservoir in the iron stove. Sarah used a small pan to ladle water into the two pans while Beth furnished several dish towels. Martha announced that she would wash. She cautioned Beth to go be seated. Becca and the other children took the table scraps out to her goats.

"Mattie, come sit beside me," Beth said. When Mattie was seated, she told her, "I've never been more excited to see all you ladies working here. It's been so nice. Thank you for your part in this day. Now, what was it you wanted to talk about? Is this private enough?"

"You're welcome, Beth. Yes, this is private enough. I just wanted to ask you if I could come out to help you serve the meal for the stagecoach next Tuesday."

Beth understood immediately and agreed. Mattie was so taken with Matt and this was the only way they could see each other. Matt would do his stage runs on Thursdays and Tuesdays and in-between that was driving the stage. He really didn't have a home - just a bunk at either Deadwood or Cheyenne. This seemed to be the only way they could spend time together.

CHAPTER SIXTY-ONE
A Message of Service

Once the dishes were done, Esther Prescott began their study with prayer. Then she asked the ladies to follow along as she read. Not everyone had their own Bible so they shared or listened to Esther as she read from her King James Bible:

> **1Peter 4:10, 11** *As every man hath received the gift, even so, minister the same one to another, as good stewards of the manifold grace of God.*
> *If any man speak, let him speak as the oracles of God; if any man minister, let him do it as of the ability which God giveth: that God in all things may be glorified through Jesus Christ, to whom be praise and dominion ever and ever. Amen*

Esther talked about the ministry of service. She said these two verses say that anyone who serves should do so with the strength provided by God, so in all things God may be praised through the Son. Then she read from Joshua 22:5:

> **Joshua 22:5** *But take diligent heed to do the commandment and the law, which Moses the servant of the LORD charged you, to love the LORD your God, and to walk in all his ways, and to keep his commandment, and to cleave unto him, and to serve with all your heart and with all your soul.*

"Be very careful to keep the commandment to love the Lord your God, to obey and follow His instruction, to hold fast to Him and to serve Him with all you heart and soul."

> **Matthew 20: 26-28** *But it shall not be so among you: but whosoever will be great among you, let him be your minister;*
> *And whosoever will be chief among you, let him be your servant: Even as the Son of man came not to be ministered unto, but to minister, and to give his life a ransom for many.*

"Jesus said whoever wants to become great must be your servant and whoever wants to be first must be your slave. Jesus did not come to earth to be served but to give His life as a ransom for many. Jesus served others in many ways during his ministry."

Esther finished the study by saying, "Who among us doesn't want to hear our Lord say to us, 'well done, thou good and faithful servant'?"

The day was soon over and Beth waved goodbye and again expressed her thanks as the ladies left in their wagons. It had been quite a day. The ladies had prepared a delicious noon meal for the stage passengers and handlers, they had cleaned up afterwards, and they all had taken part in a Bible study later in the afternoon. She felt a contentedness she had not experienced in a long time.

CHAPTER SIXTY-TWO
Tuck Helps Grey Wolf Sell Horses

It was the middle of the morning on Tuesday when Charlie came into the sheriff's office with news that Grey Wolf was down at the livery corral with a bunch of horses. Tuck decided to head down there. He was anxious to see his horses as well as offer assistance if needed in the sale.

When Tuck got to the corral, he saw Pete Ballard talking with Grey Wolf while White Eagle and Running Wolf were putting the horses in the corral.

"Hello. How is the trade going?"

Grey Wolf said, "Good. Pete want ten horses."

This was the first time Grey Wolf had dealt in cash, so he asked Tuck to help him with it. Tuck asked Pete how much he was paying for the horses and told Gray Wolf it would be a good idea to open an account at the bank, and explained to him what all was involved.

Anyway, that was a lot of money to keep on his person. He agreed to this and asked Tuck to accompany him to the bank. The bank was new to Mustang Ridge and many people were cautious but happy to have it in the town. Tuck was sure not many banks would allow an Indian to open an account, but he knew it would not be a problem at the Mustang Ridge bank. It was another sign that Mustang Ridge was a growing community.

Once Pete had paid him and Grey Wolf had made a deposit at the bank, they stopped in at the mercantile and talked to Sam. Sam had said earlier he would buy some of the horses. When they talked to him, he shook hands with Grey Wolf. *Funny that. Grey Wolf was getting accustomed to shaking hands.* People in Mustang Ridge had been shaking his hand a lot lately.

Sam bought the rest of the horses and paid him partly in cash. Grey Wolf took the rest out in trade at his store. The Shoshone bought a lot of food supplies such as beans and rice that Tuck knew his family had been without for quite a long time. This was a God-send to his family. Tuck went along with him back to the bank so he could deposit the rest of the money from Sam. He thought he would do well in the future. Tuck said goodbye to Grey Wolf, Running Wolf, and White Eagle. Grey Wolf was the exception among the Indians. Not all have been able to get on in the white settlements like he had.

It was good that he was able to sell his horses. It was good that he had traded for a supply of food. With winter coming, his family would have need for it. And speaking of winter, snowflakes were starting. Tuck looked at the sky and saw a dark cloud to the west, guessing they were in for it.

CHAPTER SIXTY-THREE
Snow Storm!

It was late Tuesday morning at Deer Creek Ranch and Beth had been busy with the food preparation for the noon stage. She heard a horse outside and saw out the window that Mattie had arrived and Thad was taking her horse to the barn. She also saw that snow was starting to blow around. She hoped the stagecoach would not get into trouble with the snow.

"My, that snow is sure coming down," Mattie commented as she hustled inside out of the bad weather. "It wasn't even snowing when I left town."

Beth looked at the sky and was troubled with what she saw. This was not going to turn out very good for anyone out in the storm, and that meant the stage. "Mattie, let's take a moment to pray for the stage."

With their heads bowed, the two women asked God to provide safety for Matt and Tom and the stagecoach. Their prayers were cut short as Becca blew in with her pail of milk. "Mama, that storm is getting bad. I could hardly see my way to the ranch-house. The wind is horrible."

Thad and Nate were in the house by the fireplace. They had finished their chores and were warming up by the fire. When Thad heard what Becca said, he went to the window to look out, concerned about the stagecoach getting through. He had the horses ready to go but had not taken them out of the barn.

Beth was keeping the food warm on the back of the stove. The biscuits were ready to pop in the oven and the apple spice cake was on the table. The occupants of the ranch-house paced back and forth to the window, which was becoming iced over. Thad scraped the ice off and peered out into the swirling mass of white.

"Ma, come look." Beth ran to the window and looked out while Thad donned his heavy coat. "I think it's here." They had not even heard the trumpet sound.

Thad helped Matt to unload the stagecoach and get the frozen men and woman into the warmth of the ranch-house. Tom went to the fireplace and held out his hands to the warmth of the fire.

"Thad, let me soak up a little of this warmth and I will help you get the horses into the barn," Tom said. "We have some ropes in the stage. We need to run a rope with us to make sure we can get back."

Beth helped Thad with the ropes. They tied several together and when Tom was ready to go out, Thad tied one end to the hitching rail. They left the stage and just unhitched the teams. Then, holding on to the guide rope, they took the teams to the barn. Beth watched from the window, praying for their safety. In the meantime, Mattie was serving the food to the five passengers and Matt.

Thad and Tom returned after some time with the aid of the rope. When they got to the stage, they took down the baggage from the top. It was obvious for everyone that they would be spending the night, snowed in. Thad and Tom then sat down to eat at the table.

Beth began making plans for overnight accommodations. Becca could sleep with Beth and Mattie could have the cot that Thad had built in her room. She would give Becca's room to the couple, the Baker's, and the three male passengers could make their beds in the loft with the boys. That left Matt and Tom, who could bed down in front of the fireplace. *I wonder how long we will be snowbound.*

When the meal was finished, Beth and Mattie cleared the table and started washing the dishes. Mrs. Baker asked if she could help since she didn't know what else to do. Beth graciously accepted her help and they visited back and forth. Matt still sat at the table, watching Mattie. When she was finished, she sat down next to Matt. Beth went to the living area and asked if the men would like some more coffee. When they said yes, she brought the tin cups and filled them from the blue and white speckled pot. She kept the coffee pot filled the rest of the day.

Becca brought out a couple of puzzles and put them on each end of the table. Matt and Mattie started working on one. Some of the others came to the table to watch them putting the puzzles together. Tom had a deck of cards in his bag and started up a game with some of the men. Others played a game of checkers.

As the afternoon wore down, Beth started getting food ready for the evening meal. She was glad for the root cellar under the kitchen which held quite a bit of their harvest. Becca came over to help her while Mattie spent her time with Matt. It was becoming darker outside, showing that the day was drawing to a close.

"Mama, what about milking Buttercup? What will we do?"

Beth discussed it with Thad and Tom. They said they could use the guide rope again to go out to the barn. They had tied it to the barn so it would give a way to get back there if needed.

"I don't think Becca should go out though," Tom said. "Thad and I can go out and get Buttercup milked."

"It will be good to have the milk with the extra mouths to feed," agreed Beth.

Thad and Tom took their coats off the pegs and prepared to go out into the white abyss. Beth handed Thad the pail for the milk. "Be careful," she cautioned.

"I'll get the other chores done while we're out there," Thad informed his mother.

Two of the passengers heard him and also offered to go along. "Wait up," one said. "We'll come along and help you with the chores."

Matt rose as if to join them, but Ralph Herman and Burt Leonard stopped him. "No, Matt. You stay and keep Mattie company. You rest for now." They laughed and slapped him on the back.

"Thanks, men. Will do."

So, three men accompanied Thad to the barn to do the chores, Tom and two passengers. Beth looked out the window as they took hold of the rope and made their way to the barn disappearing in a mass of white.

It took longer than usual to do the chores, which was to be expected. Beth kept watch out the window, waiting for some sign of them. Becca had taken on the duty of getting supper ready since she wasn't milking Buttercup. She made a fresh pot of coffee because she knew the men would need something hot to warm them up. Beth glanced back at her daughter, pleased at how she had matured into a competent young lady. Becca was an excellent cook.

"Here they come," called Beth. She scurried to open the door for the snow-covered men. As they stumbled into the open door, Thad carried the pail of milk while Tom carried a basket of fresh eggs.

"We got eggs too!" Tom held up the basket triumphantly. "Should be enough for everyone for breakfast."

"How did it go?" Beth asked. "Are the livestock going to survive this?"

"It was cold getting to the barn. That wind is awful, but the livestock are going to be okay. I don't think Buttercup liked it that someone different was milking her," Thad said.

"She likes me to sing to her," Becca said. "Did you sing to her?"

"No, I did not!" Thad laughed.

"Maybe it was because you had cold hands." Tom teased him.

"Well, there's that," replied Thad. "Looks like you got quite a few eggs though."

Nate came running to see how many eggs his chickens had laid. "How are my chickens? Are they going to live through the storm?"

Tom answered him, "Yes, Nate. They are good. There are so many animals in that barn, they have created their own heat. They're all doing fine."

Once the men had removed their coats and taken a seat at the table, Becca poured coffee for them. As they sat sipping their coffee and warming their hands around the hot cups, Beth and Becca set the table and began serving the food.

That evening the visitors of Deer Creek Ranch spent their time as they had in the afternoon. They continued working on the puzzles, playing cards, and visiting. Nate even brought out his flute which Thad had carved for him. Beth had taught him how to play it, so he played 'Jesus Loves Me', the only song he knew. Marie Baker began singing with him and Beth joined in. As Nate began to play it again, Mattie and Becca sang too. The voices of the women provided sweet entertainment to the stranded visitors.

As it neared time for everyone to call it a day, Beth stoked the fire in the kitchen stove while Thad added wood to the large fireplace in the living area. Each of the bedrooms had its own small fireplace and he also stoked them before the occupants retired.

"Good night, everyone," called Beth. "Hopefully, tomorrow will bring some sunshine. See you in the morning."

CHAPTER SIXTY-FOUR
The Day After the Storm

Beth awoke early in the morning to start the breakfast preparation but also to take a look outside. She had noticed in the night the wind had died down. Looking out the window, she saw that the snow had blown into drifts around the barn and ranch-house. It was the first snow of the season and it had blown in pretty hard.

The coffee was cooking on the stove, creating a delicious aroma. Beth started mixing the flapjacks she was going to make when everyone woke up. She also got a slab of bacon from the root cellar and sliced several strips and put in the large cast iron pan. Matt and Tom, sleeping by the big fireplace, woke to the smell of bacon and coffee. As everyone began filtering into the great room, Beth cracked the eggs into the skillet.

"I can't believe that smell is making me hungry. After all the food you gave us yesterday, I should still be full. That sure smells good, Beth." Matt came over to the stove where Beth was just as Mattie came out of Beth's bedroom.

"Good morning everyone," Mattie said to the two of them but including Tom who was also getting up.

Tom threw some more logs in the fireplace, then went to the window and looked out. Matt came over and handed a cup of coffee to Tom and drank from his own.

"Matt, do you think we'll be able to go?"

"Maybe. Let's get everyone going on breakfast, and we'll see how it goes," Matt turned from the window and saw that the over-nighters were all up and heading to the table. Even Beth's children were all up.

"Morning folks. I was just telling Tom that I think we will try to get going as soon as we have had breakfast," Matt announced to anyone who was listening.

Mattie was frying the bacon while Beth flipped the flapjacks. Mattie filled the coffee cups at the table and refilled the pot with water to make more coffee. The hungry group sat at the table and was about to start on the flapjacks when Matt said, "Wait everyone. Beth, are you going to ask the blessing?"

"Oh, yes," Beth said turning from the stove. She came over to the table and asked them to bow with her as she gave thanks.

"Dear Father in Heaven, we thank Thee for this food and Thy loving care for us. Thou hast seen us safely through a bad winter storm. I ask Thee to continue to give the passengers safety as they leave today. Be with Matt and Tom as they drive and protect the stagecoach on the way to the next stop. And keep everyone warm. Amen."

Everyone dug into the flapjacks with sorghum and the bacon and eggs with a zesty hunger. When they were finished, Thad rose and retrieving his coat from the hook, he donned it preparing to go to the barn. Tom did the same saying, "I'll go with you Thad. Looks like I can take up our rope. No need for that to get to the barn anymore. "

"Yeah, thought there would be more snow though. All that wind really fooled us."

As Thad and Tom went outside, everyone else finished eating and went to get their bags packed. Then Becca and Nate put their coats on to do their chores. Nate grabbed the egg basket and Becca got the milk pail and they went outside. Matt sat at the table having another cup of coffee with Mattie.

Beth heard Mattie softly tell Matt, "I'm glad I was here when you got snowed in."

She saw Matt pat Mattie's hand. *I should get out of here and leave those two alone for a while.*

Thad and Tom hitched the teams up to the stagecoach. Tom threw the passenger's baggage up on top and opened the door for the passengers.

A rested and satisfied group were all filing out to the stage and thanking Beth for her hospitality during the storm. Amazingly enough, no one was upset about having to stay over and losing a day of travel. On the contrary, they acted like they enjoyed themselves.

Beth had already told Matt that the passengers would only be charged for the one meal, not the rest of them. Matt thanked her and told the passengers about what Beth said and told them to make their payments to her. They would be leaving in ten minutes. However, as they paid Beth, they gave her extra saying her hospitality was worth it to them.

Mattie and Beth waved goodbye as the stagecoach pulled away. "Well, I suppose I should get ready to go too. Hopefully Pete and Esther will not have worried too much about my absence," Mattie said.

"Mattie, it was so good having you here and getting to know you." Beth laughed. "And who would have guessed you would have that much time to spend with Matt."

Mattie blushed. "You know, huh?"

"Of course. One would have to be blind not to. And I think it's great. I think you two make a great couple. I just wish there was some way for you two to have more time together," Beth said.

"I think there might be a change in that. Matt has been talking to a banker from Texas, who also has a horse ranch and goes all over buying horses. In fact, he was here for Thanksgiving Matt said. Anyway, he wants to set Matt up in a ranch as partners. Matt wants to raise cattle as well as horses."

"My goodness, that's wonderful. Wait, did you say that guy was a banker from Texas?"

"Yes, why?" Mattie asked and watched as Beth grew pale and dropped into the nearest chair. "Beth, are you all right?"

"Did--- did Matt say what town in Texas this banker was from?"

"No, he didn't. Oh, my goodness, Beth. I never thought. Do you think he might be from where you lived?"

"I don't think so. The banker in my town was someone else, unless he came after I left. I should ask Matt where that town is. Texas is a big territory. Could be hundreds of miles from my former home."

"Well, you would have known if he was. Matt said he was one of the passengers who ate Thanksgiving dinner here."

"Oh, yes. I saw him and Matt talking after mealtime."

"I hope it will be okay. Beth, I'm sorry, I have to go. I see Thad has my horse saddled and waiting out front."

"Thank you for your help, Mattie. Good luck to you and Matt. Be careful on your way back to town."

Mattie had only been gone a short while when the door opened and in walked Thad and Tuck. Beth looked up at Tuck from her rocking chair and smiled at him. It was so good to see him. She didn't know why he was here but she was glad he was.

She got up and went to get the coffee pot. "Coffee's pretty fresh yet, Tuck. How about a cup?"

"Sure," he said pulling back a chair and sitting down.

"What brings you out here?" Beth asked.

"Well," Tuck considered her question. "I've been asked that question a few times today and nobody believes me when I say it is to check on how things are after the storm. So, I guess I'll just tell the truth and say, I came out just to see you."

"Oh, Tuck. I'm so glad you did." Beth put her hand on top of Tuck's hand. Even though she had just heard what could be bad news from Mattie, and her mind was busy with possibilities--some of them not good – she still was glad to see Tuck.

"Beth, would you…" Tuck paused. "Would you mind if I courted you?"

"I would dearly love for you to court me."

CHAPTER SIXTY-FIVE
Tuck Worries About Beth

Tuck put the coffee pot on in the office. He had stayed there to sleep last night because of the storm that blew through yesterday. The winds were terrible. Tuck couldn't see across the street so he just spent the night at the jail. He hadn't slept well last night worrying about Beth and her family. The more he thought about it, the more he thought he should ride out there.

When Charlie came in he said, "Charlie, I'm heading out to Deer Creek Ranch to check on everyone."

Tuck stopped by the mercantile to talk to Sam. "I'm going out to Deer Creek Ranch. Is there anything you need to send out to Beth?"

"I don't have anything to be delivered out there," Sam said looking kind of funny at Tuck. "Was there was another reason you stopped?"

Searching for something to explain himself, he told Sam about the Texas banker and his concern for Beth. Sam understood right away and said he'd look into it, maybe send out some telegrams. Now that Mustang Ridge had its own telegraph office located in the back of the mercantile, it was easier to communicate. Tuck said he didn't know if it was the same town or not. He did know that Beth didn't seem to recognize his name. Maybe it wasn't anywhere near where Beth lived.

Tuck stopped by his room and donned a change of clothing, then rode out to the ranch. He met Mattie McLeod riding toward town and they stopped to talk for a while. She told him what had happened with the weather and the stagecoach. When Tuck asked how come she was out there when it stormed, she blushed and told him about her attraction to Matt.

Tuck smiled and asked, "Does Matt feel the same way?"

"Yes, he does. Why are you going out there, Tuck?"

"To check on the ranch for the stage line."

Mattie looked at Tuck sideways and laughed. "Yeah."

Tuck felt a little sheepish that she saw through him so clearly. When Tuck got to the ranch, Thad was coming in from the barn.

"Hello, Tuck. What brings you out here?"

"To check if there had been any damage. Did you survive the storm okay?"

"Everything was great: it was like a party with everyone house-bound."

They went into the ranch-house together. Beth looked up and saw Tuck and smiled so big, he felt like he was a youngster again. *Her smile can really make a gloomy day bright again.*

Beth asked Tuck to have coffee with her and they sat down at the table while Thad went back out to the barn with Nate. He didn't know where Becca was. He really wasn't paying much attention. The two of them talked a little then Tuck asked her something that he had no thought of asking when he went out there. But then again, maybe he really did.

Tuck stumbled all over his words but finally was able to ask Beth for permission to court her. *Can you believe it? She said yes! Imagine how happy I was when she said she'd love to have me court her.*

They just sat there at the table and talked until the children returned. Tuck guessed they were hungry; it was lunch time.

CHAPTER SIXTY-SIX
Tuck Courts Beth as the Town Looks On

It was Sunday and Beth and her family had made the trek to Mustang Ridge to go to church. Beth had not seen Tuck since he had asked to court her. She found that she was eagerly anticipating seeing him again. Questions began to form in her mind. How would he go about courting her? How would she react? What would her children say about it? In fact, how and when should she tell them? Then of course, what would her friends say? So, so many questions. *Father God, give me wisdom in all of these areas.*

Thad was tying the team's reins to the hitching rail while the rest of the family was getting down from the wagon. As Beth turned toward the wagon to climb down, she felt strong hands at her waist helping her. She turned and looked into the gentle eyes of her new suitor. Tuck took her arm in his and held his hand over hers.

"Good morning, Beth." Tuck's voice was husky and warm.

"Good morning to you too," Beth responded in kind.

"Shall we?" Tuck led her up the front steps and into the church where they stopped to visit with friends before having a seat.

"Good morning you two," said Reverend Prescott. "Good to see you."

Martha and Sam were next. Martha gushed, "Oh my. It's so good to see you two together. Bless you."

Sam saying, "Tuck, about time."

Sarah moved close and whispered in Beth's ear, "May God bless you two."

Mattie came next and said with a smile, "You too, huh?"

As Beth and Tuck walked further down the church aisle to take a seat in the pew, Beth was absolutely sure she was red as a beet. She felt the burning in her cheeks. Even though she was so uncomfortable, she felt the warmth of Tuck's arm and decided she liked that feeling even more.

Reverend Prescott opened the service with prayer and directed his congregation to stand and join him in singing "Come Thou Fount."

Come thou fount of every blessing
Tune my heart to sing thy grace
Streams of mercy never ceasing
Call for songs of loudest praise
Teach me some melodious sonnet
Sung by flaming tongues above
I'll praise the mount I'm fixed upon it
Mount of thy redeeming love

Here I raise my Ebenezer
Hither by thy help I come
And I hope by thy good pleasure
Safely to arrive at home

Jesus sought me when a stranger
Wondering from the fold of God
He, to rescue me from danger
Interposed His precious blood

O to grace how great a debtor daily I'm constrained to be!
Let thy goodness like a fetter, bind my wandering heart to thee
Prone to wander Lord I feel it, prone to leave the God I love
Here's my heart, O take and seal it, seal it for thy courts above

As Beth's melodious voice sang those precious words, her prayer to God echoed the last words to the song; *"Here's my heart, O take and seal it, seal it for thy courts above."*

As Beth and Tuck walked to the wagon, Beth asked Tuck if he would care to come to Sunday dinner with them at the ranch. He answered in the affirmative and they ended up with Thad riding Irish while Tuck drove the wagon, sitting with Beth on the wagon's front seat and Becca and Nate on the second seat.

The family ate dinner together when they arrived. The venison roast that Beth had in the oven with carrots and potatoes from the root cellar smelled delicious as they opened the door to the ranch-house. Before long, Beth and Becca had the food on the table and called everyone to the table to eat. Tuck offered the blessing.

CHAPTER SIXTY-SEVEN
Matt Takes a Week Off

It was Thursday and the last stagecoach of the week was due to arrive. Beth had dinner ready as she heard the trumpet sound as it neared the ranch. She pulled her shawl around her shoulders and stepped out to the porch. She was surprised to note that Matt was not driving the stagecoach today. Instead, Will Barrett was the Whip.

Worried about Matt, Beth asked, "What happened to Matt?"

"Don't worry, Mrs. Eastman. He's fine. He just took a few days off to take care of a personal matter." Will Barrett assured her as he dismounted from the box.

"Oh?" said Beth, curious.

"Now, Mrs. Eastman. You know I can't tell you anything if I don't know," Will said. "He didn't tell me even though I asked."

She turned to her passengers and went about serving the noon meal. Later, when Will called, "All aboard," Beth waved goodbye to the passengers. She still pondered why Matt needed the days off from the stage line. Had his shoulder acted up again? Was he in too much pain? Was it something else?

The answer came next Sunday when the Eastman family arrived for church. As Tuck and Beth were walking into the church, arm in arm, they met Matt and Mattie also walking arm in arm. Since it was time for church to begin, Matt quickly confided in Tuck that he needed to talk to him afterwards. Beth heard the interchange, and she became even more curious.

Later, after the conclusion of the service, Mattie and Matt came to Tuck and Beth by their wagon.

"So, Matt. What's this all about?" asked Tuck. "Something wrong?"

"No," Mattie answered for him. "In fact, everything is wonderful."

Mattie continued with a look at Matt, "Matt and I are going to be married next Sunday afternoon. We've already asked Reverend Prescott to perform the service."

Matt continued, "And we want you two to stand up with us when we get married."

Beth flew to Mattie's side, hugging her. "This seems so sudden. Are your sure you don't need more time to get to know each other?

"I'm sure, Beth. Besides, we are both widowed and I've found that out west, things move faster," Mattie answered her.

"Well then, I will be pleased to stand up for you. I'm so happy for you two."

Tuck nodded and shook Matt's hand. "I accept the offer to stand up with you. Congratulations, Matt."

"Where will you live?" Beth asked.

"That's another part of our surprise. Remember the fella from Texas on Thanksgiving Day? Well, he and I have been talking since then. He bought a ranch southwest of Mustang Ridge and wants to go into partnership with me in establishing a horse and cattle ranch," Matt said, warming to the subject. "Eventually, I'll buy him out and have complete ownership. It's something I have always wanted to do."

"That's great news! So, you'll go right there after the wedding?" Tuck asked.

"Yes. I took some days off to go get the ranch-house ready to live in. There's not a lot there, but Mattie brought a lot of furnishings out in her wagon, so we can put those to good use."

Mattie looked at Beth who had been quiet during Matt's excited explanation of their plans. "Beth, are you not happy for us?"

"Oh, Mattie dear. Of course, I am. I saw from the beginning that you two were meant for each other. It's that I just got to know you and take you into my heart as a dear friend, and now you will be going far away."

"Beth, it's only about 30 miles away. We'll still be able to visit occasionally," Matt offered.

"Yes, I suppose so," Beth said, not really convinced.

Tuck squeezed Beth's hand. "We can help you move your things down there," he said looking at Beth.

"That would be great, but I don't think we can do it in one day. It would be late when the wedding and reception is done."

"We'll work something out. Maybe we will have to wait until the next Friday when you are free."

"That would probably work out great," Mattie said. "I don't think I can fit everything into my wagon. I have more furniture since I came to Mustang Ridge."

"There, you see? I knew we could work something out," Tuck squeezed Beth's hand again.

CHAPTER SIXTY-EIGHT
Tuck Gets Ready for Matt and Mattie's Wedding

Tuck sure was excited for Matt. It didn't come as a complete surprise though. Beth had told him about Mattie coming out to the ranch to help with the stage dinner, just so she could see Matt, and he had seen her riding away from the ranch after the storm. He was happy for Matt too, that he would be able to get away from driving the stage. What with his shoulder acting up in bad weather, it was not comfortable for him anymore. Driving a 6-up requires a lot of shoulder strength. He's a great guy and a great stage driver. Tuck hoped that Will Bennett would do as good a job.

Beth sure got quiet thinking about Mattie moving away. But that's how life goes. Tuck hoped that a promise to take Mattie's extra furnishings down would help her. Besides, he was anxious to see Matt's ranch operation himself.

He hoped it would be good weather and speaking of weather, Tuck thought if that stage should happen to get stranded at Deer Creek Ranch again, it sure would be nice if there was more room for people to sleep. It was good there were only five passengers that time, but it could easily have been more.

Right now, the weather had warmed considerably and there was hardly any trace of snow, but he knew that wouldn't last. He'd have to talk to Sam about building on a couple more rooms or so. Then Tuck supposed he should tell Beth his little secret about Deer Creek Ranch. It's time.

Tuck talked to Sam about it Monday and Sam thought it was a good idea to build on to the ranch-house.

"We should get right on that Tuesday before the weather turns cold again," Sam said. "We have to see about lining up some men to help with the job and get out there. I'll line up a work crew."

While Tuck was at the mercantile, he bought a small side table for a wedding present for Matt and Mattie. He hoped it would be something they could use. He couldn't take all the credit as Sam advised him.

Tuck made another purchase too. One of a personal nature. Sam promised to keep quiet about it, though he couldn't seem to wipe that silly smile off his face.

CHAPTER SIXTY-NINE
Additions to Deer Creek Ranch House

Beth wasn't sure she understood how the stage line could approve the building of the addition to the ranch-house at Deer Creek Ranch. However, who was she to argue with their generosity. As she watched the men at work on the building project, she thanked God for this additional blessing in their lives.

Tuck, Sam, and three other men had come out first thing Tuesday morning with the building materials. She was amazed at how quickly they worked. They brought boards and logs from town, which had been curing for several months. Their plan was to halve the logs, strip the bark, and place them on top of the boards so they would match the rest of the ranch-house. The men began work on building the frames for the two rooms, then putting in the individual fireplaces.

Although Beth had not been asked to, she prepared dinner for the working men in addition to that for the stage. She fed them before the stage arrived, so there would be room for them to sit at the table. Becca, Nate, and Thad ate at that time also. As she served them the venison stew she had made, she was introduced to the three men. They were Simon Wesley, Wilber Lloyd, and Gus Stanley. They were young men who were hired on by the stage line to do things like building construction, so they knew their work and were very accomplished in doing it.

"This is real good stew, Mrs. Eastman," Wilber Lloyd complimented her.

"I agree," Gus Stanley responded.

"Mrs. Eastman, I don't believe I've eaten a finer stew."

"Well, you boys are welcome," Beth replied, blushing. "Your compliments will go to my head if I'm not careful." Secretly, Beth relished the compliments from these men and from the stage passengers. It helped her to keep on cooking.

Following dinner, all the men went back to work; this time laying the boards on the frames Sam and Tuck had built. By evening, they had all the walls done and the openings cut for the doors into the main ranch-house. They would return to work on the roof the next day and to chink the log halves so they would match the rest of the building.

As they left the table to get back to work, Beth heard the trumpet blow.

"That was good timing," Tuck commented.

"Indeed," Beth said.

Beth opened the ranch-house door and welcomed Will, Tom, and the six stage passengers into her home for their dinner.

Will and Tom went directly to the fireplace and stood warming their hands. "Sure gets cold up there in the box with the wind rushing by," Tom grumbled.

"Here, boys, wrap your hands around some hot coffee," Beth invited, pouring some for the rest of the people.

"Thanks, Mrs. Eastman. I appreciate it," said Tom as they took the proffered hot coffee.

"So, how was this trip, Will? Any trouble with the Sioux?" Beth asked.

"Not this time. They seem to have settled down."

"That's good."

"So, how's Matt? Heard he's getting married."

"Yes, next Sunday. He and Mattie will leave afterwards to go to his ranch 30 miles south of Mustang Ridge," replied Beth.

"Yeah, heard he was going into ranching. Good for him. Miss him though," Tom said.

"You got some kind of building going on here?" Will asked.

"Yes, the stage line thought after the blizzard that stranded the stage here, we should have more room to put up the passengers, so they are adding two rooms onto the ranch-house."

"Well I'll be. Imagine that." Tom pondered a moment, and then commented. "Folks, we will be leaving in ten minutes. Pay Mrs. Eastman and take care of any other things you need to do and meet me out front."

Thad had been hitching the fresh teams to the stage. Tom climbed up into the box while Will helped the passengers into the stagecoach. Swinging up into the box, Will took up the reins and waving goodbye to Beth, he urged the teams forward. Another stage stop was over.

"Ma, do you suppose I could help the men work on the building?" Thad asked.

"Of course, Thad. Go ahead."

So, with the work crew increased by one man, the project sped along until they called it a day. They would be back to finish the roof on Wednesday.

CHAPTER SEVENTY
Rooms Are Added to the Ranch-house

Although Tuck didn't get to see much of Beth while they worked on the new rooms, just being near her as she served their noon meal was enough to stir his heart. But he wanted to spend time alone with her.

That first day of work they completed even more than they thought. Tuck knew in the afternoon when Thad came out to help, that Beth was in the ranch-house attending to the schooling of Becca and Nate. So close and yet so far.

They came back the next day to finish with the roof. Tuck believed the cold was even worse, or maybe it was because they were up so high. Beth kept them supplied with warming coffee throughout the day.

When the day ended, the men had done what they set out to do and all was ready for Beth to move things in. Thad had made four cots to put in the rooms and Tuck knew that Beth and Becca had been sewing curtains for the two windows. He was sure if the stage were snowbound again, there would be sleeping room for the passengers. However, that was only a secondary part of his plan. He wanted Nate and Thad to each have a room and not have to sleep in the loft every night.

After the work was done, he told Sam to go on with the men. He was going to stay a while. Sam said goodbye, and Tuck thanked him for the help. Tuck had thought it would be nice to spend some time with Beth and maybe get an invite to try out one of those new beds Thad had made.

Beth and Tuck sat near the big fireplace after supper was over. They talked about the future of the stage line, the station, and then moved on to Matt and his wedding. It was hard to talk of more serious things with Beth when her children were within hearing distance but it was turning too cold to go outside.

That night Tuck helped the children with their chores. He enjoyed being with them, even when Becca and Nate got into a gigantic fight. He wasn't sure what it was about, but it was really upsetting the horses so Thad sent them packing back to the house. He and Tuck finished their chores.

As the children started to get ready for bed, it finally came – Beth's invitation for Tuck to spend the night. He supposed it wasn't in good taste to spend the night, but he didn't care. And he also didn't care that the children would be there at breakfast as he enjoyed being with them too. One day soon, he hoped they would all be together as a family.

The next morning Tuck helped with the chores again. *I could get used to this.* When they trouped into the ranch-house bearing a basket of fresh eggs and a bucket of milk, Beth greeted them with the delicious-aroma of her flapjacks and bacon. This woman sure knew the way to a man's heart.

After Tuck finished his third cup of coffee, Beth had to continue her dinner preparations, so he decided it was past time for him to head back into town. After all, he did have a job and probably should attend to it.

CHAPTER SEVENTY-ONE
Matt and Mattie's Wedding

Beth scurried around the ranch-house, her excitement catching. She had prepared an early breakfast and it was time to head out the door. Thad had the 2-seater hitched up to Bullet and Lightning and was waiting out front. Beth still wasn't happy with how she looked. She was standing up for Mattie and she wanted to look her best.

Becca came into her mother's room and observed her looking in the mirror. She said, "Mama, do you still have that pretty lace collar? That would look nice on your dress."

"Yes, I do! Perfect idea. Thanks Becca."

She rummaged in her dresser drawer until she found it and laid it over her dress collar. The pretty blue cotton dress that she had recently made looked lovely with the white lace on the collar. She looked in the dresser mirror and was satisfied. She rushed out of her bedroom to see if everyone else was ready.

Becca was wearing the blue and white checked gingham that Beth had made for her birthday. Nate and Thad were wearing their church clothes. She picked up the wedding gift that she had wrapped and announced that they were ready. They loaded into the 2-seater and headed to town.

After the morning service, Beth stood next to Mattie in front of the altar, holding the bridal bouquet. Mattie looked so nice and so did Matt. A happier couple she had not seen. Tuck at Matt's side looked so solemn. Reverend Prescott was asking the couple to repeat the vows after him. Then it was time for the ring. Matt placed the wedding band on Mattie's finger and Reverend Prescott said, "I pronounce you man and wife."

Everyone stood and applauded the newlyweds. The pews were pushed back and the ladies of the church set up a lunch for all to partake. The wedding gifts were brought to the couple to open while they ate. The side table from Tuck was revealed and a set of seven dishcloths from Beth which she had embroidered with the days of the week. The couple received a lot of other useful gifts as well.

After the gifts were all opened, the town gave the couple a happy send-off as they prepared to board their wagon and head to their new home. Beth and Mattie hugged goodbye. A few tears were seen on both their faces.

Beth stood back and Tuck came to her side, and reached for her hand. She looked up at him and smiled. *I love this man. I really do.*

CHAPTER SEVENTY-TWO
Evil Comes to Deer Creek Station

It had been a busy week, and Beth was tired. She had the meal almost ready when she heard horses ride up to the front of the ranch-house. Looking out the window, she saw two men she had never seen before dismount and head for the door. They barged into the ranch-house without knocking, with guns drawn.

"What is this? What do you want?" Beth demanded in alarm. She was thankful that Nate and Becca were up in the loft. Becca had promised to play a game with Nate and he had it up there. At the noise of the unwanted visitors, she saw Becca peer over the edge of the loft. Beth shook her head ever so slightly. Becca seemed to understand and pulled Nate back and kept him quiet. *Oh, why couldn't this have been a day when Tuck was here?*

"Who else is here?" demanded the leader.

"No one," Beth answered.

"What about the hostler?" he demanded again.

"He's out in the barn getting the horses ready for the noon stage. It's almost noon so I need to finish preparing the meal."

"No!" he shouted. "Nobody will be eating."

"Why are you doing this?" Beth asked.

"I want the gold the stage is carrying," he answered.

"But that stage doesn't carry gold. It's only a passenger stage," Beth argued.

"Not today, Missy. I got word that they are carrying a strongbox of gold bars, so you just shut up."

Beth heard the trumpet blast signifying the arrival of the stage. "What's that?" the leader demanded.

"The stage trumpet telling me to have the food ready and Thad to have the horses ready," Beth answered him.

"Who's Thad?"

"The hostler," she answered.

He came up behind Beth, and grabbing her with his arm around her neck, he dictated orders to her. "When the driver gets in tell him to bring the strongbox in."

He held his crooked arm tight to her neck so she couldn't speak. She tried to tell him the passengers came in first and the shotgun helped unhitch the horses, but she couldn't.

Please Father, get us safely through this situation. Be with my children, keep them safe.

The passengers started coming in, which surprised the robbers, but the leader waved his gun with his other hand for them to go to their left. The second robber also pointed them over. Beth was glad they were on that side. It put them opposite Becca and Nate. When Will came into the ranch-house, he had a questioning look on his face because Beth was usually at the door and welcoming the passengers. Then he saw why Beth wasn't at the door.

"What's going on?" Will asked.

"You the driver?"

"Yes, what do you want?"

"I want you to get that strongbox from the stage."

"What? Are you crazy? This is a passenger stage. We don't carry strong boxes," Will said. "Now let her go so she can feed these passengers."

Beth could tell this man who had a gun on her and everyone else was hesitating. Things were not going as he had planned. Would he let her go, or would he kill them all?

Finally, he said to his partner, "Go out and find that hostler. You. Driver. Get over there with the passengers."

Will moved slowly over to the wall. "Beth, you all right?" he asked her.

She tried to speak but of course, couldn't since the robber still had her tight by the neck, so she tried to nod.

"Listen fella. You hurt her or any of these passengers, your life isn't going to be worth spit," Will threatened.

"Shut up!" the robber yelled at Will.

Will saw a movement up at the loft. Becca, big-eyed, peered over the edge. When the robber looked away, Will shook his head at Becca. She got the message and ducked back down again.

"Where's that shotgun?" the leader suddenly asked.

"He's down at the barn helping the hostler," Will supplied.

"My partner will take care of him. Just keep still while we wait for him to come back."

As they told about it later, when Tom went into the barn to help Thad, he mentioned that his mother had not been at the door to greet the passengers. Tom didn't feel right about it,

especially since there were two horses tied to rail. Neither did Thad. They cracked the barn door to look out and saw the second robber heading to the barn with his gun drawn. They waited for him to enter the barn and jumped him the moment he came in. Then tied him up, so he couldn't move.

Thad showed Tom how to go out the back door of the barn so he could enter the ranch-house by the back door. Meanwhile, Thad went up to the ranch-house and entered like he usually would. While attention was turned on him, Tom entered from the rear door, took a board to the back of the leader's head, and knocked him out cold. Beth, close to passing out, fell to the floor. Thad rushed to her side while Tom grabbed the robber's gun.

"Ma! Are you all right?" Thad was panicked, fearing that his mother had been hurt. One of the female passengers, Mrs. Caldwell rushed over to help Beth.

"I'm fine," Beth whispered hoarsely.

As he bent to tie the robber's hands behind his back, Will called up to the loft, "Becca, you and Nate can come down now."

Becca rushed to her mother's side and threw her arms around her.

"What was going on here?" Tom asked Will.

"They had the idea that our stage was carrying a gold shipment in the strongbox."

"We don't even have a strongbox," Tom said. "Wonder where they got that idea."

Mrs. Caldwell had gone to the stove and brought the food over to the table. "We might as well eat the food she has prepared since it is ready."

Mr. Caldwell and the other three passengers went to have a seat at the table. Will helped Tom to bind up the robber. Then Thad and Tom went down to the barn to hitch up the fresh horses. They decided to leave the other robber down at the barn. No sense in putting them under the same roof.

"What shall we do about these bandits?" Tom asked Will after they had grabbed a bite.

"They are going to take a cold ride up top. We'll tie them to the top of the stage and make a detour into Mustang Ridge to the sheriff's office."

Thad, Tom, and two of the passengers helped Will get the unhappy thugs on top of the stage and tied down. When Will called ten minutes until the stage left, the passengers paid Beth over her objections. They told her she deserved it and besides, she had prepared the food.

Later that afternoon, Beth was resting on the sofa near the fireplace. Her voice was still a little hoarse. Her children were waiting on her, not wanting to leave her side. Nate was snuggled close under his mother's arm when they heard a horse galloping into the yard at a good clip.

"Oh no. Not again," Becca cried.

"It's Tuck," Thad called from the window.

Tuck threw open the ranch-house door. He looked around and saw Beth on the sofa and rushed over to her. He sat next to her and took her in him arms. "How are you? Are you hurt?" he asked in a husky voice.

"No, Tuck. I'm fine. Especially now that you are here."

"You children? You're okay?" he asked.

"Yes. Tom and Will helped with it all," Thad said.

At that point, Thad motioned for Becca and Nate to leave them alone. He was glad he had because as he was herding his siblings into his bedroom, he saw Tuck get down on one knee and pull a small box from his vest pocket. He smiled to himself. It would be a good day for his mother after all.

"Beth Eastman, will you do me the honor of becoming my wife?"

CHAPTER SEVENTY-THREE
She Said Yes

Beth was walking on air. Tuck had asked her to marry him and of course, she said yes.

She and Tuck sat holding each other for as long as they could. But then noises began issuing from the bedroom where the children were. Tuck smiled down at Beth and kissed her cheek.

"Shall we?" Tuck nodded toward the bedroom.

She nodded her head yes.

"Thad, would you bring Becca and Nate out here?"

When the children came out, they sat around Tuck and Beth. They were smiling and snickering. Beth knew they probably were aware of what was going on. Tuck smiled at them and said, "Your mother and I have some news for you. I asked her to marry me, and she said yes."

"Yahoo!" Nate exclaimed. He jumped up and danced around in a circle, joined by his brother and sister.

"That is such great news, Tuck. I am so glad," Becca exclaimed.

They were all making so much noise, they almost failed to hear the knock on the door, but Tuck heard it. "Thad, the door. I'm kind of tied up here." Nate was on Tuck's knee and Beth was hugging him like she would never let go.

Thad went to the door and discovered Sam and Martha Garrison. They had ridden up in their buggy and no one inside had heard them.

"Sam, Martha. Come in," Thad said holding the door wide.

"What's all the noise in here? I had to knock twice to get someone to hear me," Sam asked.

"Welcome, Sam, Martha. We are celebrating, aren't we Beth?"

"We are, shall I tell them?"

"Well, somebody better tell us!"

"I asked Beth to marry me, and she said yes," Tuck explained.

Martha let out a scream of joy. "Beth, Tuck, I'm so happy for you two. I've been hoping this would happen."

Sam shook Tuck's hand once he had gotten free from Beth. "Congratulations. That is good news indeed."

"So, what brings you folks out here?" Beth asked.

"When I saw the stage come into town with those two thugs on top, I ran out and helped the men get them down and to the jail. I heard Will tell you how they held Beth hostage. I went right away to get Martha and we came out here. I'm so sorry you had to go through this, Beth," Sam explained.

"Oh Beth, how awful for you. Praise the Lord, you weren't hurt," Martha cried.

After lengthy tales of what had occurred while the robber held Beth hostage; how Becca and Nate hid in the loft the whole time; how Thad and Tom suspected trouble because Beth didn't open the door; how Tom came around back while Thad provided the distraction so he could knock out the leader; they started talking again about the engagement.

"So, have you set a date yet?" Martha asked.

"No," Beth laughed. "We just told the children, and then you knocked on the door. I don't know about the date. Tuck and I will have to talk about it when we are alone."

"Point taken," Martha laughed. "But I was so worried about you when I heard. You're sure you weren't hurt in anyway?"

"Just a little hoarse from him holding me around my neck," Beth explained.

"How awful and here it was all for nothing. The robbers said they were told there would be gold on the stage? I wonder where they got their information. Why did they think this stage carried gold?"

Sam said, "I need to look into it on that end. Somebody spoke out of turn. It could have been deadly."

Becca had gone to the stove and was busy fixing supper. "Would you folks like to stay to supper? I'll have it ready in a few minutes" Becca invited.

"Oh of course, Becca," said Martha. "Let me help you dear."

So, the good friends enjoyed supper together, celebrating the news of Tuck and Beth's engagement and the good outcome of a nasty situation earlier.

CHAPTER SEVENTY-FOUR
Tuck is Angry

When Will drove the stage up in front of the sheriff's office and told Tuck what had taken place at the stage station, Tuck was nearly overcome with rage directed toward the two robbers tied up on top of the stage. He helped get them down from the top and they firmly deposited them in two of the cells. They complained about how cold they were, having been tied to the top of the stage coming in. Tuck really didn't want to give them a blanket, he was so mad at them. But his faith won out and he asked Charlie to get the blankets for them.

Will had never learned what their names were, so Tuck questioned them after the stage left. They were not very forthcoming, and Tuck had the feeling that the names they gave were only aliases. The mouthy one, apparently the leader, said his name was Clive

Jones and his partner was actually his brother, Dade Jones. Clive Jones was an obnoxious sort and even locked in a jail cell, he was still making wisecracks about "the pretty dame" at the stage station. That only managed to incense Tuck further. Both Clive and Dade could not seem to believe that they were guilty of anything. They just thought that they had been let down by the informant who gave them such bad information.

As soon as Tuck had the prisoners processed, he opened the safe and took out a package with his name on it and put it in his vest pocket inside his heavy coat. He left the prisoners in the capable hands of his deputy and mounting Irish, rode hard and fast to Deer Creek Ranch.

If they had hurt his Beth in any way, he'd...! Well, he hoped he didn't have to face that. If only he had been there when it happened, he could have been there to prevent harm to her. His thoughts slammed around in his head while he rode. What would he find when he got there? Was he only halfway there? Was Beth hurt? Never had the ranch seemed so far from town as he raced toward Beth.

When Tuck arrived at the ranch, he didn't even bother to knock. He hurried through the door, looked for Beth and found her in front of the fire surrounded by her children. He raced to her side and asked if she was okay. She nodded and her voice was so hoarse when she spoke. He noticed her neck was red, and it made him angry all over again.

Nate snuggled under her arm and Becca sat at her side. Thad came over and hovered behind them, as though to protect his family. Tuck knelt at her feet and held her hand.

Tuck was aware that Thad had taken Becca and Nate into another room, so he took the opportunity as long as he was down on one knee. He pulled the package out of his vest pocket and removed the engagement ring. He'd bought the ring shortly after they began courting, but now he couldn't take any chance that something worse may happen to his sweetheart. He asked her to be his wife.

Tuck had to admit, he was a little afraid Beth might not accept his proposal. After all, they had only been courting a short time. All the way to the ranch, he thought of what he would do if she said no. But she said yes! He should have been thinking about what to do if she said yes, because he was left not knowing what to do next, so they sat together and held hands.

Just after they told the children, who by the way, were pretty excited, Sam and Martha came visiting. Sam must have run right home to get Martha. Knowing her, she didn't waste any time.

She probably threw a coat on and was out the door before Sam was. And bless Martha, she came bearing a pie.

CHAPTER SEVENTY-FIVE
Date for Wedding and Secret Revealed

"We should set a date for our wedding," Tuck said after the Garrison's had left. "When would you like to be married?"

"I was thinking a spring wedding would be nice."

"Why so far away?" asked Tuck. He was thinking about his reason for asking her today, wanting to hurry it up.

"It's not that long to wait. After all, it will soon be Christmas. Winter travel will be a problem."

"Whatever you say," he said, but Tuck really didn't believe what he was saying to her. He wanted to be next to her now—to protect her.

"Perhaps around Resurrection Sunday would be good. We could talk to Reverend Prescott about it before we decide for sure."

"Yes," Tuck said.

"Tuck?" Beth snuggled closer.

"Yes?"

"Where will we live when we are married?"

"Why, right here at Deer Creek Ranch." Tuck knew it was time to tell Beth who owned the ranch.

"You see, this was my parent's ranch. When they passed on, I inherited it. So, you are marrying the owner of Deer Creek Ranch."

Beth pulled away from Tuck to better look at him straight on. "But why did you never say anything?"

"Sam and I agreed before you came, that we would keep me out of it and then there just wasn't a perfect time to tell you."

"Well, no wonder you were so eager to build on to the barn and the pasture, not to mention the ranch-house."

"I'm sorry; I probably should have told you sooner," Tuck said, his confidence weakening.

Thinking of her very own circumstances and the truth she withheld for so many months, Beth was humbled. "I am not in the position to judge you for a secret you withheld; so yes, I'm all right with it, Tuck. Will you continue to be sheriff?"

"For a time probably - until they can find someone to replace me. In the meantime, I want to start growing a cattle operation. That's what

my folks had here at one time. There is room to the south to pasture cattle so Thad can still have his horse operation to the north. We'd have to add on to the corral to utilize it for both of us though."

"How exciting that will be. I can hardly wait," Beth exclaimed.

"Want to make it earlier?" Tuck half joked.

Beth smiled and patted Tuck's hand.

CHAPTER SEVENTY-SIX
Tuck and Beth Set a Date?

Beth wants it to be married around Resurrection Sunday. That's almost four months away! Tuck wanted to be married right away, so he could protect her from danger like she had faced earlier in the day. But he gave in and agreed with Beth even though inside he longed to make it now.

When Beth asked where they would live when they were married, he knew it was time to tell her the truth about who owned Deer Creek Ranch. Tuck was afraid of her reaction to knowing he owned it. When she said she was not in a position to judge him about keeping a secret, he felt right there that they had been in similar circumstances, and he understood in a new way what she had gone through when he reacted so badly. He gave thanks to God that this wonderful woman loved him!

When Tuck returned to Mustang Ridge, he went first to the office.

"Howdy, Tuck. Everything is quiet here. Still have those two robbers in the cells, and nothing happening on the streets. Even the saloon is quiet."

"I think I'll run over to the telegraph office and see if we have any notices."

"All right-ee, Tuck. Later then."

The telegraph office used to have a corner in the mercantile, but as use of it increased, Sam built a small office next door to his store. The full time operator, Walt Grimes, lived in the back.

When Tuck went to the telegraph office, Walt was just locking the door. "Come in, Tuck. I have some telegrams for you."

Usually, wanted posters came through the US mail, but occasionally something was sent by telegraph especially since the mail was brought by the freight wagons from Fort Laramie. One day, they would have rail traffic to Deadwood and would get their mail that way.

When Tuck got back to the office, he sat down and sorted through the telegrams. They consisted of the usual sort of things. But one in particular grabbed his attention and nearly took his breath away. As he read:

Wanted: Information regarding Elizabeth Caruthers traveling with 3 children, Thaddeus, Rebecca, & Nathaniel. Contact Carlyle Caruthers.

Beth had never said what their last name had been, but this had to be her family with names like that.

Tuck's heart seemed to constrict within his chest. He had to move fast on this. He hoped no one else would see it, but those Beth met up with on the wagon train might put two and two together. Tuck folded the telegram and put it in his pocket.

"Charlie, I'm leaving. See you tomorrow."

Tuck went to Sam Garrison's. His store was closed for the day, so Tuck headed to Sam's home. When he knocked, Sam answered the door and invited him in.

"Well, I can tell by the expression on your face that all is not well. What has happened since we left you at the ranch? Is Beth all right?"

Tuck handed him the folded telegram. As Sam unfolded it, Tuck felt Sam's eyes on him. He watched his face as he silently read the telegram. Tuck saw his Sam's eyes grow big. "Oh, my goodness!"

Martha entered the room. "What is it, Sam? What has happened?"

Sam handed her the telegram. "Oh no! What are you going to do, Tuck?

"Well, I'm not going to respond, for one thing. But there could be others along the wagon train route or even passengers on the stage that might. Right now, I want to get married immediately instead of next spring and adopt the children. I need to get some legal advice."

"I can't help you with the legal advice, but I do think it is wise to get married as soon as possible and to adopt those children. I do know for a fact that you have to be legally married to Beth first," Sam offered.

"Do you know when the circuit judge is due to come through?" Martha asked.

Sam and Tuck looked at each other. Tuck hadn't even thought about an adoption process.

"I'll have to send a telegram," he said.

"What will you tell Beth?" Martha asked.

"Just what I told you," Tuck replied.

"Tell her we think your wedding should take place as soon as possible," Sam said.

"Thanks for your advice. I'd appreciate your prayers too," Tuck said.

Tuck didn't sleep much that night. He kept planning what he needed to do first thing in the morning. Send the telegram to the circuit judge, talk to Reverend Prescott, go to Deer Creek Ranch, and tell Beth and the children the bad news. He wasn't looking forward to putting that fear into their lives, especially since they had all been so joyful when he saw them last. Back in a far corner of his mind was the thought that they wouldn't have to wait until spring to be married.

CHAPTER SEVENTY-SEVEN
Terrifying News

Friday morning the chores had been done and Beth was setting the table for breakfast when she heard a horse ride up. "Thad, who is that who just rode up?"

"Tuck. Early for him to visit, isn't it? Maybe he can't stay away from you," he teased.

"All right, everyone to the table. I'll set another place. Thad, let him in."

"Hi, Tuck. Come on in. We are just about to set down to breakfast. Ma set another place for you."

"I'll just have coffee, Beth. I'm not very hungry," Tuck said taking a chair.

"This must be serious, Tuck, for you not to be hungry." Beth was beginning to be worried. Something really was wrong. Did Tuck want to back out of marrying her? She poured him a cup of coffee.

"Please sit down. I have something to share with you."

"Do you want to be alone? Should we leave the room?" Thad inquired. He looked worried too. Tuck shook his head no.

As Beth sat down, Tuck pulled the folded telegram from his pocket. "I received this telegram when I got back to town last night. Wanted you all to hear what it says because it concerns us all," He read it aloud to them.

Wanted: Information regarding Elizabeth Caruthers traveling with 3 children, Thaddeus, Rebecca, & Nathaniel. Contact Carlyle Caruthers.

Beth's eyes opened wide. The children all three turned to look at their mother, fear pasted on their faces. Tuck saw the apprehension his reading of the telegram had provoked.

"Don't worry. I'm not going to respond; however, there may be those along your trip out here, or even some of the stage passengers, that will remember you and your children and contact Caruthers hoping for a reward."

"So, what should we do?" Beth asked.

"I talked to Sam and Martha about it and we all think you and I should get married right away and then I can move to adopt the children, if that is acceptable with you...," Tuck responded, looking to everyone involved.

The children were ecstatic, everyone nodding. "I think that would be wonderful," Becca responded. "That means I would be Becca Tucker. I love it."

Thad and Nate agreed. "How long would it take to make an adoption final?" asked Thad.

"It would have to be heard in front of the circuit judge when he comes to judge those two robbers who are still in my jail. If we aren't married when he comes to Mustang Ridge, we will have to wait until he comes through again in about a month or more."

"Oh my," said Beth. She took a deep breath. "Then I think we need to take care of wedding plans first. Should we go see Reverend Prescott?"

"I stopped by to see him before I came here. He is expecting us anytime that is convenient for us. I also sent a telegram to the circuit judge asking him for any information on what we need to do ahead of time concerning adopting the children."

Beth wiped her hands on her apron and then rubbed her temples. She realized time was short. "Let's finish breakfast and all go see Reverend Prescott," she said. As she dished up the bacon and eggs, she noticed Tuck eyeing them. "Hungry now, Tuck?"

He laughed but it wasn't his usual hearty laughter. He was nervous about how this would all fall into place—or not. However, he held out his plate with a smile. "Yup. Worked up an appetite." He didn't want to cause Beth or her children any more worry than necessary.

Following breakfast and once the dishes were washed, Thad hitched up Bullet and Lightning to the 2-seater and they rode into Mustang Ridge accompanied by Tuck on Irish. When they arrived in Mustang Ridge, they went directly to the parsonage.

"Hello, folks, come on in the parlor and have a seat. Mrs. Prescott has some milk and cookies for the children. Some coffee for you and Beth?" he asked Tuck.

They both nodded while Esther provided the refreshments for the young people with Becca's help.

"So, Tuck, I take it that Beth and the children are in agreement with the need for this hurry-up wedding, or they wouldn't be here." Tuck nodded.

"Are they also all right with the adoption?" the reverend asked.

"Yes! We are!" Thad interjected into the conversation as he re-entered the parlor.

Reverend Prescott laughed. "Before I look at my schedule, let's look to our Father for guidance."

After a short time of prayer, the minster asked, "Would you be open to Sunday afternoon?"

Beth gasped. "The day after tomorrow?"

"Yes."

"Then Sunday it is," Beth said looking at Tuck who nodded his agreement.

"That acceptable with you children?" Tuck asked. They each confirmed their acceptance of the plan with nods. Their initial excitement was replaced by the realization of the seriousness of the timing of both a wedding and an adoption.

"I need to work with Esther in preparing the church, and you probably need to notify your guests." Reverend Prescott rose as if to dismiss them.

"Yes!" Beth responded.

As they left the parsonage and boarded the 2-seater, they talked about whom to notify. Tuck said he would ride down to Matt and Maggie's ranch to issue the invite to them. Beth said she would notify those in Mustang Ridge.

"Before I go, I want to ask my best friend to be my best man," Tuck said. "Nate would you be my best man?"

"Me! You want me to be your best man?" Nate couldn't believe his ears.

"Yes, I do," answered Tuck. "I can't think of anyone I want more than you, Nate."

"And I will talk to Sarah about being my bride's maid," Beth said, watching Nate still reacting.

Tuck left on his horse while Beth and her children went to the mercantile and told Sam about their plans. She knew that Tuck had already spoken to Sam, so now she told him the details of the wedding event. She asked him to be sure and let Martha know also, which she knew he would anyway.

"Do you have a special dress to wear, Beth?" Sam asked her.

"No Sam. I don't have one," she answered

"Come here and look at the new dresses I got in on the freight wagons last week. I bet there might be something that would fit you."

Sam then showed her three different dresses to choose from.

"Oh, Sam. This red one with the white trim is beautiful. I'll take this one." Beth tried to pay him, but Sam said, "My gift to the bride."

Again, thanking him for thinking of it, she asked Sam to let any church members who came into the mercantile know about the wedding details.

"Sam, there is something else I'd like to ask you," Beth said.

"Sure, what's that?" Sam looked up from the dress he was wrapping for her.

"Would you be able to walk me down the aisle?"

Sam almost blushed. "Beth, my dear. Nothing would give me greater pleasure."

"Thank you, Sam. See you Sunday."

They drove the wagon to the Wells home. While Beth talked to Sarah, Thad and Becca talked with Izzy. Nate and Ben found some things to talk about also

Sarah squealed with joy when Beth told her the news and said she would for sure stand up for her. She could hardly wait.

"What will you wear?" Sarah asked. So, Beth showed her the dress she had just bought at the mercantile.

"I'll fix up something for you to wear on your head with a short train," Sarah told her. "I will bring it Sunday."

"Thank you, Sarah. I appreciate it." She took the package with her dress and went out to the wagon where her children joined her. She knew Tuck would let Charlie know too. Apparently, she had talked to everyone she needed to. She and her children drove home to prepare their clothing for the wedding.

CHAPTER SEVENTY-EIGHT
Tuck and Beth Make Plans

Tuck had just left Matt and Mattie's ranch after issuing them a wedding invitation. He told Matt about the telegram and the children's grandfather searching for word on their where-a-bouts. For that reason, Beth and Tuck were getting married as soon as possible so Tuck could legally adopt the children. Matt understood the situation. They were enthusiastic about coming and said they would be there. Matt said they would bring the wagon and pick up Mattie's furniture so Tuck wouldn't have to worry about it.

Tuck rode back to Mustang Ridge and went right to the mercantile. He needed to talk to Sam. He shook Sam's hand when he arrived. Sam said Beth had been there and told him about the wedding. He was telling anyone who came that went to the church about the time for the wedding. Sam also said that Martha was already baking up a storm to furnish cake for the reception. That made Tuck smile. Of course, she was.

Tuck told Sam he needed to buy a white shirt and a string tie. He had both and after making his purchase, Tuck went over to the jail where Charlie was on duty watching the two robbers. Tuck told him about the wedding and invited him.

"Was there was any word yet from the circuit judge?" he asked Charlie upon his return to the jail.

"There is a telegram on your desk from Judge Carmody." Charlie said. "Nothing about when he's coming, but he answered your inquiry about the adoption."

Tuck opened the telegram and read the judge's answer. Carmody said he would take care of the adoption when he came to conduct the trial for the two prisoners. He would send another telegram to let Tuck know when he would be in Mustang Ridge. Tuck hoped it would be soon for two reasons. The most important reason was to accomplish the adoption of Beth's children. The second reason was to get rid of those stage robbers. Every time he looked at them or heard them whining, he was reminded all over again of the way they had treated his Beth.

Tuck went to his rented room and hung his shirt on the hook on the back of the door so the wrinkles would come out. Didn't have anything to iron it with so this would have to do. He sat down and took a deep breath. *I'm getting married the day after tomorrow!* Had he told everyone that needed to be notified? His head was all mixed up inside. He might have forgotten something or someone. What else did he need to do?

It was supper time, so Tuck went to the Silver Star to get supper for himself and the prisoners. He guarded Charlie while he gave them the food, then Charlie left to get his own food and take the evening off. Tuck sat down and ate his own supper while the prisoners ate. Saloon food sure didn't stand up to Beth's cooking or even Martha's, that's for sure.

Tomorrow Tuck would have duty until midnight; then John would be in to watch the prisoners. John Mussman was the part-time deputy who had been hired to fill in when they needed someone to watch the prisoners. On Sunday Charlie would take over until 10:00 and John would take it the rest of the day. That way Charlie could go to church and come to the wedding.

It was Saturday and Tuck had some last-minute things to take care of concerning the wedding. He rode over to the Wells and asked them if Becca could stay with Izzy after the wedding for a day or two. Next, he went back to the mercantile to talk to Sam. Tuck asked him if he and Martha would take the boys for a day or two. Funny thing about that is both Sarah and Sam told Tuck that Beth had already talked to each of them about that. Tuck smiled. *That's my Beth.*

CHAPTER SEVENTY-NINE
Beth and Tuck Get Married

Sunday morning was a scurry of activity at the Deer Creek Ranch. The wedding was to take place following the morning church service. So everyone was putting on their best clothing. Becca was helping her mother to look her best and pack her new dress.

"You children pack some extras to take. I asked Sarah if you could stay with Izzy for a day or two," Beth told Becca. "The boys will stay with the Garrisons."

The children looked at each other and rolled their eyes. Beth had already told them the day before a couple of times, so they were already packed and ready.

Thad went out to hitch up Bullet and Lightning to the 2-seater and saddle up Buck. He would keep Buck with him until Tuesday so he could come out to hitch up the stage.

"All right everyone, to the wagon. It's time to go to church," Beth called. She climbed onto the wagon and took up the reins. "Giddy up, Bullet, Lightning." she called to the horses.

Beth was so nervous she could barely drive the horses. She loved Tuck with all her heart. It wasn't a fear of that. She was in fear for her children. *What if Tuck isn't able to adopt them in time and Caruthers comes and takes them away again?*

Beth shook it off and smiled for the sake of her precious children. She had done all that she could for them. She would not let them see her fear now that they were so close. *Dear Father, take my fear and weakness and give me Thy strength instead.*

Unfortunately, Beth didn't hear much of the sermon. Her mind was in other places. She turned and looked at Tuck sitting beside her. What a handsome man he was. She heard Reverend Prescott when he invited everyone to her and Tuck's wedding at 1:00. Her stomach took a leap as she heard the announcement.

After the service, Sarah helped Beth to take off her church dress and put on the new red dress. She had brought the head piece with a short train trailing behind. As she set it on Beth's head and fluffed the train into place, she said, "Beth, you look beautiful. I'm so happy that I can be here to share in this glorious day."

Beth hugged her friend," I'm so glad you and your family turned off the Oregon Trail when we did."

Once she was dressed, Beth went looking for Nate so she could make sure he was looking all right, but she couldn't find him.

"What's wrong, Mama?" asked Becca.

"I'm looking for Nate."

"Mama, Thad is taking care of him. Besides, he's in the same room as Tuck and you need to stay out of there. The bride and groom aren't supposed to see each other before the wedding."

Beth laughed, "We just saw each other in church."

"Doesn't matter, you look a little different with your new dress and head piece."

Beth laughed. Becca had become a capable young woman in the last few months. She was proud of her daughter.

Soon Grace Norby began playing the church piano and Sam came up and took Beth's arm. "Are you ready, Beth?" he inquired.

Beth patted his arm and Sam began walking her down the aisle. She looked to the altar where her husband-to-be stood waiting for her. He looked so handsome standing there with his best man. Little Nate was looking so grown-up and so proud. What a wonderful thing Tuck did in asking Nate to be his best man. *Well, here I am at the end of the aisle. I'm ready to become Mrs. Adam Tucker.*

"Welcome friends. We are here to join in holy matrimony two of our dear friends, Beth Eastman and Adam Tucker. Join me in prayer, please."

"Father, we thank Thee for Thy loving kindness in bringing this man and this woman together. We give Thee the glory for their love for each other. We ask Thee to help this family as they grow together. Amen"

Reverend Prescott looked over the congregation—many of the same parishioners he had just preached to a couple of hours ago. However, their faces were beaming with expectancy of something good about to happen. He had to smile, if only they would feel the same way about listening to one of his sermons on a Sunday morning. But back to the business at hand. He had a wedding to perform.

"Adam Tucker, will you have this woman to be your wife, to live together in holy marriage? Will you love her, comfort her, honor, and keep her in sickness and in health, and forsaking all others, be faithful to her as long as you both shall live?"

"I will," Tuck stated firmly.

"Beth Eastman, will you have this man to be your husband, to live together in holy marriage? Will you love him, comfort him, honor, and keep him in sickness and in health, and forsaking all others, be faithful to him as long as you both shall live?"

"I will," Beth responded.

"You may place the ring on her finger," Reverend Prescott said after Beth and Tuck repeated their vows after him.

Tuck turned to look at his best man. Nate took the gold band out of his pocket and handed it to Tuck, who placed the ring on Beth's finger, repeating, "With this ring I thee wed."

"Adam and Beth, through their promises to each other today, have been joined together in holy wedlock. Because they have exchanged their vows before God and these witnesses, and have pledged their commitment each to the other, I now pronounce that they are husband and wife. Those whom God hath joined together, let no one put asunder. You may now kiss your bride!"

Tuck kissed his bride tenderly. The music began once again and Tuck and Beth turned to walk down the aisle and to begin their lives as Mr. and Mrs. Adam Tucker.

Beth noticed Sam take Nate in tow as they headed down the aisle too. Sarah had made a bridal bouquet for Beth. They weren't real flowers since it was December but she had done a beautiful job using her dressmaker flowers. Now Sarah handed the bouquet back to Beth as they walked back.

The congregation pushed the pews to one side, so they could make room for refreshments. Martha enlisted the help of Becca and Thad to carry in the cakes she had prepared. Tuck and Beth stood at the table, which held the cakes and cut the bridal cake together: there were no plates, so the guests simply took their piece of cake in their hands.

Friends brought their gifts to Beth and Tuck. Many brought canned goods. Sam and Martha gave them a crate of oranges which had just come in on the freight wagons from California a few days ago.

The wedding was over and everyone went their separate ways, the boys with the Garrisons and Becca with Izzy. The bride and groom headed out to Deer Creek Ranch in the 2-seater with Irish tied behind.

A Safe Haven for Beth/Karen Carr

CHAPTER EIGHTY
Back to Business

The bride and groom spent their wedding night and all of Monday enjoying their time together. After breakfast, the two of them went out to take care of the chores. Tuck took care of the horses while Beth fed the chickens and goats and milked Buttercup. Tuck gathered the eggs while Beth laughed as he jumped when one particular hen pecked his arm. They did the same thing with the evening chores except Tuck made Beth gather the eggs.

#

Tuesday morning Beth got up to make breakfast and start dinner for the stagecoach passengers. It was hard for her to concentrate because Tuck kept kissing her on the back of her neck. Not that she didn't enjoy it; she just had work to do. It wasn't long before she heard Thad ride up on Buck. He had come to get the horses ready for the stage. He came into the ranch house first to say hello to his mother and Tuck.

"Is it safe to come in?" he called. He kissed his mother on the cheek.

"Yes," Beth laughed. "Come have some breakfast."

Later that afternoon, Sam and Martha drove out to the ranch with both Nate and Becca. Beth thanked them for picking up Becca and coming out with both children.

"Martha, I appreciate all the work you did on the cakes. That was so nice of you," Beth told her. "They were delicious."

"You're very welcome. I enjoyed doing it."

CHAPTER EIGHTY-ONE
Tuck Takes His Bride to Shoshone Camp

Wednesday - Tuck and Beth had been married for three days now. Tuck felt like he was dreaming yet. He had to keep telling himself that Beth was his wife now.

After breakfast was over, Beth and Tuck rode into town on their horses to take care of some business. Tuck didn't get to see Beth on a horse very often; she usually drove the 2-seater. *She knows how to sit a horse, that's for sure.*

Tuck wanted to be at the ranch more than the time being sheriff would allow. He and Beth had talked about that and his enlarging the ranch to raise cattle, so he was going to talk to Sam about his resignation from the job of sheriff since he was the town leader.

Then Tuck also wanted to talk to Charlie to see if he would have an interest in taking the job of full-time sheriff. He knew Charlie would do a good job so he planned to recommend Charlie to Sam for the job. He would stay on as sheriff though until a replacement was found.

When they stopped at the mercantile, Sam was grinning ear to ear when they arrived. Sometimes Tuck wondered about him. Sam made some funny remarks about them having to get away from the children already to be alone. *Funny man, Sam.*

While Beth did some shopping, which mainly consisted of looking around, Tuck talked to Sam about resigning.

"I'm not surprised, but you will have to put it before the town at the next meeting, which isn't until next week.

"I'll be there. We're going over to the sheriff's office to talk to Charlie about the position. I think Charlie would be a good sheriff," Tuck said.

"Yes, Charlie would make a good sheriff," Sam agreed.

"Beth and I are going to ride out and see Grey Wolf and his family as long as the snows haven't built up yet. Could be the last chance we would have to go out there. I want to tell Grey Wolf I'm not going to be sheriff anymore and why. Beth had never been out to their home."

"Hold up. I have something I'd like you to take to them." Sam came back with a basket.

"I'll see to it they receive it." Tuck didn't ask Sam what was in it and he didn't tell him but it had a big red bow on it. Tuck's guess was it was a Christmas present for the family.

"Are you ready to go, Beth?"

"Yes, I just have this spool of thread I need."

Tuck took the ten cents out of his pocket and paid for it.

Later, they went to the sheriff's office. Charlie told Tuck he had a telegram for him from the circuit judge. He was coming to Mustang Ridge next Monday. Tuck was glad it would be a day when there was no stage, so they all could be there. After telling Charlie the news about his resigning, they left him contemplating if he wanted to be sheriff instead of deputy; then they headed out to Grey Wolf's camp. They ate an early lunch on the way of jerky and some of Thad's pemmican and water from their canteens.

When they arrived at their camp, White Eagle as usual was there to meet them and ride in with them. Tuck wondered if they kept him as lookout or if he was just attuned to Tuck's arrival. Tuck told him that Beth was his new wife. His family had met Beth at church when they had visited, but once the cold weather arrived, they stayed close to camp.

Grey Wolf invited Tuck and Beth into their hogan. Tuck was surprised at how warm it was inside. This made him even happier that he had helped build it. Prairie Flower invited them to sit. Beth gave them the basket from Sam she had been carrying on her horse. She said Sam had sent it to her family.

Tuck asked Grey Wolf how it was going with breaking horses. He said he had four horses that were broke and ready to sell. He wondered if Tuck would take them to Pete at the Livery. Tuck knew that Pete was expecting delivery and had sent the money with Tuck.

Grey Wolf said he spent most of his time now hunting. Just last week he had shot an antelope. Prairie Flower and Singing Butterfly had been making jerky and pemmican out of the meat. She also made utensils out of the bone, such as spoons and needles for sewing. Beth marveled at how they didn't let anything go to waste on an animal. Even the hide would be made into a blanket to ward off the winter cold.

When Beth and Tuck were ready to go, Grey Wolf gave him the string of mustangs and he led them behind him as they started down the trail for Mustang Ridge. It had been a busy day for Beth and Tuck, and they were ready to be home.

Tuck's backside was sore from sitting in the saddle all day. He could only imagine how Beth's felt.

CHAPTER EIGHTY-TWO
Circuit Judge Comes to Mustang Ridge

Beth and the children all went into town with Tuck Monday morning. They sat in while Judge Carmody heard the case of the two stage robbers at the sheriff's office. Beth and Thad testified about the events of that terrible day. When it was done, the judge passed sentence for them to be incarcerated at the Territorial Prison at Lancaster in the Nebraska Territory. He ordered that they remain in the Mustang Ridge jail until they could be taken there by Marshalls. Then he turned to Tuck and his new family.

"It is nice to meet you folks. I hope that I can put your minds at ease regarding any rights of the paternal grandfather," Judge Carmody greeted them. "Sheriff Tucker has given me the details about your plight. I must say, I admire you and your children, Mrs. Tucker, for how you

took matters into your own hands and escaped from this situation. Thad, I'm sorry you had to be put through this treatment. Now then, did you folks bring your marriage certificate with you?"

"Yes, here it is." Beth pulled it out of her handbag.

"So--let's get on with the process. We'll finish with the paperwork and signatures."

"Adam Tucker, as an adopting step-parent who wants to become a legal parent to the three children in question, you will assume all parental responsibilities for Beth Eastman-Tucker's children."

"A step-parent adoption is a legal process where the step-parent becomes the legal parent of the child. This relationship becomes permanent, and you will be taking over the legal and financial responsibilities for these children."

"Since the biological father is deceased, we will not need to get his permission. Once you adopt Thad, Becca and Nate Eastman, these children are as much yours and as much your responsibility as if they were yours biologically."

"After the age of 14, the child's consent is usually required if the child's natural parents no longer have parental rights. As this is not the case since the biological father is deceased and the mother is not giving up her rights, it is a moot point. However, I will be asking all three children to voice and sign their consent to the adoption to ensure against any others coming forward with a desire to infringe upon these adoption proceedings."

"So, let's move on to the signatures. Adam and Beth, please sign here," he said handing them the pen. After they had both signed, he moved on to the children.

"First, Thad, since you are over 14, is it your desire to be legally adopted by your step-father, Adam Tucker?"

"Yes, sir. It is," answered Thad.

"Please sign under your mother and father's name to agree to the proceedings," the judge directed.

"Next, Becca, is it your desire to be legally adopted by your step-father, Adam Tucker?"

"Yes, sir. It is," answered Becca.

"Please sign under your brother's name to agree to the proceedings," the judge directed.

"Nate, is it your desire to be legally adopted by your step-father, Adam Tucker?"

"Yes, sir. It is," answered Nate.

"Please sign under your sister's name to agree to the proceedings," the judge directed.

After the paper work was completed, the judge said, "You are now Thad, Becca, and Nate Tucker. Congratulations."

"I will file this paperwork as soon as I return to Omaha but it is legal as of today," the judge said as he replaced the papers in his briefcase.

"Hooray!" Nate yelled jumping up and down.

"Does this mean we're safe from Grandfather?" Becca asked timidly.

"Legally, yes young lady," Judge Carmody said.

Beth heard the judge say 'legally' but she also heard what he wasn't saying. She didn't want to ask him in front of the children, so she waited until they went outside to the 2-seater.

"Judge Carmody, I have a question."

"Yes, Mrs. Tucker?"

"You said they are safe legally. Is there some other way he can harm them?"

"Yes, he could kidnap them, but I don't see that as a problem given how well-known he is," answered the judge.

So, it was done. Beth and Tuck were married and the children had all been adopted by Tuck. They could breathe a sigh of relief.

CHAPTER EIGHTY-THREE
News from Boston

Thursday the stagecoach coming from Cheyenne arrived and Beth served her guests as usual. Will and Tom entered the ranch-house with the passengers while Tuck directed them to the privy and the wash basin. Will thought it a joy to call her Mrs. Tucker instead of Mrs. Eastman. "Mrs. Tucker will be serving your meal to you," he directed, with a smile towards Beth. "She is an excellent cook."

During the meal, Beth became engaged in conversation with one of the passengers, Harvey Mintz. She noticed he carried a Boston newspaper and wanting to take a look at it, she also didn't want to draw attention to herself. So, she took up the coffee pot and going around the table, she began refilling their cups. When she came to him, she asked, "More coffee, Mr. Mintz?"

"Yes, please."

Pouring the coffee into his cup, she commented on the newspaper lying next to his plate, "Is that really a Boston newspaper?"

"It is. Would you care to look at it?"

"Yes, I would," Beth stated. "I always like to read the news from the states. We don't often get newspapers from back east out here."

He handed her the newspaper and she went to sit down and read it, giving Becca the nod to serve the dessert. Back in her chair in front of the fireplace, she scanned the pages looking for anything that might point toward her situation. She found it on the second page, though it had not been what she had in mind. The headlines drew her attention:

Funeral Held for Local Boston Banker

She read on to discover that it was indeed her father-in-law who had passed away the previous month. It stated that he left no living relatives to mourn his passing, and went on to say that he had been an influential banker, starting many banks throughout the east.

Beth felt guilty by the relief that washed over her, but it meant that they were free of his dominance for good. Was it a hidden blessing to know that she and her family no longer needed to look over their shoulders, to worry about being found out? *Father, forgive me for feeling joy over the death of this man.*

Beth returned the newspaper to Mr. Mintz, thanking him for allowing her to read it. After the stage had left, Tuck said to her. "Okay, Beth. What did you find in the Boston newspaper?"

Three pairs of eyes widened as they turned to look at their mother. They had not been aware of the newspaper, but Tuck had been sharing the meal with them and observed his wife's subtly in reading the paper.

"Carlyle Caruthers is dead. We don't have to worry about him anymore." She saw their expressions and knew they felt the same response as she had. She told them what the article stated about him, including his leaving no living relatives. Even though her children feared him and wanted nothing to do with him, she could see the sadness they felt that he did not count them as family.

"Well," said Tuck. "I think this is something we can now put behind us. God protected you as you traveled out here. He used these events to bring us together so we might become a family. I am grateful to God for that part. We can now get on with our lives, with being a family."

"Yes," Thad agreed, "the Tucker family."

CHAPTER EIGHTY-FOUR
Searching for a Tree

Christmas Eve was a few days away and last night had been the first snow since the stage had been stranded at the ranch-house. However, the cold temperatures and high winds were just as bad. Hearing the sounds of laughter outside, Beth went to the window and looked out. Tuck and Nate were rolling around in the snow, throwing snowballs at each other, building a distorted snowman - all kinds of snowy fun.

It made her smile to see how Tuck and Nate got on together. You would never know that they weren't biologically father and son. *Father, thank you for bring Tuck into my life. I love that man so much.*

Beth went back to her Christmas baking. She was making cookies and candies to take to the Christmas Eve pageant at church tomorrow night. It would be her family's first Christmas at Mustang Ridge, and her excitement was nearly as high as Nate and Becca's. Becca was singing a solo. She was pretty nervous and so was Beth, but she knew Becca's youthful voice was perfect for the song. Nate was excited too because he was to be one of the wise men in the Nativity pageant.

In addition to Christmas Eve services, Deer Creek Ranch was hosting a dinner on Christmas Day. It would be a full house. Sam and Martha Garrison; Reverend and Esther Prescott; Jacob and Sarah Wells and Izzy and Ben would be sharing their Christmas bounty with them. Everyone was bringing lots of food. Tuck and Thad had constructed an even longer table and some benches, so there would be plenty of table room and seating.

Beth was pleased she didn't have to juggle around stagecoach dinners. Tuck had insisted that the stagecoach stop be moved into Mustang Ridge when they started again in the spring, and Sam had made it happen. After the hostage situation with Beth, Tuck wanted Beth to be safe. Especially since there was talk that the line would be adding a strong box to the coaches, so they would be carrying gold. Pete Ballard would in charge of the teams of horses, and Sally's Café would serve the dinner to the passengers.

Becca was practicing her solo in her bedroom with the door closed. She made sure that if the menfolk came in, that Beth would immediately let her know so she could stop. When she was all practiced out, she came out to help her mother with the baking.

Beth set aside the baking and started dinner preparation. She had browned a rabbit Thad had shot earlier that morning and it now finished baking in the oven. She had been baking potatoes around the cookies, so when that was done, she called everyone to come eat. She hadn't seen Thad since he brought in the cleaned rabbit early in the morning. Apparently, he had some kind of project going on in the barn, and no one was allowed to enter.

While they ate their dinner, Tuck shared with the children his desire to go up to the foothills and cut a pine tree for their Christmas tree. Needless to say, Nate wanted to go right away, and even Becca was thrilled at the prospect.

"Thad, will you be able to go with us?" Tuck inquired. He knew Thad was working hard to complete a project in the barn.

"Yeah, I'll be able to," he responded.

"How about you, Beth? Can you come along?"

"Yes, I think that would be fun for the whole family to do," Beth said. "It will be a brand-new family tradition."

Dinner was over and Beth and Becca did the dishes while Thad and Tuck saddled the horses including an extra horse (Blaze) to carry the tree. Thad had his rifle in its scabbard on Buck and Tuck his shotgun on Irish. Beth rode Lightning, Becca rode Copper, and Nate rode Bullet. They led the horses up to the ranch- house and tied them to the hitching rail. Tuck wanted to get one last cup of coffee before they departed, so they entered to see that Beth and Becca both wore their coats and were about to head out the door.

"Are we ready to go?" Beth inquired.

"Almost," laughed Thad. "Papa Tuck here had to get one last cup of coffee."

Beth turned to the stove to pour him one. "It's hot. Be careful."

But Tuck slugged it down in no time, and said, "That's better. Let's go."

The foothills of the Mustang Mountains, normally green year-around, were mostly white now. Last night's snowfall had stuck to the trees giving them a festive spirit. Beth thought it a beautiful sight. She was glad she had come along even though there was much work to do.

It was then she noticed that both Tuck and Thad carried their rifles in their scabbards. "Why do you have your rifles? Is there a threat of bears?"

"No, bears are in hibernation by now. I thought I might be able to do some hunting while we are out here," explained Thad.

"Mine is a shotgun," Tuck said. "I just like to be prepared when going to the foothills." Neither of them mentioned the fact that several ranchers had complained of wolves killing their calves.

"Isn't this pretty?" Becca marveled at the beauty the snow gave the landscape. Everyone agreed with her. *God had painted the dull-colored ground and trees with his majestic white,* Beth thought.

As they neared the smaller trees on the foothills, Beth could see sign of rabbits, even deer. She saw Thad loosen his rifle as a deer bounced away.

The horses were beginning to have a hard time of getting through the snow because it was so deep. Tuck thought they ought to stop and see about getting one of the trees where they were before the horses tired out completely. He dismounted and gave the reins to Beth. "Don't let the reins drop," he cautioned everyone. "They are skittish with this deep snow, so they may run off.

Tuck went to Blaze and removed the axe from the pack. "All right-ee. Which one do you want me to chop down?"

After they agreed upon a certain tree, Tuck began to chop the tree. As the blows of his axe rang out in the crisp, cold air, the horses did show they were a little skittish. Beth patted Lightning's neck. "There, there Lightning. Stay calm, boy." Becca did the same with her horse and Nate did with his.

Tuck fastened the tree to Blaze's back and put the axe back in the pack. "Are we ready to head back down now?" he asked.

At that moment the sound of a wolf howling further up the mountainside sent shivers down Beth's back. The horses began to prance about nervously.

"Yes, Tuck. Let's go," Beth said with apprehension.

"Thad, lead the way down. I'll bring up the rear," Tuck directed. "Keep a tight rein on your horses. If they rear and buck you off, it will be a long walk back to the ranch."

No one spoke as they made their way down from the foothills. Once they were down, they didn't need to ride single file. Tuck pulled up next to Beth. "Exciting, huh?"

"Foreboding is more the word I would use," Beth stated emphatically. "That howl nearly petrified me."

"I'm sorry, Beth. I think we are safe now. He was much further from us than he sounded." Tuck was genuinely sorry Beth had been frightened. He attempted to ease her fear. "Are you still frightened?"

"I'm fine, Tuck. Is it natural for wolves to be down this low?"

Tuck and Thad exchanged looks. "What is it?" Beth asked seeing that exchange. "What aren't you telling me?"

Tuck sighed. "They have come down and attacked some of the ranchers' cattle," he explained. "Not ours, but on the other side of Mustang Ridge."

"Oh, dear God!" Beth said in horror. "We shouldn't have come out here."

"We were safe. Besides there are two crack shots riding with you," Tuck said grinning.

"Rascal!" said Beth.

"Thad. Deer - to your left," Tuck directed.

Thad removed his rifle from the scabbard and in one swift move, sighted the deer with his weapon and fired. The deer dropped in its tracks. Thad dismounted and handed his reins to Becca. Pulling his hunting knife from its sheath at his waist, he began to field dress his kill.

Tuck had been watching the trail behind them while Thad dressed the deer. He swung back to Thad with urgency in his voice. "Call it done, Thad. Now!"

With one final move, Thad firmly gripped the entrails and pulled down hard. He packed up the carcass and threw it over Blaze's back. He tied a rope under the horse's belly to the front and back legs. Jumping onto Buck's back and grabbing the reins from Becca, he was ready to ride.

They took off at a pretty fast clip since they were now on the flats, leaving the foothills behind them. Beth looked behind them and saw that about four wolves had descended upon the site of the field dressing and were ravenously eating what had been left behind. She shuddered.

Arriving at Deer Creek Ranch, they rode the horses right into the barn. Becca and Beth unsaddled Lightning and Copper while Tuck help Nate unsaddle Bullet. He then assisted Thad in hoisting the deer carcass up by a rope to one of the rafters where it would hang before he skinned it and transferred it to the root cellar. Thad finished the cleaning that he was unable to do in the field. Tuck unsaddled his and Thad's horses. He took the tree, saying. "Are you ready to go up to the ranch-house?

"Sure. I'll take your shotgun since you have your hands full," Thad responded.

They took the tree inside and Beth pointed out where the best spot would be. Tuck put his arm around his wife's waist as they stood and looked at the tree. "It's a beautiful tree, isn't it?"

CHAPTER EIGHTY-FIVE
Christmas Eve Service

Beth and Becca were packing up the Christmas goodies which would be served following the pageant. Tuck and Thad had gone out to hitch up Lightning and Bullet to the 2-seater, so they could go into town. It was a tight fit now that there were five of them, but Nate was still small enough that three could fit on one seat.

Tuck came into the ranch-house saying, "Better get some of those antelope skins to put on our legs. It's getting mighty cold out there."

Beth handed him the baskets of food, and he took them out and tied them to the back of the 2-seater. Thad took the antelope hides out to the wagon followed by his mother and sister. Nate had already claimed his spot on the second seat.

Tuck and Thad sat in front with Tuck driving. The rest sat in the second seat with Nate in the middle. Tuck took up the reins saying, "Hy yup."

The church was lit up with candles and kerosene lanterns and lamps. Pine boughs were draped around the entrance and again along the sides of the pews. Beth deposited her baskets of food on the table where Martha was arranging everything.

"Merry Christmas, Beth," said Martha. "Sure is cold tonight, isn't it?"

"Yes, it is! Merry Christmas to you too, Martha."

"It's a good thing we are having this early, so everyone can get home before it really gets cold!" remarked Tuck.

Beth grimaced at the thought of this cold getting any worse. Wyoming cold was much colder than Boston cold, if that was even possible.

The Tucker family took their seats as Reverend Prescott approached the platform in the front of the church. "Welcome everyone and Merry Christmas. I think we are ready to get started on our pageant. Please join me in prayer."

"Holy Father above, we come to Thee tonight to worship Thee in song and to tell the story of the birth of Thy Son, Jesus Christ. As we praise Thee for sending Thy Son to cleanse us of our sins, we thank Thee for this grace Thou hast given us, an adoption to become Thy children. Thanks be to Thee, our Everlasting Father and Thy Son. Amen."

The pageant followed, with the children acting out the roles of the Nativity. Nate preformed perfectly, in Beth's eyes anyway, as one of the wise men. As the night wore to an end, Becca stepped to the platform to sing. Beth was the only one who knew about it. As Tuck looked to Beth, she smiled at him, placing her hand in his. Grace Norby began playing the piano as Becca stepped forward. Her beautiful voice began to sing "O Christmas Tree."

O Christmas tree, O Christmas tree
How lovely are thy branches
O Christmas tree, O Christmas tree
How lovely are thy branches
Your boughs so green in summertime
Stay bravely green in wintertime
O Christmas tree, O Christmas tree
How lovely are thy branches

There were cheers and clapping following her song. Beth could see Becca's face turn red and tears were streaming down Beth's cheeks. Then Grace began playing again, this time ever so softly while Becca spoke.

"On Christmas Eve in 1818 a blizzard stranded the small town of Ogledorf in the Austrian mountains. The people there found that their church organ was broken. So, the priest and organist began composing a song that could be sung without an organ yet one that would express their Christmas joy. All day and all night they worked and at midnight the sweet carol Silent Night was born."

Becca then began singing the carol, "Silent Night."

Silent night, holy night!
All is calm, all is bright.
Round yon Virgin, Mother and Child.
Holy infant so tender and mild,
Sleep in heavenly peace,
Sleep in heavenly peace

Silent night, holy night!
Shepherds quake at the sight.
Glories stream from heaven afar
Heavenly hosts sing Alleluia,
Christ the Savior is born!
Christ the Savior is born

Silent night, holy night!
Son of God love's pure light.
Radiant beams from Thy holy face
With dawn of redeeming grace,
Jesus Lord, at Thy birth
Jesus Lord, at Thy birth

"What a beautiful voice to bring us a beautiful message of God's love for us," Reverend Prescott said as Becca left the platform.

"Now, in closing our program for tonight, I would invite all of you to partake in the Christmas goodies provided by the women of our church. Thank you, ladies."

The pews were pushed back to make room for the folks to eat. Beth was amazed at how quickly the containers were emptied. Beth packed up her empty plates and put them in the baskets for Tuck to take out to the 2-seater.

"We need to get going," he said to Sam. "We have a ways to go tonight in this cold."

"See you tomorrow then. Have a safe trip."

"Becca, your songs were beautiful and heartfelt. Thank you for sharing your talent with us," Esther Prescott told her as they were leaving the church.

"Thank you, Mrs. Prescott."

The eight miles to the ranch seemed longer than ever to Beth. The cold was bone-cold, as the men on the wagon train would say. Beth was thankful for the warmth of the hides. She thought they would never get home but finally they pulled up to the ranch-house. Beth took the baskets with Becca and Nate's help and Tucker and Thad drove the 2-seater to the barn and unhitched the horses. They put them in their stalls and gave them an extra amount of hay.

Beth made some hot cocoa to warm everyone. It was something she was able to order from Sam. They had it in Boston but not out here. Her family enjoyed the taste and the warmth it provided. *A Christmas Eve treat*, she thought. Stoking the fires more, they all prepared to retire for the night. As Beth lay in Tuck's arms, she sighed. *What a glorious service it was, Lord. I thank Thee for the warmth and love tonight.*

CHAPTER EIGHTY-SIX
Christmas Day at Deer Creek Ranch

Beth woke to the sounds of Christmas. Becca calling, "Merry Christmas," Nate calling, "Its Christmas!" and Thad coming in from outside shouting – "Merry Christmas, Tucker family! Wake up all you lazy bones!"

As Beth snuggled closer to her husband, the sounds diminished to whispers and shushes. Beth felt rather than heard a soft chuckle emanate from Tuck. She turned to look at him.

"Merry Christmas, Mrs. Tucker," Tuck said nuzzling Beth's cheek with his unshaven beard. "I think we should get up, don't you?"

"It's too early. I want to sleep some more."

Both Beth and Tuck were startled out of their sleepiness by a pounding on their bedroom door. "Mama! Tuck! Wake up, it's Christmas."

"Well," Tuck said pulling off the covers, "I guess that is that. Rise and shine, beautiful."

"When you talk like that, of course I will get up. We'll be out in a bit, children."

Tuck and Beth were surprised to find out that Thad had arisen quite early to do the chores. He had fed and watered all the livestock, milked Buttercup, and gathered the eggs. By the time they exited their bedroom, Becca had breakfast well underway. Nate was sitting on the rug in front of the Christmas tree, slyly checking out the packages underneath.

"Okay, now that breakfast is over, lets head for the tree," Thad directed, surprising his parents at his eagerness.

As all were seated, Thad said he wanted to give his gifts first. Each one of them received a package wrapped in brown paper and tied with a string. "Everyone open them at the same time."

"Oooo, Thad. They are beautiful! Thank you," exclaimed Becca, the first to get into her package.

Beth was almost overcome when she beheld the softest pair of mittens she had ever seen. After everyone had their packages opened and express their awe and thanks to Thad, Beth said, "How, what…?"

"They are made from deer hide. I took my hides to Grey Wolf and he and his family cured and tanned them for me. When they were finished, I brought them back here and have been working on them in the barn all this time."

"My goodness, Thad. These are so beautiful. You must have worked really hard on them," Beth remarked.

"How did they get them so soft and where is the hair?" asked Becca.

"I don't think you really want to know," warned her brother, "but it involves using the brains of the deer."

"You're right. I really don't want to know," Becca responded. "I'll just want to feel the softness of my new mittens. Thank you, Thad."

Other gifts were exchanged and as they came to an end, Tuck asked Thad to help him bring something in from the barn. Becca stood at the door ready to open it when they returned. Beth gasped as she saw them bring in a piece of furniture covered with a quilt. Once the quilt was removed, Beth saw that it was a china cupboard.

"Where would you like us to put it?" Tuck asked.

She pointed out the place and they moved it there. Beth hugged her husband. "Thank you, dear."

"You're welcome, Beth. I was worried Sam wouldn't get it in before Christmas, but it came a few days ago with the last freight."

"Now that we've all opened our gifts, I think it is time to start getting this ranch-house ready for a big Christmas dinner," Beth reminded her family. And so they did. Tuck and Thad set up the tables and seating; Becca and Beth began the food preparation; Nate even helped set up the chairs. They were all making ready for the big day.

"Here comes Sam and Martha!" hollered Nate from the window. He was accompanied by the frantic barking of Bandit. Beth wondered if there would ever be a time when Nate wouldn't announce visitors so loudly. Laughing she said, "Do you remember what you are to do

"Yes. I say 'Merry Christmas' and ask to take their coats."

"Well, they are at the door. Perform your task."

Nate was so excited that when he opened the door, he forgot half the words and yelled, "Christmas! Coats!"

Fortunately, they knew what he meant. Sam removed his wife's coat and handed it to Nate. "Merry Christmas to you too, Nate. Here's Martha's coat and now mine. Thank you very much."

"Merry Christmas, Martha, Sam. Sure glad the sun came out strong today and is warming things up," Beth said, "Here, I'll show you what to do with that," she said pointing at the basket Martha had brought. It contained extra table settings to use, knowing that Beth didn't have enough for everyone.

Bandit began barking at the window. Nate had missed that one. "It's the Wells," he announced. Sam and Martha both laughed.

This time, Nate had it right as he opened the door. "Merry Christmas! May I take your coats?"

Sarah went to the kitchen with a basket of food. "Merry Christmas, Beth, Merry Christmas Martha," she said.

Thad helped Izzy to remove her coat and handed it to Nate, then did the same with Sarah's coat.

"And here come the Prescotts." Nate announced.

Tuck had been helping the men take their horses to the barn for warmth. He now approached the ranch-house and was about to open the door when he heard a horse whinny. Tuck was pleased at what he saw. It was Grey Wolf and his family all on horseback. He hadn't told anyone, but he had invited the Shoshone family. He and Grey Wolf didn't know if the weather would allow it though. Tuck had made the offer for them to spend the night if the weather was bad.

"Grey Wolf, it's so good to see you. Merry Christmas everyone. Come in." Tuck opened the ranch-house door and announced, "Grey Wolf and his family are here!"

Tuck helped them down and with their saddle bags. "Grey Wolf, come. Let's take the horses to the barn, and then we can join the rest."

Beth was warmed at the sight of the Indian family intermingling with her friends around the food. *This is the way it should be, isn't it, Lord?*

Grey Wolf and his family didn't go to their home that night. It was late and extremely cold again, so Tuck talked them into staying the night. They would all stay in the loft except for He-Who-Is-Wise. Climbing the ladder to the loft would be too hard for him, so he unrolled his bedroll in front of the fireplace.

Everyone had settled down for the night. When morning arrived and the sun came out, Beth mused on the past few weeks. All leading up to a joyful Christmas for all.

CHAPTER EIGHTY-SEVEN
Spring

Beth was breathing in the smells of April as she sat on the porch resting. She had been working in the garden, turning the soil so as to make a fertile bed for the seeds she would be planting. It was hard work, but not something she hadn't done before. In her heart, she knew why. Beth was expecting and was excited about the prospect of telling Tuck he was to be a father. *Celebrating our life together. And Thou hast given me and Tuck a new life too. I thank Thee, Father,* Beth thought as she patted her stomach. *I will tell Tuck tonight after everyone has gone to bed.*

While Beth worked in the garden, Becca took the time to create a rock garden like Izzy's. Earlier she had dug up small cacti to plant around the rocks. Beth thought it looked quite nice and told Becca well done.

Later that evening, Beth thought her children would never go to bed. Even Tuck wanted to sit at the table and work on his ranch books by the dim light of the kerosene lamp. Finally, Beth could stand it no longer. She lit a candle to take to their bedroom and turned down the light of the lamp on the table in front of Tuck.

"Hey! I'm working here," Tuck protested.

"You were working. Now you are coming to bed," she said, kissing the back of his neck.

"All right, guess I have no choice." Tuck grinned.

"That's right, Mr. Tucker. Off you go."

Even though it was spring, the nights were still chilly. Tuck threw some more logs into the fireplace before climbing into bed. He reached for his wife and they snuggled for a while before Beth said, "Tuck, I have something important to tell you."

"So that's why such a hurry to get me to come to bed. What is it?"

"Tuck, we are going to have a baby!"

"What? Are you serious?" Tuck exclaimed, raising up on his elbow.

"Yes. Isn't it grand?" Beth asked her husband. She had not been sure how he would handle the news. After all, that was the last thing they had expected at their age. Beth had believed her child-bearing days were behind her.

"Grand!" Tick shouted. "It's better than grand! When are you due?"

"Dr. Phillips said I am about three months along, so probably sometime in October."

"That's wonderful. I love you, Mrs. Tucker."

"And I love you, Mr. Tucker."

"How have you been feeling?" Tuck was concerned for her. "I noticed you were favoring your back earlier this evening."

"Oh yes. I was hoeing in the garden, and it tired me more than it should have. It's different this time, but then I'm a few years older." Beth smiled.

"All the same, I think you should let Thad and me prepare the garden for you. No arguments." Tuck saw that Beth intended to debate the point.

The weariness of a long day soon brought sleep to the couple but not for long. Beth roused from her slumber with her back hurting even more than before. Suddenly a sharp pain brought her to complete wakefulness and she cried out.

Tuck jerked awake. "What is it, Beth? What's happening?"

Beth could not answer him. All she could do was cry out as the pains continued one after the other. "Nooo." She cried out. *"Father, please don't let this happen.*

Tuck saw his beloved writhing in pain, unable to even speak to him. He climbed into his jeans and ran out to summon Thad. Thad had already awakened, hearing his mother's cries, and had done the same. "What's wrong? What's the matter with Ma?"

"Thad, I need you to ride into town and get Doc Phillips. Your mother is in a bad way. I think she is losing our baby."

"Sure. Right away." He took his coat off the hook and turned. "I didn't even know…"

"Yes, she just told me after we went to bed."

"I'll ride as fast as I can." And he was off.

Tuck wet a cloth with cool water and went into his wife. He placed it on her forehead. He didn't know if it would help her or not but at least it was taking away the beads of perspiration on her brow. He felt that touch was important to her, so she would know he was close by.

Becca had awakened by now and came to their bedroom door. "What's going on, Tuck? What's wrong with Mama?"

"She is pregnant, Becca. But something is wrong, so Thad went to get Dr. Phillips. Is Nate awake?"

"He's starting to stir, I think. I'll stay with him."

Although Tuck thought it took an awful long time for the doctor to arrive, Thad brought him back in record time. Dr. Phillips had just returned from another call and had not unsaddled his horse yet, so they both came straight away.

"How's she doing?" Dr. Phillips asked while he took his coat off.

"She doesn't seem to know I'm there. The pain must be awful; she cries out often."

Doc entered the room and began his examination of Beth. "Beth, can you hear me? It's Doc Phillips. I'm going to check things out and see what is going on."

Beth's only response was a moan. Her cries had subsided and now she just moaned. Tuck was beside himself with worry. He paced the bedroom floor until Doc told him to go out and talk to the children. They needed to know what was happening.

"But, Doc. I don't even know what is happening."

Doc put his arm across Tuck's shoulder. "My boy, she has lost the baby. I need to make sure we don't lose her too."

Tuck's intake of breath was his only answer. He hurried out to the living room where all three children were sitting wide-eyed with fear.

Becca jumped up and asked Tuck, "How is she?"

Tuck had them sit down and he told them what Dr. Phillips had told him. That she had lost the baby and the doctor was working with Beth to make sure they didn't lose her too. "We need to go to God in prayer for your mother," he urged them. He was not going to behave the way he had done when he lost Mary and their baby. He had turned from God at the first sign of trouble. Not this time. He had three children to be concerned about.

So, for the next while, Tuck and his three children spent time on their knees petitioning their Father in Heaven to spare the life of their beloved wife and mother. When at last the doctor exited the bedroom, he came upon the scene of a family on their knees, united in prayer. It did his heart good to see such faith and to hear they not only prayed for Beth but for him as well. He remembered hearing how things had been different with Tuck six or seven years ago. He sent up a quick prayer of his own, thanking God that Tuck was handling things differently this time.

Tuck became aware of Doc standing in the room. He jumped up from his knees and asked him how Beth was. The children did as well.

"Children, Tuck. Beth has had a miscarriage; she has lost the baby. But I believe that she is going to come through this."

Becca cried and held on to Nate who wasn't sure he knew what all was going on. But he knew Doc had said that his mother would be all right and that was good enough for him.

"Can we see her now?" Tuck asked.

"She's resting now which she really needs. It's been a long and exhausting night for her. But you can go in and sit with her, Tuck. The children should wait until she is awake." Turning to Becca he said, "Now Becca, suppose you roust up a cup of coffee and something to eat with it. I am suddenly famished."

Becca scurried to do as she was bidden, thankful for something constructive to do. Thad took Nate and they went out to do the chores, promising Becca they would take care of her goats too.

Tuck sat with Beth and thanked God for sparing her life.

CHAPTER EIGHTY-EIGHT
Tuck Grieves

Tuck sat at his wife's bedside watching her sleeping peacefully, thankful for each breath she took. He closed his eyes and silently thanked God that Beth was going to survive this. He prayed that God would continue to keep his mind clear for the sake of the children. He was well aware of how he had behaved when he lost Mary and the baby. Turning away from God was not something he wanted to do again. It had made him miserable. Even though he didn't understand why God would give them this hope of having a child only to snatch it away before he was even used to the idea, he didn't pretend to know God's will. Tuck asked for strength to do right by his wife and adopted children.

As Tuck sat there next to her bedside, he remembered how only a few hours ago she had told him he was going to be a father. He couldn't explain how his heart swelled up inside with the news. That they were going to have a baby!

Now... but if I dwell on that, I will be back to how I felt before. Tuck looked at Beth, her face beautiful and peaceful as she slept with no more pain. *I love you Beth, more than I have the words to say.* Although he didn't realize it, he must have whispered those words out loud, as Beth opened her eyes and smiled at him.

"I love you too," she whispered. Then she closed her eyes and went back to sleep.

Tuck rose and softly went out of the bedroom. He left the door ajar in case they needed to hear her. Doc was just finishing his breakfast and complimented Becca on her cooking. He rose from the table and asked how Beth was doing. Tuck told him she woke for a bit, and then went back to sleep. Doc said she appeared to be doing well and he would check on her again tomorrow. They thanked him for coming out and he expressed his condolences over the loss of the baby.

"Becca, where are Nate and Thad?" Tuck inquired

"They are doing chores and should be just about done."

Tuck was thankful for the work ethic they had been taught by their mother. She had done well by them. He went back to their bedroom and sat with Beth again. He was glad the children were able to take care of the chores because he really just wanted to be here with his wife. Tuck spent several minutes reflecting on when he first met Beth and how he came to understand that his own confused thoughts were a growing love for her. God had blessed them in their marriage but for some reason saw fit to take their child before it was born. It was hard for Tuck to say, not my will, but Yours Lord. But he knew deep in his soul that God's way is higher than his.

CHAPTER EIGHTY-NINE
Beth Recuperates

Beth was aware of the words Tuck whispered to her about his love. She was able to wake long enough to say she loved him too. She fell back to sleep and dreamed of the man who sat next to her bed.

Beth's dreams were of safety and warmth as she felt Tuck's nearness. He pervaded her dreams with his presence and love. But as her dreams continued, it was perhaps inevitable that she should dream of her pregnancy, of the baby who she knew was no longer inside her. Tears escaped from under her eyelids. She felt Tuck take her hand and hold on. She opened her eyes and the tears were unleashed.

Tuck reached over and gently wiped her eyes dry.

"Oh, Tuck."

"I know," he said softly. "I know."

Through the tears, Beth could see the anguish on her husband's face. He does know, she thought. This rugged sheriff-turned-rancher had a softness about him that Beth admired. She knew he would be there for her always. "I love you Tuck, with all my heart." Tuck gathered her up in his arms." I will always be thankful that you survived this crisis in our lives. I don't even want to think what it would have been like if I had lost you as well as our baby."

Beth patted his back. "Tuck, are the children near? Can I see them?"

The three of them filed into her bedroom after Tuck summoned them. They were afraid to speak. Afraid they might say the wrong thing. Beth, with a mother's wisdom, knew this and held out her hands to her children. They flew to her side, and the four of them just held each other for a time. No words had to be spoken. Tuck watched on from his chair with a new father's pride.

They were roused from their positions when Bandit began barking. Tuck rose from his chair to see what it was about. He smiled when he saw two wagons pull up to the hitching rail. One was Reverend Prescott and Esther. The second was Sam and Martha. As the women were helped from their seats, Tuck saw dishes of food being brought to the ranch house. Doc had volunteered to the tell Reverend Prescott and Sam.

"Tuck, I am so sorry for your loss," Martha said softly. She hugged him. Sam shook his hand. "How is Beth?"

"Peaceful, I guess you could say. The children were just in there with her."

"Reverend Prescott, thank you for coming."

"Becca, can you help me and Esther with this food? We brought some for dinner and there will be left overs you can have for supper." Martha brought her food containers to the table as did Esther. Sam went out to bring in more.

"Do you think you and I can go in and see Beth for a moment of prayer?" Reverend Prescott asked.

"Yes, I know she would like that, and I would too. Thank you." Tuck led the way into Beth's room.

"Beth, I am so sorry for your loss," he said taking her hand. "I wonder if you would allow me to pray over you and Tuck."

"Yes, please." Beth answered weakly.

Reverend Prescott took Beth's and Tuck's hands and submitted a prayer to God that helped lessen their sorrow and filled their aching hearts with hope, knowing that the little life that was lost during the night was now with the Father in Heaven.

CHAPTER NINETY
Spring Three Years Later

Things had moved along in the lives of those who lived at Dear Creek Ranch during the last three years. Thad increased his herd of horses by purchasing from Grey Wolf. However, he didn't want to use only mustangs, so a buying trip to Texas was planned. Tuck also planned a trip to Texas with Thad as he wanted to purchase yearling cattle to increase his herd. Thad and Tuck worked well together. They had added "Adam and Thad Tucker, Prop" to the sign over the valley road showing that visitors had entered Deer Creek Ranch. While they were gone on their buying trip, Beth and Becca were to be in charge of the horses. Before leaving, Tuck had shown Beth how to hitch up the team to the 2-seater.

Tuck had about twenty head of cattle so they needed to make sure the cattle, as well as the horses, had plenty of green grass on which to graze. The trip was to take some time. Once the livestock had been purchased, they were to be shipped by rail from the northern panhandle of Texas to Fort Laramie in the Wyoming Territory. Since there was not yet any rail service north, a trail drive was to be organized, which included drovers and a cook. This was something Tuck was familiar with, having done this sort of work before he became sheriff. Thad was looking forward to the trail drive.

#

One morning Beth, Becca, and Nate took the 2-seater into Mustang Ridge for supplies. Beth decided that she had been spoiled. It was hard work for her to harness and hitch up the team to the 2-seater. She was much better at saddling a horse. She told Becca maybe they would do that next time.

Beth got out of the 2-seater and tied the reins to the hitching rail. "You two go into the mercantile. I'm going to stop in at the telegraph office and see if there is any word from Tuck."

However, there had been no wire sent to her even though Tuck and Thad had been gone for a week. Beth wasn't worried yet. They were going to stop at Matt's on the way down to Texas to see if he had any yearlings to sell him. The entire trip could take several weeks. She went back to the mercantile. She called 'hello' to Sam as she walked through the store looking to see if there was anything she needed. Nate ogled the candy jars, and Becca looked at materials.

"Beth, what do you need today?" Sam inquired.

"I guess I really didn't need anything. I wanted to see if there was a wire from Tuck. But there wasn't."

Sam nodded. He understood. "How's things out at the ranch?"

"We're managing. I know one thing. I realize how much Thad and Tuck were doing that helped me. I shall be forever grateful to both of them."

Sam laughed. "So, you don't need anything today?"

"Afraid not, Sam. I probably should get some of what Nate is looking at in those jars though. Let's have a sack of lemon drops and one of peppermint sticks."

"We'll be back in a few days," stated Beth, "to check at the telegraph office."

# # #

Life on Deer Creek Ranch went on as before. Nate took care of his chickens, Becca her goats, and Beth and Becca cared for the horses and cattle. Beth prayed almost continuously for safety for Tuck and Thad. She knew that on a trail ride there were many dangers, but they hadn't sent word yet that they had even bought the cattle. Tuck promised he would send a wire when they were ready to load them on the train. Maybe she was expecting the buying trip to go faster, but she was getting impatient that she had received no word.

Then the day came when the three of them rode by horseback into Mustang Ridge. Beth went to the telegraph office right away. She was elated to find a wire from Tuck waiting for her. They had bought the cattle and were shipping the day he sent it. She was so relieved to hear from him. He promised to send another wire before they began the drive.

They headed back to the ranch in time to do the chores. While getting supper ready, they heard thunder and saw a great deal of lightning. The thunder really boomed and seemed to shake the ground. Beth heard the shrill whinny of one of the horses.

"That's probably Star," Beth told her children. "She gets so skittish over loud noises. I'm going out to the barn and try to calm her down, make sure she's not tangled up in her stall."

When Beth arrived at the barn, she found that Star was frantically jumping in her stall trying to get out.

"Whoa, girl. Settle down. Good girl," she soothed the frantic horse. Beth opened the stall and went in to pat her neck. She had learned in the past this calmed Star. However, just as she did, a mountain-moving clap of thunder shook the barn and Star nearly jumped the stall. As she did, her body came down close to the wall where Beth was standing and pinned her there. Beth felt an excruciating pain go through her left arm. She felt weak and light-headed and knew she might pass out from the pain. In her fuzzy brain, she knew she had to get up and out of Star's stall. Trying to avoid the flying hooves was nearly impossible, but Beth persevered knowing she had to and calling upon her Heavenly Father to help her.

Once outside of the stall, Beth collapsed on the barn floor. This time, she did pass out. She didn't know how long she lay there, but when she regained consciousness, she heard a light rain falling on the barn roof. She tried to get up to move, but promptly passed out again.

The next thing she was aware of was Becca's voice calling, "Mama? Where are you?"

Faintly, Beth tried to answer her. "On the floor."

Frantically Becca ran to her mother's side. "Mama!"

"Arm, broken. Keep passing out. Help me to the house."

It was a long and painful process, but Becca finally was able to get Beth to the ranch-house and lay her on her bed. "Mama, I'll ride into Mustang Ridge and get the doctor. I'll tell Nate to sit with you."

"Thank you, dear," Beth said weakly. She heard Becca telling Nate to go sit with his mother. As Nate came into her room and sat beside her bed, she rallied long enough to tell the frightened boy that the doctor would help her, not to worry.

Nate sat next to his mother's bedside, concern showing on his face. He remembered three years ago when she had lost her baby and he had sat beside her here. He bowed his head and asked God to heal her.

Beth later learned that Becca had saddled Rio, a mustang that Tuck had bought for her from Grey Wolf, and rode into town to get the doctor. She knew her mother would be wondering about a wire, so she stopped at the telegraph office after telling the doctor. Sure enough, there was a wire from Tuck. She pocketed the wire and was running to her pony when Sam saw her and asked what was going on. When she told him, Sam said he would let Martha know and they would come out right away. Becca ran her pony at a gallop back to the ranch. Poor Rio was winded when she got there. She knew she shouldn't have done that but was worried about her mother.

She had beaten the doctor there. She dismounted Rio and tied him at the hitching rail in front of the ranch-house and hurried in. Nate came out of Beth's room when he heard the door open. He held his finger to his lips signaling that Beth was sleeping.

"Where's the doctor," he asked her.

"He's coming in his buggy. I hurried on ahead. Sam and Martha are coming out too."

CHAPTER NINETY-ONE
Beth's Broken Arm

Dr. Phillips attended to Beth's broken arm. He said there was a lot of bruising, and the swelling had already started. He set the bone and put a splint on her arm using a couple of thin boards and wrapping them with strips of cloth.

"She will have a great deal of pain, and I have given her a dose of laudanum which should help," Dr. Phillips explained to Becca. "I'll leave a bottle of it and a dropper. I wrote down how often to give it and how much. Be very careful not to give her more as it is highly addictive."

As Dr. Phillips closed his medical bag, he said, "I'll be back out tomorrow afternoon to check on her. Do you have someone to help care for her?"

"Martha Garrison is on her way out with Sam," answered Becca.

"Good, good."

It was then Becca heard the arrival of the Garrisons. She was so thankful to have her there. When Martha was in the ranch-house, she talked to the doctor and he repeated his instructions to her.

"When the swelling goes down, I will remove the splint and apply a cast," he said.

Beth opened her eyes, vaguely aware that someone else was there as well as Dr. Phillips. She heard Martha come into the room and take her hand. "Beth, don't worry now. I'm here to help Becca. I am staying to care for you."

Beth whispered, "Thank you, Martha."

"I'll take Becca's horse to the barn," Sam informed them. "Want to come with me Nate? We'll do the chores while we are out there."

Sam and Nate headed to the barn with Rio in tow.

"Becca, do you know when Tuck and Thad will get back?" Martha inquired.

"Oh my. I forgot about the wire from Tuck." Becca ran to her jacket and retrieved it from the pocket. "I'll read it now. Tuck says they are starting the drive from Fort Laramie. They will stop at Matt's to get his yearlings and then head home. Oh wait. He sent this wire three days ago."

"I wonder how long it will take for them to get here," Martha pondered...

CHAPTER NINETY-TWO
Beth Heals

Two days later, Dr. Phillips retuned again to check on his patient. The swelling had gone down, so he was able to cast her arm. He dipped strips of cloth in Plaster of Paris which he had mixed with water and applied them to her arm, conforming to the shape of her arm.

"How is your pain, Beth?" he asked.

"Much better, Doctor. May I stop taking the laudanum now? I just had it once yesterday."

"Yes, that is a good idea," he said. "Once this cast is dry you can start to sit up in a chair for a while each day. But be sure and wear this sling whenever you are out of bed. You may need the laudanum the first couple of times you are up. I will check on you again in a couple of days."

Martha walked the doctor to the door. "Martha, I'm glad you are here to take care of her," he confided to her. "What about the chores? Are the children able to do them?"

"Mostly, although several of the men from church have been coming out to help with the cattle and horses. The children take care of their goats and chickens," Martha answered.

Later in the day, Sam returned to the ranch with another bag for Martha and a box of supplies for the household. He went to the barn to tend to the larger animals. When he returned to the house, he asked Martha, "How is she doing?"

"Much better. The doctor applied a cast today. Starting tomorrow, she can sit in a chair for a while each day."

"That's good."

"Are you staying for supper, Sam?" she inquired.

"I thought you'd never ask!" he laughed. "I miss you and I miss your cooking."

# # #

A week later, Beth was sitting up in a chair with her arm in a sling when Nate came running into the house. Martha held her finger to her lips as she noticed Beth was dozing in her chair. Nate skidded to a halt, and in a quiet voice said, "Cattle, I hear cattle."

Martha rushed to the window and saw that Nate was correct. The cattle were being driven through the corral and into the ranch by the drovers. She saw Tuck among the men but didn't see Thad at first. "Stay in the house, Nate, so you won't get in the way."

Once the cattle had been turned into the pasture, Martha saw Thad ride up with his horses. He and his drovers turned them into the horse corral. Becca saw Tuck coming toward the ranch-house. She rushed outside and threw herself into Tuck's arms followed closely by Nate.

Tuck hurried into the house looking for his Beth. He stopped when he saw her sleeping in the chair with her casted arm in a sling and resting on a pillow. He then saw Martha and asked, "What happened, Martha? What's going on?"

"She broke her arm," Martha informed him.

"Star was scared of the thunder and Mama went to settle her down," Becca contributed.

"Star knocked her against the stall and broke her arm," added Nate.

Beth heard her husband's voice and woke up. She held her good right arm up to him and he rushed to her side.

"I'm so glad you are back, Tuck."

"I'm so sorry this happened to you and while I was gone too. Does it hurt awful, honey?"

"It's better now that the cast is on," she said. "And now that you are here. Martha has been helping Becca care for me since the day it happened."

Tuck looked to Martha. "Thank you, Martha. I'm forever grateful. You too, Becca."

Nate informed Tuck that several men from church had been coming out to see to the cattle and horses.

"Becca and I take care of our chickens and goats," he informed Tuck. "I'm glad you're home, Pa."

Beth's heart swelled when she heard Nate call him "Pa." She knew from looking at Tuck's face he felt pride. Tuck hugged Nate close to him. "Me too, son. Me too."

CHAPTER NINETY-THREE – EPILOGE

A New Journal entry-April 20 in the year of our Lord 1879

I have decided to take up writing again with a brand-new journal and a brand-new life. I reached this decision mainly because I can't do anything else due to the cast on my broken left arm. Also, because Martha brought a journal from the mercantile for me. Fortunately, I am right-handed and can still write.

As I sit on the porch and look around at our home, I am reminded of many changes in our lives. The cuttings I obtained at Ash Hollow of grape vines, currents, and roses are now prolific around the ranch-house. The additions the stage line (according to Tuck) made to the ranch-house have made a wonderful home for all of us. I think I see now what Tuck was up to. I wonder too if the stage line really paid for it all. I wonder about the food too, or was that also a part of what Tuck was doing? Perhaps one day I will ask him. Perhaps not.

While Tuck and Thad are gone on their cattle and horse buying trip, Martha, bless her heart, is helping Becca with me and my household because of my broken arm. She has been a breath of fresh air in the midst of my trauma. Between the care from both her and Becca, they take good care of me. Father, I thank Thee for Martha and Becca.

It is spring and once again I feel sadness as I am reminded of the pregnancy which was cut short over three years ago. This time of year brings those painful reminders. But even though I am saddened at the loss of our baby, I also relish the tenderness Tuck showed to me at that time. I love that man so much.

First, I want to bring up-to-date the many changes which have occurred at Deer Creek Ranch and at Mustang Ridge in the past three-plus years. Tuck and I have settled in to a glorious life with our three children. I no longer run the stagecoach stop. It has been moved into Mustang Ridge. Pete takes care of the horses at the Livery, and the passengers are fed at Sally's Café run by a new-comer to town, Sally Slade.

It was Tuck's decision to move the stage stop into town. He didn't want to run the risk of me going through the same thing I did before. I'm all right with that, though I was a little sad at first, giving it up when I had just become used to the idea. However, I soon found I liked being a rancher's wife even more. Except for when I broke my arm, that is. It is good to be available to my children although they are no longer little.

Tuck resigned as sheriff and Charlie became the new sheriff. A new man was hired to help out as deputy - Ben Slade - who is married to Sally. I think Tuck is happy with that decision. He is enjoying being a full-time rancher.

Jacob Wells has grown his blacksmith business, and Sarah is teaching school in the newly built schoolhouse on the south edge of town. Both Becca and Nate attend the school there. Next year, Becca will help Sarah teach.

Reverend Prescott is still the minister of our growing church and an addition has recently been built onto the church. We like not having to move the pews back for special occasions. He and his wife, Esther are new parents of a baby boy, Daniel. Praise God for new life.

Sam and Martha continued as leaders of the community with one difference. The big change in their lives is their newly adopted four-year-old girl, Rachel. They received word from Fort Laramie of this child whose parents died on the wagon train and they immediately said they wanted to adopt her, sight unseen. I am so happy for them. What a joy she has been in their lives. Blessings on the three of them, Father.

Also, the town of Mustang Ridge elected a mayor for the first time. Sam Garrison is the first mayor. A very good choice, as he was always a community leader.

Matt and Mattie's ranch continues to grow as has their family. Mattie has given birth to a baby boy.

They named him Tucker. Tucker Cutter, a mouthful, but they will call him Little Tuck. I miss Mattie as I don't get to visit with her as much.

Grey Wolf's family still lives in the same place in the foothills of the Mustang Mountains, except for the grandfather. He-Who-Is-Wise passed on to his happy hunting ground earlier this year. Singing Butterfly took as her husband a young brave from down by Fort Laramie. He and his bride live in Grey Wolf's camp and have built their own hogan. His family moved up here too, and are building their own hogan. The Shoshone camp has really grown as well.

There is more talk of building a railroad to Deadwood now that the Indian uprisings are dying down. When that is done, there won't be much of a need for the stage line. It would probably shut down soon after the rail is open. Thad and Tuck look forward to that time as it will improve the marketability of both their horses and cattle.

Several leaders in the Territory have started talking about statehood for us. One big obstacle though is that there aren't enough people. The population has grown slowly since the Territory was established in 1869. The United States Congress uses as a guideline that a territory has to show a population of 60,000 people to qualify for statehood. The Territory of Wyoming has fewer than 55,000 people. Women had been able to vote for 20 years in the Wyoming Territory and this also seemed to be controversial with Congress.

Tuck's cattle concern has grown by leaps and bounds. Thad's horse breeding is also growing. They are the proud proprietors of Deer Creek Ranch. Tuck is proud as can be to tell people he and his son run the ranch.

Thad is twenty years old now. He is a tall and slender young man who doesn't realize how good-looking he is. And that is a good thing. I'm sure when they went to Texas on their buying trip, he melted the hearts of girls there. There is a young lady at church who is about Thad's age. Clara is her name and I think she has feelings for Thad, but he is apparently unaware of her. I have also noticed that Thad is spending time at the Wells home. Perhaps he is interested in Izzy? She has been helping Dr. Phillips in his office as she is of the mind that she would like to be a nurse. I have kept my observations of Thad and Izzy to myself. There is plenty of time for that to work itself out, as Izzy is only fifteen-years-old.

Becca is fifteen also and turning into a lovely young woman. I am not sure what she will do with her life. She talks of going east for college but just doesn't know what she would study. She continues to sing at church, weddings, and the like. She looks forward to helping Sarah next year in the school. Maybe she will become a teacher, whatever it is God's will.

Nate is nine now and about the same as he was at six! He is still loud and rambunctious but loveable all

the same. Still too early to know what Nate wants to

do, although I strongly suspect he will be a rancher. I'm not sure though if his avid interest in ranching is really because he wants to ranch someday, or if he just wants to be close to Tuck's side.

One very happy and momentous event took place for Nate during this time. He asked Jesus to be his Savior. Becca and Thad had trusted Jesus when we lived in Texas, but Nate waited until now. I feel at peace regarding my children that no matter what happens to them on this earth, no one can take away their salvation.

And me – I am enjoying my life of being a rancher's wife - except when thunder scares a horse, and I am in the stall. Hindsight tells me I should never have been in the stall in the first place. Needless to say, my Father in Heaven was protecting me that day. And I am thankful to Him for His continued protection.

God has indeed brought our family safely to the Wyoming Territory all the way from Boston. I am thankful to Him for putting us into the lives of our dear friends at Mustang Ridge, especially Adam Tucker. When I look back, I am amazed at God's promises, His faithfulness, and His kindness. He really does know what is best for us and we will eventually know too if we just completely trust in Him. He provides a Safe Haven for all who trust in Him.

RECIPES

Some of these recipes (the first 3) are ones from my family and continue to be used today. Some are recipes used by the pioneers with items we don't use today.

Mama's Noodles
Flour
1 egg
2 T warm water
¼ t salt
 Place flour on board. In well in center, break egg and add
 2 T warm water and salt. Work dough until very stiff.
Divide in two and roll as thin as possible. Cut into strips.
Let stand for 30 minutes.
In salty boiling water. boil until just tender. Drain and toss with melted butter. Serve hot.

Beth's Beef Stew
Melt bacon grease in large cast iron pot or Dutch Oven.
Braise chunks of beef. Get a good color on all side of the beef.

Remove from pot, scrape up the brownings on the bottom
and add water. Wine or apple cider may be used.
Add chopped vegetables, such as carrots and potatoes and onion.
If available, add peas. Season with any herbs available
such as sage, thyme or oregano.
Add more liquid and cover with lid. Let simmer on back of stove
until everything is tender, about three hours

Grandma Ina Pearl's Sour Cream Raisin Pie
1 cup sour cream
½ cup raisins, chopped fine
½ t. cinnamon
1 cup sugar
¼ t, cloves
3 eggs, slightly beaten
Bake in 325 degree oven till filling is set.

Be very careful not to have too hot an oven; may have to use lower temp. Can use one crust or lattice.

Beth's Johnnycake
Corn meal
Hot water
Sugar
Salt
Mix corn meal, sugar and salt together. Add hot water and Mix. Fry in bacon fat.

Fried Apples
Fry 4 slices of bacon in a Dutch oven. Remove bacon.
Peel and slice 6-8 apples (Granny Smith)
Put apples in Dutch oven with bacon grease,
Cover and cook down the apples, but not to mush.
Serve topped with butter and sugar.

Corn Mush
1cup cornmeal
4 cups boiling water
1T. bacon grease
1tsp salt
Dried currents
Put currents or other dried fruits in water and bring to a boil.
Sprinkle cornmeal into boiling water stirring
constantly, adding lard and salt. Cook for about 3 minutes.

Pour in bowls and top with milk, butter and molasses or sorghum.

Beth's Fried Cakes
1 ½ cups flour
1 cup water
Mix with fork.
With flour on hands, roll on surface to 1/4 inch thick.
Cut into 2-inch squares
Heat rendered fat in skillet and add dough squares
Brown on both sides
Sprinkle with sugar

Sorghum Cake
2 T butter
½ cup sugar
2 eggs
1 cup sorghum or molasses
½ water
½ t baking soda
2 cups flour

Cream butter and sugar. Add eggs. Mix sorghum, water and soda.
Add alternately with flour to creamed mixture.
Bake 45 minutes in 10 x 10 pan at a 350 degrees.

Wagon Train Ash Cake
Make a batter with corn meal, salt and water
Pour batter on hot hearth or outside on a hot rock. Spread ashes on top.
When bread is brown, brush off ashes.
Some ashes will penetrate the batter, but it was believed it added to the
flavor.

Soda Biscuits
1lb flour, and mix it with enough milk to make a stiff dough;
dissolve 1tsp carbonate of soda in a little milk; add to dough with a
teaspoon of salt.
Work dough well together and roll out thin; cut into round biscuits, and
bake them in a moderate oven.
The yolk of an egg is sometimes added.

Mama's Apple Shortcake
Fill a square bread tin ¾ full of sliced sour apples
Make a thick batter of ½ a cupful of sour cream
½ cupful of buttermilk
1 teaspoonful of saleratus or baking powder
A little salt & flour to make quite stiff – a little stiffer than cake
Turn this over the apples; bake 40 minutes and serve with sauce or
cream and sugar flavored with nutmeg.

ACKNOWLEGEMENTS

My appreciation to the staff members of the following who spent time sharing information with me.
The Archway – Kearney, Nebraska
Fort Kearny Park – Kearney, Nebraska
Pioneer Village – Minden, Nebraska
Chimney Rock National Monument – Bayard, Nebraska

Song Lyrics found Online
Come Thou Fount – Robert Robinson - 1757
Amazing Grace! John Newton (former slave trader wrote it in 1779)
Old Dan Tucker - Daniel Decatur Emmett. 1843
I Need Thee Every Hour – Annie S. Hawks, 1872
Pop Goes the Weasel – English nursery rhyme1853
Wait for the Wagon – New Orleans parlor song - 1850
Sweet hour of prayer! – William Walford - 1845Come Thou Fount – Robert Robinson - 1757O Christmas Tree - Ernst Anschütz - 1824Silent Night - Franz Xaver Gruber – 1818Just as I Am – text by Charlotte Elliot - 1836

About the Author

After retiring from her positon as mental health secretary in a local hospital clinic, Karen Carr has devoted her time between four grandchildren, writing, and travel, with a little fishing thrown in. She began her writing career with children's picture books written while still working full time. Once retired, she became intrigued with historical Christian fiction, which took her down a path of research and travel.

Karen enjoys book signing events, reading mysteries, fishing, and just spending time with her family.

Visit Karen on line at: www.karenmcarr.vpweb.com

Or connect with her at:

Twitter: https://twitter.com/@carrkm12

Facebook: https://www.facebook.com/karencarrauthor/

Amazon: https://www.amazon.com/-/e/B004AN327G

Also Available From Karen Carr
Children's Picture Books
Littlest Penguin – Guardian Angel Publishing
My Hot Air Balloon – Mirror Publishing
The Many Hats of Jeremiah Porter –Shapato Pub/CreateSpace.
What's That Strange Noise? –co-authored with 6-yr old granddaughter
– Guardian Angel Publishing

Mystery
Mystery at Burr Oak: A Dog Named Wang – Mirror Pub

Anthologies
Christmas Story Collection – "The Christmas House" Little Cab Press
Needle in a Haystack – "Mama's Sewing Machine" -   Shapato
Publishing

Children's Picture Books Coming
A Daisy for Sarah – Guardian Angel Publishing

Save Haven Series
#1A Safe Haven for Beth
#2 Thad Tucker Wyoming Rancher
 And coming in the future:
#3 Ben Tucker, American Soldier
#4 Ellie Tucker and White Barn Inn